"I AM A WIZARD
AND FEAR ONLY THAT WHICH
I CANNOT UNDERSTAND, BOATMAN."

"We wish to travel not to the base of the mountains but through them. Down the river as far as it will carry us and then out the other side of Zaryt's Teeth."

The frog sat back down slowly. "You realize that's just a rumor. There may not be any other side."

"That makes it interesting, doesn't it?" said Clothahump.

Fingers drummed on the table, marking time and thoughts. "One hundred gold pieces," Bribbens said at last.

"You said the fee didn't vary," Talea reminded him from the doorway. "One gold piece a league."

"That is for travel on Earth, female. Hell is more expensive country."

Books by
ALAN DEAN FOSTER

Alien
Clash of the Titans
Outland
Krull
Spellsinger
The Man Who Used the Universe
The Hour of the Gate

Published by
WARNER BOOKS

ALAN DEAN FOSTER

THE HOUR OF THE GATE

SPELLSINGER BOOK TWO

WARNER BOOKS

A Warner Communications Company

WARNER BOOKS EDITION

Copyright © 1984 *by Thranx, Inc.*
All rights reserved.

Cover art by Carl Lundgren

Map designed by Richard Oriolo

Warner Books, Inc.,
666 Fifth Avenue,
New York, N.Y. 10103

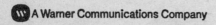 A Warner Communications Company

Printed in the United States of America

First Warner Books Printing: *February, 1984*

10 9 8 7 6 5 4 3 2 1

To

the trio that never was
But should have been.

Janis
Aretha
Billie

The ladies, bless 'em all.

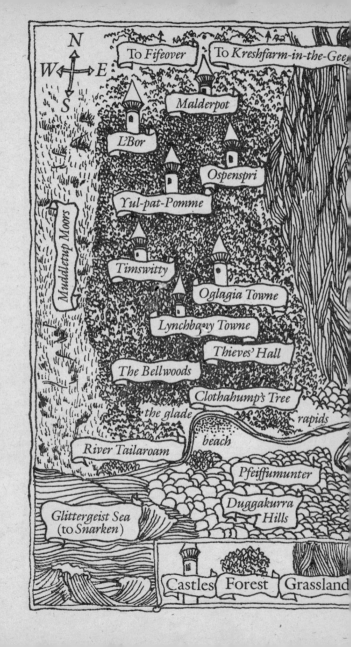

I

Jon-Tom reeled dizzily at the top of the steps. All wrong, he knew. Out of place, out of time. He was *not* standing before the entrance to this strange Council Building in a city named Polastrindu. A five-foot tall otter in peaked green cap and bright clothing was *not* eying him anxiously, wondering if he was about to witness a fainting spell. A bespectacled bipedal turtle was *not* staring sourly at him, waiting for him to regain his senses so they could be about the business of saving the world. An enormous, exceedingly ugly black bat was *not* hovering nearby, muttering darkly to himself about dirty pots and pans and the lack of workman's comp a famulus enjoyed while in a wizard's employ.

Sadly, saying these things were *not* did *not* transform the reality.

" 'Ere now, mate," the otter Mudge inquired, "don't you be sick all over us, wot?"

"Sorry," Jonathan Thomas Meriweather said apologetically. "Oral exams always make me queasy."

"Be of good cheer, my young friend," said the wizard Clothahump. He tapped his plastron. "I shall do the necessary talking. You are here to add credence to what I will say, not to add words. Come now. Time dies and the world draws nearer disaster." He ambled through the portal. As he had now for many weeks, the transposed Jon-Tom could only long for his own vanished world, hope desperately that once this crisis had passed Clothahump could return him to it, and follow the turtle's lead.

Inside they marched past scribes and clerks and other functionaries, all of whom turned to look at them in passing. The hall itself was wood and stone, but the bark-stripped logs that supported this structure had been polished to a high luster. Rich reds faded into bright, almost canary-yellow grains. The logs had the sheen of marble pillars.

They turned past two clusters of arguing workers. The arguing stopped as they passed. Apparently everyone in Polastrindu now knew who they were, or at least that they controlled the dragon who'd almost burned down the city the previous night.

Up a pair of staircases they climbed. Clothahump puffed hard to keep up with the rest. Then they passed through a set of beautiful black and yellow buckeye-burl doors and entered a small room.

There was a single straight, long table on a raised dais. It curved at either end, forming horns of wood. To the right a small bespectacled margay sat behind a drafting table. He wore brown shirt, shorts, boots, and an odd narrow cap. The quill pen he was writing with was connected by wooden arms to six similar pens hovering over a much larger table and six separate scrolls. It was a clever mechanism enabling the scribe to make an original and six copies simultaneously. An assistant, a young wolf cub, stood nearby. He was poised to change the scrolls or unroll them as the occasion demanded.

Seated behind the raised table was the Grand Council of the City, County, and Province of Greater Polastrindu, the largest and most influential of its kind in the warmlands.

Jon-Tom surveyed the councillors. From left to right, he saw first a rather foppishly clad prairie dog draped in thin silks, lace, neck chains, and a large gold earring in his right ear. Next came a corpulent gopher in pink, wearing the expected dark wraparound glasses. This redoubtable female likely represented the city's nocturnal citizens. His eyes passed impatiently over most of the others.

There were only two truly striking personalities seated behind the table. At its far right end sat a tall, severely attired marten. If not actually a military uniform, his dress was very warlike. It was black and blue and there were silver epaulets crusting his shoulders and chevronlike ripples on his sleeves. Double bandoliers of small stilettoes formed a lethal "X" across his chest. His clothing was so spotless Mudge whispered that it must have a dirt-repellent spell cast on it.

His posture matched his attire. He sat rigidly erect in his low chair, his high torso not bending even slightly across the table. His attitude was also much more attentive than that of any of the other council members.

Jon-Tom tried to analyze their states of mind as they took stock of the tiny group waiting before the long table. Their expressions conveyed everything from fear to amusement. Only the marten seemed genuinely interested.

The other imposing figure on the dais sat in the middle of the table. He was flanked by two formal perches on which rested the representatives of Polastrindu's arboreal population.

One was a large raven. At the moment he was picking his beak with a silver pick held easily in his left foot. He wore a red, green, and ocher kilt and matching vest. On the other perch was the smallest intelligent inhabitant of the warmlands Jon-Tom had yet encountered. The hummingbird was no larger than a man's head. It had a long beak, exquisite plumage, and heavily jeweled kilt and vest. It might have flown free from the treasure vaults of Dresden.

Gold trim lined the kilt, and a necklace of the finest gold filigree hung around the ruby-throated neck. He also wore a tiny cap similar to an Australian bush hat. It was secured on the iridescent head with a gold strap.

Jon-Tom marveled at the hat. Slipping it on over that curving beak would be a considerable project, unless the strap joined at a tiny buckle he couldn't see.

All inhabitants and stretches of the province were thus represented. They were dominated by the motionless figure of the marten on the far right, and by the stocky individual in their center.

It was that citizen who commanded everyone's attention as he pushed back his chair and stood. The badger wore spectacles similar to Clothahump's. His fur was silvered on his back, indicating age.

He had very neatly trimmed claws. Despite his civilized appearance Jon-Tom was grateful for the manicure, knowing the reputation badgers had for ferocity and tenacity in a fight. Deep-set black eyes stared out at them. He wore a stiff, high-collared suit marked only by a discreet gold flower on his lapel. One paw slammed down hard on the table. Jon-Tom hadn't known what to expect, but the instant angry outburst was not the greeting he'd hoped for.

"Now what do you mean by bringing this great narsty fire-breathing beastie into the city limits and burning down the harbor barracks, not to mention disrupting the city's commerce, panicking its citizenry, and causing disruption and general dismay among the populace?!?" The voice rose immediately to an angry pitch as he shook a thick warning finger down at them.

"Give me one reason why I should not have the lot of you run into the lowest jails!"

Jon-Tom looked at Mudge in dismay. It was Clothahump who spoke patiently. "We have come to Polastrindu, friend, in order to—"

"I am Mayor and Council President Wuckle Three-Stripe!" snorted the badger, "and you will address me as befits my titles and position!"

"We are here," continued the wizard, unperturbed and unimpressed, "on a mission of great consequence to every inhabitant of the civilized world. It would behoove you to listen closely to what I am about to tell you."

"Yeah," said Pog, who had settled on one of the numerous empty perches ringing the room, "and if ya don't, our good buddy da dragon will burn your manure pile of a rat-warren down around your waxy ears!"

"Shut up, Pog." Clothahump glared irritably at the bat.

While he was doing so the unctuous gopher leaned over and spoke to the badger in a delicate yet matronly voice. "The creature is undiplomatic, Mayor-President, but he has a point."

"I will not be blackmailed, Pevmora." He looked down the other way and asked in a less belligerent tone, "What do you say, Aveticus? Do we disembowel these intruders now, or what?"

The marten's reply was so quiet Jon-Tom had to strain to make it out. Nevertheless, the creature conveyed an impression of cold power. As would any student interested in the law, Jon-Tom noticed that all the other council members immediately ceased picking their mouths, chattering to each other, or whatever they'd been doing, in order now to pay attention.

"I think we should listen to what they have to say to us. Not only because of the threat posed by the dragon, against whose breath I will not expend my soldiers and whom you must admit we can do nothing about, but also because they speak as visitors who mean us nothing but good will. I cannot yet pass on the importance of what they may say, but I think we can safely accept their professed motivations. Also, they do not strike me as fools."

"Sensibly put, youngster," said Clothahump.

The marten nodded once, barely, and ignored the fact that he was anything but a cub. He smiled as imperceptibly as he'd nodded, showing sharp white teeth.

"Of course, good turtle, if you are wasting our time or do indeed mean us harm, then we will be forced to take other measures."

Clothahump waved the comment away. "You give us credit for being other than fools. I return the compliment. Now then, let us have no more talk of motivations and time, for I have none of the last to spare." He launched into a long and by now familiar explanation of the danger from the Plated Folk and their preparations, from their massed armies to their still unknown new magic.

When he'd finished the badger looked as bellicose as before. "The Plated Folk, the Plated Folk! Every time some idiot seer panics, it's 'the Plated Folk are coming, the Plated Folk are coming!'" He resumed his seat and spoke sarcastically.

"Do you think we can be panicked by tales and rumors that mothers use to scare their cubs into bed? Do you think we believe every claim laid before us by every disturbed would-be leader? What do you think we are, stranger?"

"Stubborn," replied Clothahump patiently. "I assure you on my honor as a wizard and member in good standing of the Guild for nearly two hundred years that everything I have just told you is true." He indicated Jon-Tom, who until now had been silently watching and listening.

"Last night, this young spellsinger actually encountered an envoy of the Plated Folk. He was here to foment trouble among local human citizens, and according to my young associate he was well disguised."

That brought some of the more insipid members of the council wide awake. "One of *them* . . . here, in the city . . . !"

"He was attempting to begin war between the species," reiterated the wizard. More mutters of disbelief from those behind the long table.

"He wanted me to join with his puppets," Jon-Tom explained. "The humans he'd recruited say the Plated Folk have promised to make them the overlords and administrators of all the warmlands the insects conquer. I didn't believe it for a minute, of course, but I think I've studied more about such matters than those poor deluded people. I don't think they have many followers. Nevertheless, the word should be spread. Just letting it be known that you know what the Plated Folk are trying to do should discourage potential recruits to their cause."

The muttering among the councillors changed from nervous to angry. "Where is he?" shouted the hummingbird, suddenly buzzing over the table to halt and hover only inches from Jon-Tom's face. "Where is the insect offal, and his furless dupes?" Tiny, furious eyes stared into larger human ones. "I will put out their eyes myself. I shall . . ."

"Perch down, Millevoddevareen," said Wuckle Three-Stripe, the badger. "And control yourself. I will not tolerate anarchy in the chambers."

The bird glared back at the Mayor, muttered something under his breath, and shot back to his seat. His wings continued to whirr with nervous energy. He forced himself to calm down by preening them with his long bill.

"Such fringe fanatics have always existed among the species," the Mayor said thoughtfully. "Humans have no corner on racial prejudice. These you speak of will be warned, but they are of little consequence. When the time for final choices arrives, common sense takes precedence over emotion. Most people are sensible enough to realize they would never survive a Plated Folk conquest." He smiled and his mask fur wrinkled.

"But no such invasion has ever succeeded. Not in tens of thousands of years."

"There is still only one way through Zaryt's Teeth," proclaimed a squirrel, "and that is by way of the Jo-Troom Pass. Two thousand years ago Usdrett of Osprinspri raised the Great Wall on the site of his own victory over the Plated Folk. A wall which has been strengthened and fortified by successive generations of fighters. The Gate has never been forced open, and no Plated Folk force has ever even reached the wall itself. We've never let them get that far down the Pass."

"They're too stratified," added the raven, waving a wing for emphasis. "Too inflexible in their methods of battle to cope with improvisation and change. They prepare to fight one way and cannot shift quickly enough to handle another. Why, their last attempt at an invasion was among the most disastrous of all. Their defeats grow worse with each attack. Such occasional assaults are good for the warmlands: they keep the people from complacency and sharpen the skills of our soldiers. Nor can we be surprised. The permanent Gate contingent can hold off any sudden attack until sufficient reinforcements can be gathered."

"This is no usual invasion," said Clothahump intently. "Not only have the Plated Folk prepared more thoroughly and in greater numbers than ever before, but I have reason to believe they have produced some terrible new magic to assist them, an evil we may be unable to counter and whose nature I have as yet been unable to ascertain."

"Magic again!" Wuckle Three-Stripe spat at the floor. "We still have no proof you're even the sorcerer you claim to be, stranger. So far I've only your word as proof."

"Are you calling me a liar, sir?"

Concerned that he might have overstepped a trifle, the Mayor retreated a bit. "I did not say that, stranger. But surely you understand my position. I can hardly be expected to alarm the entire civilized warmlands merely at the word of a single visitor. That is scarcely sufficient proof of what you have said."

"Proof? I'll give you proof." The wizard's fighting blood was up. He considered thoughtfully, then produced a couple of powders from his plastron. After tossing them on the floor he raised both hands and turned a slow circle, reciting angrily.

"Cold front, warm front, counteract my affront.
Isobars and isotherms violently descend.
Nimbus, cumulus, poles opposizing,
Ions in a mighty surge my doubters upend!"

A thunderous roar deafened everyone in the room and there was a blinding flare. Jon-Tom dazedly struggled back to a standing position to see Clothahump slowly picking himself up off the floor and readjusting his glasses.

Wuckle Three-Stripe lay on the floor in front of him, having been blown completely across the council table. His ceremonial chair was a pile of smoking ash. Behind it a neat hole had been melted through the thick leaded glass where the tiny lightning bolt had penetrated. The fact that it was a cloudless day made the feat all the more impressive.

The Mayor disdained the help of one of the other councillors. Brushing himself off and rearranging his clothing, he waddled back behind the table. A new chair was brought and set onto the pile of ash. He cleared his throat and leaned forward.

"We will accept the fact that you are a sorcerer."

"I'm glad that's sufficient proof," said Clothahump with dignity. "I'm sorry if I overdid it a mite. Some of these old spells are pretty much just for show and I'm a little rusty with them." The scribe had returned to his sextupal duplicator and was scribbling furiously.

"Plated envoys moving through our city in human disguise," murmured one of the councillors. "Talk of interspecies dissension and war, great and strange magic in the council chambers. Surely this portends unusual events, perhaps even a radically different kind of invasion."

The prairie dog leaned across the table, steepling his fingers and speaking in high-pitched, chirping tones.

"There are many forms of magic, colleagues. While the ability to conjure thunder and lightning on demand is most impressive, it differs considerably from divination. Do we then determine that on the basis of a flash of power we cease all normal activities and place Polastrindu on war alert?

"Should the call go out on that basis to distant Snarken, to L'bor and Yul-pat-pomme and all the other towns and cities of the warmlands? Must we now order farmers to leave their fields, young men their sweethearts, and bats their nightly hunts? Commerce will come to a halt and fortunes will be lost, lives disrupted.

"This is a massive question, colleagues. It must be answered by more than the words and deeds of one person." He gestured deferentially with both hands at Clothahump. "Even one so clearly versed in the arts of wizardry as you, sir."

"So you want more proof?" asked Jon-Tom.

"More specific proof, yes, tall man," said the prairie dog. "War is no casual matter. I need hardly remind the other participants of this council," and he looked the length of the long table, "that if there is no invasion, no unusual war, then it is our bodies that will provide fertilizer for next season's crops, and not those of our nomadic visitors." He looked back out of tiny black eyes at Jon-Tom. "Therefore I would expect some sympathy for our official positions."

A mild smattering of applause came from the rest of the council, except for Millevoddevareen the hummer. He continued to mutter, "I want those traitorous humans. Put their damn perverted eyes out!" His colleagues paid him no attention. Hummingbirds are notoriously more bellicose than reflective.

"Then you shall have more conclusive proof," said the weary wizard.

"Master?" Pog looked down solicitously at the turtle. "Do ya really tink anodder spell now, so close ta da odder, is a good idea?"

"Do I seem so tired then, Pog?"

The bat flapped idly, said without hesitation, "Yeah, ya do, boss."

Clothahump nodded slowly. "Your concern is noted, Pog. I'll make a good famulus out of you yet." The bat smiled, which in a bat is no prettier than a frown, but it was unusual to see the pleased expression on the fuzzy face of the normally hostile assistant.

"I expect to become more tired still." He looked at Jon-Tom, then around him at Mudge. "I'd say you represent the lower orders accurately enough."

"Thanks," said the otter drily, "Your Sorcererness."

"What would it take to convince you of the reality of this threat?"

"Well, if'n I were ignorant o' the real situation and I

needed a good convincin'," Mudge said speculatively, "I'd say it were up t' you t' prove it by showin' me."

Clothahump nodded. "I thought so."

"Master . . . ?" began Pog warningly.

"It's all right. I have the capacity, Pog." His face suddenly went blank, and he fell into a deep trance. It was not as deep as the one he had used to summon M'nemaxa, but it impressed the hell out of the council.

The room darkened, and curtains magically drew themselves across the back windows of the chambers. There was nervous whispering among those seated behind the long table, but no one moved. The marten Aveticus, Jon-Tom noted, did not seem in the least concerned.

A cloud formed at the far end of the chamber, an odd cloud that was flat and rectangular in shape. Images formed inside the cloud. As they solidified, there were gasps of horror and dismay from the council members.

Vast ranks of insect warriors marched across the cloud. They bore aloft an ocean of pikes and spears, swords and shields. Huge Plated generals directed the common troops, which stretched across misty plains as far as the eye could see. Tens of thousands paraded across that cloud.

As the view shifted and rolled, there was anxious chatter from the council. "They seem better armed than before . . . look how purposefully they drill. . . . You can feel the confidence in them . . . never saw that before. . . . The numbers, the numbers!"

The scene changed. Stone warrens and vast structures slid past in review. A massive, bulbous edifice began to come into view: the towering castle of Cugluch.

Abruptly the view changed to one of dark clouds, fluttered, and vanished. There was a thump, the cloud dissipated, together with the view, and light returned to the room.

Clothahump was sitting down on the floor, shaking his

head. Pog was hovering above him, fumbling with a vial. The wizard took a long sip of the liquid within, shook his head once more, and wiped the back of his mouth with an arm. With the bat's help he stood and smiled shakily at Jon-Tom.

"Not a bad envisioning. Couldn't get to the castle, though. Too far, and the inhibitory spells are too strong. Lost the damn vertical hold." He started to go down, and Jon-Tom barely got hold of an arm in time to keep the turtle from slumping back to the floor.

"You shouldn't have done it, sir. You're too weak."

"Had to, boy." He jerked his head toward the long table. "Some hardheads up there."

The councillors were babbling among themselves, but they fell silent when Clothahump spoke. "I tried to show you the interior of the castle keep, but its secrets are too well protected by powerful spells I cannot pierce."

"Then how do you know this great new magic exists?" asked the ever skeptical prairie dog.

"I summoned M'nemaxa."

Mutters of amazement mixed with disbelief and awe.

"Yes, I did even that," Clothahump said proudly, "though the consequences of such a conjuration could have been fatal for me and all those in my care."

"If you did so once, could you not summon the spirit once more and learn the true nature of this strange evil you feel exists in Cugluch?" wondered one of the councillors.

Clothahump laughed gently. "I see there are none here versed in wizardly lore. A pity no local sorcerer or ess could have joined us in this council.

"It was remarkable that I was able to conduct the first conjuration. Were I to try it again I could not bind the M'nemaxa spirit within restrictive boundaries. It would burst free. In less than a second I and all around me would be reduced to a crisp of meat and bone."

"I withdraw the suggestion," said the councillor hastily.

"We must rely on ourselves now," said Clothahump. "Outside forces will not save us."

"I think we should . . ." began one of the other members. He fell silent and looked to his left. So did the others.

The marten Aveticus was standing. "I will announce the mobilization," he said softly. "The armies can be ready in a few months' time. I will contact my counterparts in Snarken and L'bor, in all the other towns and cities." He stared evenly at Clothahump.

"We will meet this threat, sir, with all the force the warmlands can bring to bear. I leave it to you to counter this evil magic you speak of. I dislike fighting something I can't see. But I promise you that nothing which bleeds will pass the Jo-Troom Gate."

"But General Aveticus, we haven't reached a decision yet," protested the gopher.

The marten turned and looked down his narrow snout at his colleagues. "These visitors," and he indicated the four strangers standing and watching nearby, "have made their decision. Based upon what they have said and shown to us, I have made mine. The armies will mobilize. Whether they do so with your blessing is your decision. But they will be ready." He bowed stiffly toward Clothahump.

"Learned sir, if you will excuse me. I have much work to do." He turned and strode out of the room on short but powerful legs. Jon-Tom watched his departure admiringly. The marten was someone he would like to know better.

After an uncomfortable pause, the councillors resumed their conversation. "Well, if General Aveticus has already decided so easily . . ."

"That's right," said the hummingbird, buzzing above the table. "Our decision has been made for us. Not by these people," and he gestured with a wing, though it was so fast Jon-Tom couldn't swear he'd actually noticed the gesture so much as imagined it, "but by the General. You all know how conservative he is.

"Now that we are committed, there must be no dissension. We must act as one mind, one body, to counter the threat." He soared higher above the floor.

"I shall notify the air corps of the decision so that we may begin to coordinate operations with the army. I will also send out the peregrines with messages to the other cities and towns that the Plated Folk are again on the march, stronger and more voracious than ever. This time, brothers and sisters, we will deal them a defeat, give them a beating so bad they will not recover for a thousand years!"

Words of assent and a few cheers echoed around the council chamber. One came from the cub manipulating the scrolls. His scribe looked at him reprovingly, and the youngster settled back down to his paper shuffling as Millevoddevareen left via an opened window.

"It seems that your appeal has accomplished what you intended," said the gopher quietly, preening an eyelash. Gems sparkled around her thick neck and from the rings on every finger. "At least among the military-minded among us. All the world will react to your cry of alarm." She shook her head and smiled grimly.

"Heaven help you if your prediction turns out to be less than accurate."

"I can only say to that, madam, that I would much rather be proved inaccurate than otherwise in this matter." Clothahump bowed toward her.

There were handshakes and hugs all around as the councillors descended from their dais. In doing so, they left behind a good deal of their pomposity and officiousness.

"We'll finish the slimy bastards this time!"

"Nothing to worry about . . . be a good fight!"

There was even grudging agreement from the Mayor, who

was still irked that General Aveticus hadn't waited for the decision of the council before ordering mobilization. But there was nothing he could do about it now. Given the evidence Clothahump had so graphically presented, he wasn't sure he wanted to try.

"You'll advise us immediately, sir," he said to Clothahump, "if you learn of any changes in plan among the Plated Folk."

"Of course."

"Then there remains only the matter of a new and perhaps more elegant habitation for you until it's time to march. We have access to a number of inns for the housing of diplomatic guests. I suppose you qualify as that. But I don't know what we can do with your great flaming friend back in the courtyard, since he so impolitely burned down his quarters."

"We'll take care of him," Jon-Tom assured the Mayor.

"Please see that you do." Wuckle Three-Stripe was recovering some of his mayoral bearing. "Especially since he's the only *real* danger we've been certain of since you've appeared among us."

With that, he turned to join the animated conversation taking place among several members of the council.

Once outside the chambers and back in the city hall's main corridor Jon-Tom and Mudge took the time to congratulate Clothahump.

"Aye, that were a right fine performance, guv'nor," said the otter admiringly. "Cor, you should o' seen some o' those fat faces when you threw that army o' bugs up at 'em!"

"You've done what you wanted to, sir," agreed Jon-Tom. "The armies of the warmlands will be ready for the Plated Folk when they start through the Jo-Troom Pass."

But the wizard, hands clasped around his back, did not appear pleased. Jon-Tom frowned at him as they descended the steps to the city hall courtyard.

"Isn't that what you wanted, sir? Isn't that what we've come all this way for?"

"Hmmm? Oh, yes, my boy, that's what I wanted." He still looked discouraged. "I'm only afraid that all the armies of all the counties and cities and towns of all the warmlands might not be enough to counter the threat."

Jon-Tom and Mudge exchanged glances.

"What more can we do?" asked Mudge. "We can't fight with wot we ain't got, Your Magicalness."

"No, we cannot, good Mudge. But there may be more than what we have."

"Beggin' your pardon, sor?"

"I won't rest if there is."

"Well then, you give 'er a bit of some thought, guv, and let us know, won't you?" Mudge had the distressing feeling he wasn't going to be able to return to the familiar, comfortable environs of Lynchbany and the Bellwoods quite as soon as he'd hoped.

"I will do that, Mudge, and I will let you know when I inform the others. . . ."

II

The quarters they were taken to were luxurious compared to the barracks they'd spent their first night in. Fresh flowers, scarce in winter, were scattered profusely around the high-beamed room. They were ensconced in Polastrindu's finest inn, and the decor reflected it. Even the ceiling was high enough so Jon-Tom could stand straight without having to worry about a lamp decapitating him.

Sleeping quarters were placed around a central meeting room which had been set aside exclusively for their use. Jon-Tom still had to duck as he entered the circular chamber.

Caz was leaning back in a chair, ears cocked slightly forward, a glass held lightly in one paw. The other held a silver, ornately worked pitcher from which he was pouring a dark wine into a glass.

Flor sat on one side of him, Talea on the other. All were chuckling at some private joke. They broke off to greet the newcomers.

"Don't have to ask how it went," said Talea brightly, resting her boots on an immaculate couch. "A little while ago this party of subservient flunkies shows up at the barracks and tells us rooms have been reserved for us in this gilded hole." She sipped wine, carelessly spilled some on a finely woven carpet. "This style of crusading's more to my taste, I can tell you."

"What *did* you tell them, Jon-Tom?" wondered Flor.

He walked to an open window, rested his palms on the sill, and stared out across the city.

"It wasn't easy at first. There was a big, blustery badger named Wuckle Three-Stripe who was ready to chuck us in jail right away. It was easy to see how he got to be mayor of as big and tough a place as Polastrindu. But Clothahump scorched the seat of his pants, and after that it was easy. They paid serious attention.

"There was a general named Aveticus who's got more common sense than the rest of the local council put together. As soon as he'd heard enough he took over. The others just slid along with his opinion. I think he likes us personally, too, but he's so cold-faced it's hard to tell for sure what he's thinking. But when he talks everybody listens."

Down below lay a vast black and purple form coiled in the shade of a high stone wall. Falameezar was apparently sleeping peacefully in front of the inn stables. The other stable buildings appeared to be deserted. No doubt the riding lizards of the hotel staff and its guests had been temporarily boarded elsewhere.

"The armies are already mobilizing, and local aerial representatives have been dispatched to carry the word to the other cities and towns."

"Well, that's all right, then," said Talea cheerfully. "Our job's finished. I'm going to enjoy the afterglow." She finished her considerable glass of wine.

"Not quite finished." Clothahump had snuggled into a low-seated chair across from her couch.

"Not quite, 'e says," rumbled Mudge worriedly.

Pog selected a comfortable beam and hung himself above them. "The master says we got ta seek out every ally we can."

"But from what has been said, good sir, we are already notifying all possible allies in the warmlands." Caz sat up in his chair and gestured with his glass. Wine pitched and rolled like a tiny red pond and he didn't spill a drop.

"So long as the city fathers and mothers have seen fit to grant us these delightful accommodations, I see no reason why we should not avail ourselves of the local hospitality. Polastrindu is not so very far from Zaryt's Teeth and the Gate itself. Why not bivouac here until the coming battle? We can offer our advice to the locals."

But Clothahump disagreed. "General Aveticus strikes me as competent enough to handle military preparations. Our task must be to seek out any additional assistance we can. You just stated that all possible warmland allies are being notified. That is so. My thoughts concerned possible allies elsewhere."

"Elsewhere?" Talea sat up and looked puzzled. "There is no elsewhere."

"Try tellin' 'is nib's 'ere that," said Mudge.

Talea looked curiously at the otter, then back at the wizard. "I still don't understand."

"There is another nation whose aid would be invaluable," Clothahump explained energetically. "They are legendary fighters, and history tells us they despise the Plated Folk as much as we do."

Mudge circled a finger near one ear, whispered quietly to Jon-Tom. "Told you 'e was vergin' on the senile. The lightnin' an' the view conjurin' 'as sent him off t' balmy land.''

The most unexpected reaction came from Pog, however. The bat left his beam and hovered nervously overhead, his eyes wide, his tone fearful.

"No, Master! Don't tink of it. Don't!"

Clothahump shrugged. "Our presence here is no longer required. We would find ourselves lost among the general staffs of the assembling armies. Why then should we not seek out aid which could turn the tide of battle?"

Jon-Tom, who had returned from his position by the open window, listened curiously and wondered at Pog's sudden fright.

"What kind of allies were you thinking about, sir? I'm certainly willing to help recruit." Pog gave him an ugly look.

"I'm talking about the Weavers, of course."

The violence of the response to this announcement startled Jon-Tom and Flor.

"Who are these 'Weavers'?" she asked the wizard.

"They are thought to be the most ferocious, relentless, and accomplished mountain fighters in all the world, my dear."

"Notice he does not say 'civilized' world," said Caz pointedly. Even his usually unruffled demeanor had been mussed by the wizard's shocking pronouncement. "I would not disagree with that appraisal of Weaver fighting ability, good sir," continued the rabbit, his nose twitching uncontrollably. "And what you say about them hating the Plated Folk is also most likely true. Unfortunately, you neglect the likely possibility that they also despise us."

"That is more rumor and bedtime story than fact, Caz. Considering the circumstances, they might be quite willing to join with us. We do not know for certain that they hate us."

"That's for sure," said Talea sardonically, "because few who've gone toward their lands have ever come back."

30

"That's because no one can get across the Teeth," Mudge said assuredly. "'Ate us or not don't matter. Probably none of them that's tried reachin' Weaver lands 'as ever reached 'em. There ain't no way across the Teeth except through the Gate and then the Pass, and the Weavers, if I recall my own bedtimey stories aright, live a bloody good ways north o' the Greendowns."

"There is another way," said Clothahump quietly. Mudge gaped at him. "It is also far from here, far from the Gate, far to the north. Far across the Swordsward."

"Cross the Swordsward!" Talea laughed in disbelief. "He *is* crazy!"

"Across the great Swordsward," the sorcerer continued patiently, "lies the unique cataract known as the Sloomaz-ayor-la-Weentli, in the language of the Icelands in which it arises. It is The-River-That-Eats-Itself, also called the River of Twos, also the Double-River. In the language and knowledge of magic and wizardry, it is known as the SchizoStream."

"A schizoid river?" Jon-Tom's thoughts twisted until the knot hurt. "That doesn't make any sense."

"If you know the magical term, then you know what you say is quite true, Jon-Tom. The Sloomaz-ayor-la-Weentli is indeed the river that makes no sense."

"Neither does traveling down it, if I'm following your meaning correctly," said Caz. Clothahump nodded. "Does not The-River-That-Eats-Itself flow through the Teeth into something no living creature has seen called The Earth's Throat?" Again the wizard indicated assent.

"I see." Caz ticked the relevant points off on furry fingers as he spoke. "Then all we have to do is cross the Swordsward, find some way of navigating an impossible river, enter whatever The Earth's Throat might be, counter whatever dangers may lie within the mountains themselves, reach the Scuttleteau, on which dwell the Weavers, and convince them not only that we come as friends but that they should help us instead of eating us.''

"Yes, that's right," said Clothahump approvingly.

Caz shrugged broadly. "A simple task for any superman." He adjusted his monocle. "Which I for one am not. I am reasonably good at cards, less so at dice, and fast of mouth, but I am no reckless gambler. What you propose, sir, strikes me as the height of folly.''

"Give me credit for not being a fool with my own life," countered Clothahump. "This must be tried. I believe it can be done. With my guidance you will all survive the journey, and we will succeed.'' There was a deep noise, halfway between a chuckle and a belch. Clothahump threw the hanging famulus a quick glare, and Pog hurriedly looked innocent.

"I'll go, of course," said Jon-Tom readily.

The others gazed at him in astonishment. "Be you daft too, mate?" said Mudge.

"Daft my ass." He looked down at the otter. "I have no choice.''

"I'll go," announced Flor, smiling magnificently. "I love a challenge.''

"Oh, very well." Caz fitted his monocle carefully, his pink nose still vibrating, "but it's a fool's game to draw and roll a brace of twelves after a muntle-star pays out.''

"I suppose I'll come too," said Talea with a sigh, "because I've no more good sense than the rest of you.''

All eyes turned toward Mudge.

"Right then, quit staring at me, you bloody great twits!" His voice dropped to a discouraged mutter. "I 'ope when we find ourselves served up t' the damned Weavers for supper that I'm the last one on the rottin' menu, so I can at least 'ave the pleasure o' watchin' 'em eat you arse'oles first!''

"To such base uses we all eventually come, Mudge," Jon-Tom told him.

"Don't get philosophical with me, mate. Oh, you've no choice for sure, not if you've a 'ope o' seeing your proper 'ome again. Old Clothahump's got you by the balls, 'e as. But as for me, I can be threatened so far and then it don't matter no more."

"No one is threatening you, otter," said the wizard.

"The 'ell you ain't! I saw the look in your eye, knew I might as well say yes voluntary-like and 'ave done with it. You can work thunder and lightnin' but you can't make the journey yourself, you old fart! You don't fool me. You *need* us."

"I have never tried to deny that, Mudge. But I will not hold you. I have not threatened you. So behind all your noise and fury, why *are* you coming?"

The otter stood there and fumed, breathing hard and glaring first at the turtle, then Jon-Tom, then the others. Finally he booted an exquisite spittoon halfway across the room. It bounced ringingly off the far wall as he sat down in a huff.

"Be billy bedamned if I know!"

"I do," said Talea. "You'd rather travel along with a bunch of fools like the rest of us than stay here and be conscripted into the army. With Clothahump and Jon-Tom gone, the local authorities will treat you like any other bum."

"That's bloody likely," snorted Mudge. "Leave me alone, then, won't you? I said I'd go, though I'd bet heavy against us ever comin' back."

"Optimism is better than pessimism, my friend," said Caz pleasantly.

"You. I don't understand you at all, mate." The otter shoved back his cap and walked across the carpet to confront Caz. "A minute ago you said you weren't no reckless gambler. Now you're all for agoin' off on this charmin' little suicide trot. And of all o' us, you'd be the one I'd wager on t' stay clear o' the army's clutches.''

The rabbit looked unimpressed. ''Perhaps I can see the larger picture, Mudge.''

''Meanin' wot?''

''Meaning that if what our wise friend Clothahump knows to be true indeed comes to pass, the entire world may be embarking on that 'trot' with us.'' He smiled softly. ''There are few opportunities for gambling in a wasteland. I do not think the Plated Folk will permit recreation as usual if they are victorious. And I have other reasons.''

''Yeah? Wot reasons?''

''They are personal.''

''The wisdom of pragmatism,'' said Clothahump approvingly. ''It was a beneficial day indeed when the river brought you among us, friend Caz.''

''Maybe. But I think I would be still happier if I had not misjudged the placement of those dice and been forced to depart so precipitately from my ship. The happiness of the ignorant is no less so than any other. Ah well.'' He shrugged disarmingly. ''We are all of us caught up in momentous events beyond our ability to change.''

They agreed with him, and none realized he was referring as much to his previously mentioned personal reasons as to the coming cataclysm. . . .

The city council provided a three-axle wagon and a dray team of four matched yellow-and-black-striped lizards, plus ample supplies. Some among the council were sorry to see the wizard and spellsinger depart, but there were others who were just as happy to watch two powerful magicians leave their city.

Talea handled the reins of the wagon while Flor, Jon-Tom, Mudge, Clothahump, and Caz sorted living quarters out of the back of the heavily loaded vehicle. Thick canvas could be drawn across the top to keep out the rain. Ports cut in the slanting wooden walls provided ventilation and a means for firing arrows at any attacker.

Aveticus, resplendent in a fresh uniform and as coldly correct as ever, offered to provide a military escort at least part of the way. Clothahump declined gracefully, insisting that the less attention they attracted the better their chance for an uneventful traverse of the Swordsward.

Anyway, they had the best protection possible in the form of Falameezar. The dragon would surely frighten away any possible assailants, intelligent or otherwise.

It took the dray lizards a day or two to overcome their nervousness at the dragon's presence, but soon they were cantering along on their strong, graceful legs. Bounding on six solid rubber wheels the wagon fairly flew out of the city.

They passed small villages and farms for another several days, until at last no sign of habitation lay before them.

The fields of golden grain had given way to very tall light green grasses that stretched to the ends of the northern and eastern horizons. Dark wintry rain clouds hovered above the greenery, and there were rumblings of distant thunder.

Off to their right the immense western mountain range known as Zaryt's Teeth rose like a wall from the plains. Its lowermost peaks rose well above ten thousand feet while the highest towered to twenty-five thousand. Dominating all and visible for weeks to come was the gigantic prong of Brokenbone Peak, looking like the ossified spine of some long-fossilized titan.

It was firmly believed by many that in a cave atop that storm-swept peak dwelt the Oracle of All Knowledge. Even great wizards had been unable to penetrate the winds that howled eternally around that inaccessible crag. For by the time any grew wise enough to possibly make the journey, they had also grown too old, which might explain why isolated travelers sometimes heard monstrous laughter avalanching down Brokenbone's flanks, though most insisted it was only the wind.

The Swordsward resembled a well-manicured field. Patches of other vegetation struggled to rise above the dense grass, were only occasionally successful. Here and there small thickets that were either very thin flowering trees or enormous dandelions poked insolently above the waving green ocean.

Despite Clothahump's protests General Aveticus had given them a mounted escort to the boundary of the wild plains. The soldiers raised a departing cheer as the wagon left them behind and started out through the grass.

There were no roads, no paths through the Swordsward. The grass that formed it grew faster than any bamboo. So fast, according to Caz, that you could cut the same patch bare to the earth four times in a single day, and by nightfall it would be as thick as ever. Fortunately the blades were as flexible as they were prolific. The wagon slid over them easily.

Each blade knew its assigned place. None grew higher than the next and attempted to steal the light from its neighbor. Despite the flexibility of the grass, however, the name Swordsward had not been bestowed out of mischief or indifference. While Falameezar's thick scales were invulnerable, as were those of the dray lizards, the others had to be careful when descending from the wagon least the sharp edges of the tall blades cut through clothing and skin.

Jon-Tom learned quickly enough. Once he'd leaned over the back of the wagon to pluck a high, isolated blue flower. A quick, sharp pain made him pull back his hand. There was a thin line of red two inches long across his palm. It felt as if someone had taken a piece of new paper and drawn it fast across his skin. The wound was narrow and bled only for a minute, but it remained painful for days.

Several times they had glimpses of lanky predators like a cross between a crocodile and a greyhound. They would pace the wagon for hours before slinking off into the green.

"Noulps," Caz told him, peering out the arrowport behind him. "They would kill and eat us if they could, but I don't think that's likely. Falameezar scares them off."

"How can you tell?"

"Because they leave us. A noulp pack will follow its quarry for weeks, I'm told, until they run it down."

Days became weeks that passed without trouble. Each day the black clouds massing in the west would come nearer, their thunder more intimate. They promised more severe weather than the steady, nightly rain.

"It is winter, after all," Clothahump observed one day. "I worry about being caught out here in a really bad storm. This wagon is not the cover I would wish."

But when the full storm finally crested atop them, even the wizard was unprepared for its ferocity. The wind rose until it shook the wagon. Its huddled inhabitants felt like bugs in a box. Rain and sleet battered insistently at the wooden sides, seeking entry, while the lizards lay down in a circle in the grass and closed their eyes against the driving gale.

The wagon was wide and low. It did not leak, did not tip over. Jon-Tom was even growing used to the storm until, on the fourth day, a terrible scream sounded from outside. It faded rapidly, swallowed up by the wind.

He fumbled for a candle, gave up, and used his sparker. Flame flashed off emerald eyes.

"What's the matter?" Talea asked him sleepily. The others were moving about beneath their blankets.

"Someone screamed."

"I didn't hear anything."

"It was outside. It's gone now."

Heads were counted. Flor was there, blinking sleep from

37

her eyes. Nearby Caz leaned up against the inner wall. Mudge was the last to awaken, having displayed the unique ability to sleep soundly through thunder, screaming, and wind.

Only Clothahump looked attentive, sensing the night smells.

"We're all here," said Flor tiredly. "Then who screamed?"

Clothahump was still listening intently, spoke without moving head or body. "The lowliest are always missed the last. Where is Pog?"

Jon-Tom looked toward the back of the wagon. The hanging perch in the upper left corner was empty. Rain stained the wood, showing where the canvas backing had been unsnapped. He moved to inspect it. Several of the sealing snaps had been broken by the force of the gale.

"He's been carried off in his sleep," said Clothahump. "We have to find him. He cannot fly in this."

Jon-Tom stuck his head outside, immediately drew it back in. The ferocity of rain and wind drowned both skin and spirits. He forced himself to try again, called the bat's name several times.

A massive, damp skull suddenly appeared close by the opening. Jon-Tom was startled, but only for a moment.

"What's the matter, Comrade?" Falameezar inquired. "Is there some trouble?"

"We've . . . we've lost one of the group," he said, trying to shield his face against the battering rain. "Pog, the bat. We think he got caught by a freak gust of wind and it's carried him off. He doesn't answer, and we're all worried. He can't walk well in the best of weather and he sure as hell can't fly in this gale. Also, there don't seem to be any trees around he could catch hold of."

"Never fear, Comrade. I will find him." The massive armored body turned southward and bellowed above the wind, "Comrade Pog, Comrade Pog!"

That steady, confident voice echoed back to them until even it was overwhelmed by distance and wind. Jon-Tom watched until the black shadow shape faded into the night, then drew back inside, wiping water from his face and hair.

"Falameezar's gone after him," he told the anxious watchers. "The storm doesn't seem to be bothering him too much, but I doubt he's got much of a chance of finding Pog unless the storm forced him down somewhere close by."

"He may be leagues from here by now," said Caz dolefully. "Damn this infernal wind!" He struck in frustration at the wooden wall.

"He was impertinent and disrespectful, but he performed his duties well for all his complaining," said Clothahump. "A good famulus. I shall miss him."

"It's too early to talk in the past tense, wizard." Flor tried to cheer him up. "Falameezar may still find him. *Quien sabe;* he may be closer than we think."

"Your words are kind, my dear. Thank you for your thoughtfulness."

The wagon rattled as another blast of near hurricane force whistled about them. Everyone fought for balance.

"But as our young spellsinger says, the weather is not encouraging. Pog is not very resourceful. I don't know. . . ."

There was no sign of the bat the next day, nor of Falameezar, and the storm continued without abating. Clothahump worried now not only that Pog might never be found but that the dragon might become disoriented and not be able to relocate the wagon. Or that he might find a river, decide he was bored with the entire business, and simply sink out of sight.

"I don't think the last likely, sir," argued Jon-Tom. "Falameezar's made a political commitment. We're his comrades. He'll be back. It would take some kind of personal crisis to make him abandon us, and there isn't much that can affect him."

"Nevertheless, though I would like to have both of them back with us, time is becoming too important." The turtle let out a resigned sigh. "If the weather breaks tomorrow, as I believe it may, we will wait one additional day. Then we must be on our way or else we might as well forget this entire mission."

"Praise the weather," murmured Mudge hopefully, and turned over in his blankets. . . .

III

When Jon-Tom woke the following morning, his first sight was of the rear canvas panel. It had been neatly pinned up, and sunlight was streaming brilliantly inside. Flor knelt and stared outward, her black hair waterfalling down her back. She seemed to sparkle.

He sat up, threw off his covers. It was eerie after so many days of violence not to hear the wind. Also absent was the persistent drumming of raindrops overhead. He leaned forward and peered out. Only a few scattered storm clouds hung stubbornly in an otherwise clear sky.

He crawled up alongside her. A gentle breeze ruffled the Swordsward, the emerald endlessness appearing as soft and delicate as the down on a young girl's legs. The distant yellow puffballs of dandelion trees looked lonely against the otherwise unbroken horizon.

"Good morning, Jon-Tom."

"*Buenos dias. Que pasa,* beautiful?"

"Not much. Just enjoying the view. And the sunshine. A week in that damn wagon." She fluffed her hair out. "It was getting a little squirrelly."

"Also smelly." He breathed deeply of the fresh air, inhaled the rich sweet smell of the rain-swept grasses. Then he stepped out onto the rear wagon seat.

Slowly he turned a circle. There was nothing but green sward and blue sky in all directions. Against that background even a distant Falameezar would have stood out like a truckload of coal in a snowbank. But there was no sign of the dragon or of his quarry.

"Nobody. Neither of 'em," he said disappointedly, turning back to look down into the wagon. Talea had just raised her head from beneath a pile of blankets and blinked at him sleepily, her red curls framing her face like the scribbles of a playful artist.

"I am most concerned," said Clothahump. He was seated at the front end of the wagon, stirring a pot of hot tea. The little copper kettle squatted on the portable stove and steamed merrily. "It is possible that—" He broke off, pointed toward Jon-Tom, and opened his mouth. Jon-Tom heard only the first of his comment.

"I do believe there is someone be—"

Something yanked hard at Jon-Tom's ankles. Arms windmilling the air, he went over backward off the platform. He landed hard, the grass cushioning him only slightly.

Blackness and colorful stars filled his vision, but he did not pass out. The darkness was a momentary veil over his eyes. By the time his head cleared his hands had been drawn above his hair, his ankles placed together, and tough cords wrapped around them. Looking down at his feet, he saw not only the bindings but a remarkably ugly face.

Its owner was perhaps two and a half feet tall, very stocky, and a perversion of humanity. Jon-Tom decided it looked like a cross between an elf and a wino. The squat creature boasted an enormous, thick black beard.

Out of this jungle peered two large brown eyes. They flanked a monstrous bulbous nose and were in turn framed by a pair of huge, floppy ears that somehow managed to fight their way out of the wiry hair. There were hints of clothing beneath the effervescent mass.

Thick, stubby fingers made sure of Jon-Tom's bonds. A set of sandals large enough for the recumbent youth floored enormous feet.

Tying the other knots was a slightly smaller version of the first ugly, except he was blond instead of dark-haired and had watery blue eyes.

Something landed on Jon-Tom's chest and knocked the wind out of him. The newcomer was solid as iron and extremely muscular. It was not the build of a body builder but instead the seamlessly smooth and deceptively porcine musculature of the power lifter.

The one on his chest now was female. Only a few red whiskers protruded from her chin. She was no less gruesome in appearance than her male counterparts. She was shaking a fist in his face and jabbering at high speed. For the first time since arriving in Mudge's meadow words had no meaning to him.

He turned his head away from that indifferently controlled fist. Angry noises and thumping sounds came from the wagon. He looked to his right, but the grass hid whatever was happening there.

Of only one thing was he certain: the sward was alive with dozens of the fast-moving, excited creatures.

The dray lizards wheezed and hissed nervously as the little monsters swarmed onto harness and reins. Mixed in with the beelike babbling of their assailants Jon-Tom could make out other voices. Most notable was that of Caz, who was speaking in an unfamiliar language similar to that of their captors. Mudge could be heard alternately cursing and bemoaning his fate, while Talea was railing at an attacker, warning that if he didn't get his oversized feet off her chest she was going to make a candlewick out of his beard.

A pole was brought and neatly slipped between the bindings on Jon-Tom's ankles and the others at his wrists. He was lifted into the air. Clearing the ground by only a few inches, he was borne off at considerable speed through the grass. He could see at least half a dozen of his captors shouldering the pole, three at his feet and three above his head. Although his sense of speed was artificially accelerated by his proximity to the ground, he fervently prayed that his bearers' sense of direction was as efficient as their deltoids. The sharp grass did not seem to bother them.

With a creak he saw the wagon turn and follow.

He had resigned himself to a long period of jouncing and bumping, but it hardly seemed he'd been picked up when he was unceremoniously dumped on the ground. Flor was dropped next to him. One by one he watched as the rest of his companions were deposited alongside. They mashed down the grass so he could see them clearly, lined up like so many kabobs. The similarity was not encouraging.

Clothahump had evidentally retreated into his shell in an attempt to avoid being moved. They had simply hefted him shell and all to carry him. When he finally stuck arms and legs out again, they were waiting with lassos and ropes. They managed to snare only a leg before he retreated in on himself.

Mutterings issued from inside the shell. This produced excited conversation among the creatures. They kicked and punched at the impervious body frantically.

The activity was directed by one of their number, who displayed a variety of metal ornaments and decorative bits of bone in hair and beard. Under his direction a couple of the creatures poked around inside the shell. They were soon able to drag the protesting, indignant turtle's head out. With the aid of others they shoved several bunches of dried, balled-up grass into his mouth and secured the gag tightly. Clothahump reached up to pull the stuffing out, and they tied his arms also. At that point he slumped back and looked exhausted.

The creature resplendent in bone and metal jumped up and down happily, jabbing a long feather-encrusted pole at the now safely bound and gagged turtle. Evidently the fashion plate was the local witch doctor or wizard, Jon-Tom decided. He'd recognized that Clothahump had been starting a spell inside his shell and had succeeded in rendering his opponent magically impotent.

Jon-Tom lay quietly and wondered if they would recognize the sorceral potential of his singing, but the duar was inside the wagon and he was firmly tied on the ground.

Moans came from nearby. Straining, he saw another of their captors idly kicking Talea with considerable force. Each time she'd curse her tormentor he'd kick her. She would jerk in pain and it would be several minutes before she regained enough strength to curse him again.

"Knock it off!" he yelled at her assailant. "Pick on somebody your own size!"

The creature responded by leaving Talea and walking over to stare curiously down into Jon-Tom's face. He jabbered at him experimentally.

Jon-Tom smiled broadly. "Same to you, you sawed-off shithead."

It's doubtful the creature followed Jon-Tom's meaning, but he accepted the incomprehensible comment with equanimity and commenced booting the lanky youth in the side instead. Jon-Tom gritted his teeth and refused to give the creature the satisfaction of hearing him groan.

After several kicks produced nothing but a steady glare, his attacker became bored and wandered off to argue with some of his companions.

In fact, there appeared to be as much fighting taking place between members of the tribe as there'd been between them and their captives. Jon-Tom looked around and was astonished to see tiny structures, camp fires, and ugly, hairless smaller versions of the adults, which could only be children. Small green and blue lizards wore backpacks and suggested scaly mules. There was consistent and unrelenting activity taking place around the six bound bodies.

Camp fires and buildings gave every appearance of having been in place for some time. Jon-Tom tried to estimate the distance they'd traveled.

"Christ," he muttered, "we couldn't have been camped more than a couple of hundred yards from this town, and we never even saw them."

"The grass conceals the Mimpa," Caz told him. Jon-Tom looked to his right, saw rabbit ears pointed in his direction. "They move freely among it, completely hidden from most of their enemies."

"Call 'em what you like. They look like trolls to me." His brow twisted in thought. "Except I always thought trolls lived underground. Singularly unlovely bunch, too."

"Well, I know naught of trolls, my friend, but the Mimpa live in the sward."

"Like fleas," Mudge snorted from somewhere nearby. "An' if I could get loose I'd start on a little deinfestation, wot!"

Now Jon-Tom could just see the otter's head. His cap was missing, no doubt knocked off during the struggle for the wagon. The otter was jerking around as if he were wired, trying to break free.

Of them all he was the only one who could match their captors for sheer energy, but he could not break the ropes.

Jon-Tom turned his attention back to the rabbit. "Can you talk to them, Caz?"

"I believe I can understand their language somewhat," was the reply. "A well-traveled animal picks up all sorts of odd knowledge. As to whether I can 'talk' to them, I don't think so. Talking takes two, and they strike me as particularly nonconversant with strangers."

"How is it they speak a language we can't follow?"

"I expect that has something to do with their being violently antagonistic to what we think of as civilized life. They're welcome to their isolation, so far as I am concerned. They are incorrigibly hostile, incorrigibly filthy, and bellicose to the point of paranoia. I sincerely wish they would all rot where they stand."

"Amen to that," said Flor.

"What are they going to do with us, Caz?"

"They're talking about that right now." He gestured with an unbound ear. "That one over there with the spangles, the chap who fancies himself something of a local dandy? The one who unfortunately forestalled Clothahump's spell casting? He's arguing with a couple of his equals. Apparently they function as some sort of rudimentary council."

Jon-Tom craned his neck, could just see the witch doctor animatedly arguing with two equally pretentious and noisy fellows.

One of them displayed the mother of all Fu Manchu mustaches. It drooped almost to his huge splayed feet. Other than that he was entirely bald. The third member of the unkempt triumvirate had a long pointed beard and waxed mustachio, but wore his hair in a crew cut. Both were as outlandishly clad as the witch doctor.

"From what I can make out," said Caz, "Baldy thinks they ought to let us go. The other two, Flattop and Bigmouth, say that since hunting has been poor lately they should sacrifice us to the gods of the Sward.''

"Who's winning?" Flor wanted to know. Jon-Tom thought that for the first time she was beginning to look a little frightened. She had plenty of company.

"Can't we talk to them at all?" he asked hopefully. "What about the one who had Clothahump gagged? Do you know his real name?"

"I already told you," said Caz. "His name is Bigmouth. Flattop, Baldy, and Bigmouth: that's how their names translate. And no, I don't think we can talk to them. Even if I knew the right words I don't think they'd let me get a word in edgewise. It seems that he who talks loudest without letting his companions make their points is the one who wins the debate."

"Then if it's just a matter of shouting, why don't you give it a try?"

"Because I think they'd cut out my tongue if I interrupted them. I am a better gambler than that, my friend."

It didn't matter, because as he watched the debate came to an end. Baldy shook a threatening finger less than an inch from Bigmouth's proboscis, whereupon Bigmouth frowned and kicked the overly demonstrative Baldy in the nuts. As he doubled over, Flattop brought a small but efficient-looking club down on Baldy's head. This effectively concluded the discussion.

Considerable cheering rose from the excited listeners, who never seemed to be standing still, a condition duplicated by their mouths.

Jon-Tom wondered at the humanoid metabolism that could generate such nonstop energy.

"I am afraid our single champion has been vanquished," said Caz.

"I don't want to die," muttered Flor. "Not here, not in this place." She started reciting Hail Marys in Spanish.

"I don't want to die either," Jon-Tom yelled at her in frustration.

"This isn't happening," she was saying dully. "It's all a dream."

"Sorry, Flor," he told her unsympathetically. "I've already been that route. It's no dream. You were enjoying yourself until now, remember?"

"It was all so wonderful," she whispered. She wasn't crying, but restraining herself required considerable effort. "Our friends, the quest we're on, when we rescued you that night in Polastrindu . . . it's been just as I'd always imagined this sort of thing would be. Being murdered by ignorant aborigines doesn't fit the rest. Can they actually kill us?"

"I think they can." Jon-Tom was too tired and afraid even to be sarcastic. "And I think we'll actually die, and actually be buried, and actually be food for worms. If we don't get out from here." He looked across at Clothahump, but the wizard could only close his eyes apologetically.

If we could just lower the gag in Clothahump's mouth when they're busy elsewhere, he thought anxiously. Some kind of spell, even one that would just distract them, would be enough.

But while the Mimpa were uncivilized they were clearly not fools, nor quite so ignorant as Caz believed. That night they confidently ignored all their captives except the carefully watched Clothahump.

At or near midnight they were all made the centerpiece of a robust celebration. Grass was cut down with tiny axes to form a cleared circle, and the captives were deposited near the center, amid a ground cover of foul-smelling granular brown stuff.

Flor wrinkled her nose, tried breathing through her mouth

instead. "*Mierda* . . . what have they covered the ground here with?"

"I believe it is dried, powdered lizard dung," said Caz worriedly. "I fear it will ruin my stockings."

"Part of the ceremony?" Jon-Tom had grown accustomed to strange smells.

"I think it may be more than that, my friend. It appears to retard the growth of the Sward grasses. An efficient if malodorous method of control."

Small fires were lit in a circle, uncomfortably near the bound prisoners. Jon-Tom would have enjoyed the resultant celebration for its barbaric splendor and enthusiasm, were it not for the fact that he was one of the proverbial pigs at the center of the banquet table.

"You said they'd sacrifice us to the gods of the Sward." As he spoke to Caz he fought to retain both confidence and sanity. "What gods do they have in mind?" His thoughts were of the lithe, long-limbed predators they'd seen sliding ribbonlike through the grass their first week out of Polastrindu.

"I have no idea as yet, my friend." He sniffed disdainfully. "Whatever, I'm sure it will be a depressing way for a gentleman to die."

"Is there another way?" Even Mudge's usually irrepressible good humor was gone.

"I had hoped," replied the rabbit, "to die in bed."

Mudge let out a high whistle, some of his good spirits returning. "O' course, mate. Now why didn't I think o' that right off? This 'ole miserable situation's got me normal thinkin' paths crossed whixwize. And not alone, I'd wager."

"Not alone your whixwized thoughts, or dying in bed?" asked Caz with a smile.

"Sort o' a joint occasion is wot I'd 'ave in mind." Again the otter whistle, and they both laughed.

"I'm glad somebody thinks this is funny." Talea glared at them both.

"No," said Caz more quietly, "I don't think it's very funny at all, glowtop. But our hands and feet are bound, I can reach no familiar salve or balm from our supplies though I am bruised all over. I can't do anything about the damage to my body, but I try to medicate the spirit. Laughter is soothing to that."

Jon-Tom could see her turn away from the rabbit, her badly tousled hair even redder in the glow from the multiple fires. Her shoulders seemed to droop and he felt an instinctive desire to reach out and comfort her.

Odd the occasions when you have insights into the personalities of others, he thought. Talea struck him as unable to find much laughter at all in life, or, indeed, pleasure of any kind. He wondered at it. High spirits and energy were not necessarily reflective of happiness. He found himself feeling sorry for her.

Might as well feel sorry for yourself, an inner voice reminded him. If you don't slip loose of these pygmy paranoids you soon won't be able to feel sorry for anyone.

Unable to pull free of his bonds, he started working his way across the circle, trying to come up against a rock sharp enough to cut them. But the soil was thick and loamy, and he encountered nothing larger than a small pebble.

Failing to locate anything else he tried sawing patiently at his ropes with fingernails. The tough fiber didn't seem to be parting in the least. Eventually the effort exhausted him and he slid into a deep, troubled sleep. . . .

IV

It was morning when next he opened his eyes. Smoke drifted into the cloudy sky from smoldering camp fires, fleeing the still, swardless circle like bored wraiths.

Once more the carrying poles were brought into use and he felt himself lifted off the ground. Flor went up next to him, and the others were strung out behind. As before, the journey was brief. No more than three or four hundred yards from the site of the transitory village, he estimated.

Quite a crowd had come along to watch. The poles were removed. Mimpa gathered around the six limp bodies. Chattering among themselves, they arranged their captives in a circle, back to back, their legs stuck out like the spokes of a wheel. Arms were bound together so that no one could lie down or move without his five companions being affected. A large post was placed in the center of the circle, hammered exuberantly into the earth, and the prisoners shoulders bound to it.

They sat in the center of a second clearing, as smelly as the first. The Mimpa satisfied themselves that the center pole was securely in the ground and then moved away, jabbering excitedly and gesturing in a way Jon-Tom did not like at the captives ringing the pole.

Despite the coolness of the winter morning and the considerable cloud cover, he was sweating even without his cape. He'd worked his nails and wrists until all the nails were broken and blood stained the restraining fibers. They had been neither cut nor loosened.

Along with other useless facts he noted that the grass around them was still moist from the previous night's rain and that his feet were facing almost due north. Clothahump was struggling to speak. He couldn't make himself understood around the gag and in any case didn't have the strength in his aged frame to continue the effort much longer.

"We can move our legs, anyway," Jon-Tom pointed out, raising his bound feet and slamming them into the ground.

"Actually, they have secured us in an excellent defensive posture," agreed Caz. "Our backs are protected. We are not completely helpless."

"If any of those noulps show up, they'll find out what kind of legs I have," said Flor grimly, kicking out experimentally with her own feet.

"Lucky noulps," commented Mudge.

"What a mind you have, otter. *La cabeza bizzaro*." She drew her knees up to her chest and thrust out violently. "First predator that comes near me is going to lose some teeth. Or choke on my feet."

Jon-Tom kicked outward again, finding the expenditure of energy gratifying. "Maybe they'll be like sharks and have sensitive noses. Maybe they'll even turn toward the Mimpa, finding them easier prey than us."

"Mayhap," said Caz, "but I think you are all lost in wishful thinking, my friends." He nodded toward the muttering, watchful nomads. "Evidently they are not afraid of whatever they are waiting for. That suggests to me a most persistent and myopic adversary."

In truth, if they were anticipating the appearance of some ferocious carnivore, Jon-Tom couldn't understand why the Mimpa continued to remain close by. They appeared relaxed and expectant, roughly as fearful as children on a Sunday School picnic.

What kind of devouring "god" were they expecting?

"Don't you hear something?" At Talea's uncertain query everyone went quiet. The attitude of expectancy simultaneously rose among the assembled Mimpa.

This was it, then. Jon-Tom tensed and cocked his legs. He would kick until he couldn't kick any more, and if one of those predators got its jaws on him he'd follow Flor's suggestion and shove his legs down its throat until it choked to death. They wouldn't go out without a fight, and with six of them functioning in tandem they might stand an outside chance of driving off whatever creature or creatures were coming close.

Unfortunately, it was not simply a matter of throats.

By straining against the supportive pole Jon-Tom could just see over the weaving crest of the Sward. All he saw beyond riffling tufts of greenery was a stand of exquisite blue- and rose-hued flowers. It was several minutes before he realized that the flowers were moving.

"Which way is it?" asked Talea.

"Where you hear the noise." He nodded northward. "Over there someplace."

"Can you see it yet?"

"I don't think so." The blossoms continued to grow larger. "All I can see so far are flowers that appear to be coming toward us. Camouflage, or protective coloration maybe."

"I'm afraid it's likely to be rather more substantial than

that." Caz's nose was twitching rapidly now. Clothahump produced a muffled, urgent noise.

"I fear the kicking will do us no good," the rabbit continued dispiritedly. "They apparently have set us in the path of a Marching Porprut."

"A what?" Flor gaped at him. "Sounds like broken plumbing."

"An analogy closer to the mark than I think you suspect, night-maned." He grinned ruefully beneath his whiskers. "As you shall see all too soon, I fear."

They resumed fighting their restraints while the Mimpa jabbering rose to an anticipatory crescendo. The assembled aborigines were jumping up and down, pounding the ground with their spears and clubs, and pointing gleefully from captives to flowers.

Flor slumped, worn out from trying to free herself. "Why are they doing this to us? We never did anything to them."

"The minds of primitives do not function on the same cause-and-effect principles that rule our lives." Caz sniffed, his ears drooping, nose in constant motion. "Yes, it must be a Porprut. We should soon be able to see it."

Another sound was growing audible above the yells and howls of the hysterical Mimpa. It was a low pattering noise, like small twigs breaking underfoot or rain falling hard on a wooden roof or a hundred mice consuming plaster. Most of all it reminded Jon-Tom of people in a theater, watching quietly and eating popcorn. Eating noises, they were.

The row of solid Sward grass to the north began to rustle. Fascinated and horrified, the captives fought to see beyond the greenery.

Suddenly darker vegetation appeared, emerging above the thin, familiar blades of the Sward. At first sight it seemed only another type of weed, but each writhing, snakelike olive-colored stalk held a tiny circular mouth lined with fine fuzzy teeth. These teeth gnawed at the Sward grass. They ate slowly, but there were dozens of them. Blades went down as methodically as if before a green combine.

These tangled, horribly animate stems vanished into a brownish-green labyrinth of intertwined stems and stalks and nodules. Above them rose beautiful pseudo-orchids of rose and blue petals.

At the base of the mass of slowly moving vegetation was an army of feathery white worm shapes. These dug deeply into the soil. New ones were appearing continuously out of the bulk, pressing down to the earth like the legs of a millipede. Presumably others were pulled free behind as the creature advanced across the plain.

"'Tis like no animal I have ever heard of or seen," said Talea in disgust.

"It's not an animal. At least, I don't think it is," Jon-Tom murmured. "I think it's a plant. A communal plant, a mobile, self-contained vegetative ecosystem."

"More magic words." Talea fought at her bonds, with no more success than before. "They will not free us now."

"See," he urged them, intrigued as he was horrified, "how it constantly puts down new roots in front. That's how it moves."

"It does more than move," Caz observed. "It will scour the earth clean, cutting as neat and even a path across the Swordsward as any reaper."

"But we're not plants. We're not part of the Sward," Flor pointed out, keeping a dull stare on the advancing plant.

"I do not think the Porprut is much concerned with citizenship," said Caz tiredly. "It appears to be a most indiscriminate consumer. I believe it will devour anything unable or too stupid to get out of its path."

Much of the Porprut had emerged into the clearing. The Mimpa had moved back but continued to watch its advance

57

and the effect it produced in its eventual prey. It was much larger than Jon-Tom had first assumed. The front was a good twenty feet across. If the earth behind it was as bare as Caz suggested, then when the creature had finished with them they would not even leave behind their bones.

It was particularly horrible to watch because its advance was so slow. The Porprut traveled no more than an inch or two every few minutes at a steady, unvarying pace. At that rate it would take quite a while before they were all consumed. Those on the south side of the pole would be forced to watch, and listen, as their companions closer to the advancing plant were slowly devoured.

It promised a particularly gruesome death. That prospect induced quite a lot of pleasure among the watchful Mimpa.

Jon-Tom dug his feet into the soft, cleared earth and kicked violently outward. A spray of earth and gravel showered down on the forefront of the approaching creature. The writhing tendrils and the mechanically chewing mouths they supported took no notice of it. Even if the prisoners had their weapons and freedom, it still would have been more sensible to run than to stand and fight.

It was loathesome to think you were about to be killed by something neither hostile nor sentient, he mused. There was nothing to react to them. There was no head, no indication of a central nervous system, no sign of external organs of perception. No ears, no eyes. It ate and moved; it was supremely and unspectacularly efficient. A basic mass-energy converter that differed only in the gift of locomotion from a blade of grass, a tree, a blueberry bush.

In a certain perverse way he was able to admire the manner in which those dozens of insatiable mouths sucked and snapped up even the least hint of growth or the tiniest crawling bug from the ground.

"Fire, maybe," he muttered. "If I could get at my sparker,

or make a spell with the duar. Or if Clothahump could speak.'' But the wizard's struggles had been as ineffective as his magic was powerful. Unable to loosen his bonds or his gag, he could only stare, helpless as the rest, as the thousand-rooted flora edged toward them.

"I don't want to die," Flor whispered, "not like this."

"Now, we been through all that, luv," Mudge reminded her. " 'Tis no use worryin' about it each time it seems about t' 'appen, or you'll worry yourself t' death. Bloody disgustin' way t' go, wot?''

"What's the difference?" said Jon-Tom tiredly. "Death's death, one way or the other. Besides," he grinned humorlessly, "as much salad and vegetables as I've eaten, it only seems fair."

"How can you still joke about it?" Flor eyed him in disbelief.

"Because there's nothing funny about it, that's how."

"You're not making any sense."

"You don't make any sense, either!" he fairly screamed at her. "This whole world doesn't make any sense! Life doesn't make any sense! Existence doesn't make any sense!''

She recoiled from his violence. As abruptly as he'd lost control, he calmed himself. "And now that we've disposed of all the Great Questions pertaining to life, I suggest that if we all rock in unison we might be able to loosen this damn pole and make some progress southwestward. Ready? One, two, three . . ."

They used their legs as best they could, but it was hard to coordinate the actions of six people of very different size and strength and would have been even if they hadn't been tied in a circle around the central pole.

It swayed but did not come free of the ground. All this desperate activity was immensely amusing to the swart spectators behind them. As with everything else it was ignored by the patiently advancing Porprut.

It was only a foot or so from Jon-Tom's boots when the proverbial sparker he'd wished for suddenly appeared. Amid shouts of terror and outrage the Mimpa suddenly melted into the surrounding Sward. Something blistered the right side of Jon-Tom's face. The gout of flame roared a second time in his ears, then a third.

By then the Porprut had halted, its multiple mouths twisting and contorting in a horrible, silent parody of pain while the falsely beautiful red and blue blooms shriveled into black ash. It made not a sound while it was being incinerated.

A winged black shape was fluttering down among the captives. It wielded a small, curved knife in one wing. With this it sliced rapidly through their bonds.

"Damn my ears but I never t'ought we'd find ya!" said the excited Pog. His great eyes darted anxiously as he moved from one bound figure to the next. "Never would have, either, if we hadn't spotted da wagon. Dat was da only ting dat stuck up above da stinking grass." He finished freeing Clothahump and moved next to Jon-Tom.

Missing his spectacles, which remained in the wagon, Clothahump squinted at the bat while rubbing circulation back into wrists and ankles. The woven gag he threw into the Sward.

"Better a delayed appearance than none at all, good famulus. You have by rescuing us done the world a great service. Civilization owes you a debt, Pog."

"Yeah, tell me about it, boss. Dat's da solemn truth, an' I ain't about ta let civilization forget it."

Free again, Jon-Tom climbed to his feet and started off toward the wagon.

"Where are you going, boy?" asked the wizard.

"To get my duar." His fear had rapidly given way to

anger. "There are one or two songs I want to sing for our little friends. I didn't think I'd have the chance and I don't want to forget any of the words, not while they're still fresh in my mind. Wait till you hear some of 'em, Clothahump. They'll burn your ears, but they'll do worse to—"

"I do not have any ears in the sense you mean them, my boy. I suggest you restrain yourself."

"Restrain myself!" He whirled on the wizard, waved toward the rapidly carbonizing lump of the Porprut. "Not only were the little bastards going to feed us slowly to that monstrosity, but they were all sitting there laughing and having a hell of a fine time watching! Maybe revenge isn't in the lexicon of wizards, but it sure as hell is in mine."

"There's no need, my boy." Clothahump waddled over and put a comforting hand on Jon-Tom's wrist. "I assure you I bear no misplaced love for our hastily departed aboriginal associates. But as you can see, they *have* departed."

In truth, as he looked around, Jon-Tom couldn't see a single ugly arm, leg, or set of whiskers.

"It is difficult to put a spell on what you cannot see," said the wizard. "You also forget the unpredictability of your redoubtable talents. Impelled by uncontrolled anger, they might generate more trouble than satisfaction. I should dislike being caught in the midst of an army of, say, vengeful daemons who, not finding smaller quarry around, might turn their deviltry on us."

Jon-Tom slumped. "All right, sir. You know best. But if I ever see one of the little fuckers again I'm going to split it on my spearpoint like a squab!"

"A most uncivilized attitude, my friend," Caz joined them, rubbing his fur and brushing daintily at his soiled silk stockings. "One in which I heartily concur." He patted Jon-Tom on the back.

"That's what this expedition needs: less thinking and more bloodthirstiness. Cut and slash, hack and rend!"

"Yeah, well . . ." Jon-Tom was becoming a bit embarrassed at his own mindless fury. It was hardly the image he held of himself. "I don't think revenge is all that unnatural an impulse."

"Of course it's not," agreed Caz readily. "Perfectly natural."

"What's perfectly natural?" Flor limped up next to them. Her right leg was still asleep. Despite the ordeal they'd just undergone, Jon-Tom thought she looked as magnificent as ever.

"Why, our tall companion's desire to barbeque any of our disagreeable captors that he can catch."

"*Si*, I'm for that." She started for the wagon. "Let's get our weapons and get after them."

This time it was Jon-Tom who extended the restraining hand. Now he was truly upset at the manner in which he'd been acting, especially in front of the dignified, sensible Caz.

"I'm not talking about forgiving and forgetting," he told her, shivering a little as he always did at the physical contact of hand and arm, "but it's not practical. They could ambush us in the Sward, even if they hung around."

"Well we can damn well sure have a look!" she protested. "What kind of a man are you?"

"Want to look and see?" he shot back challengingly.

She stared at him a moment longer, then broke into an uncontrollable giggle. He laughed along with her, as much from nervousness and the relief of release as from the poor joking.

"Hokay, hokay," she finally admitted, "so we have more important things to do, *si*?"

"Precisely, young lady." Clothahump gestured toward the wagon. "Let us put ourselves back in shape and be once more on our path."

But Jon-Tom waited behind while the others reentered the wagon and set to the task of organizing the chaos the Mimpa had made of its contents.

Walking back to the cleared circle which had so nearly been their burial place, he found a large black and purple form bending over a burned-out pile of vegetation. Falameezar had squatted down on his haunches and was picking with one massive claw at the heap of ash and woody material.

"We're all grateful as hell, Falameezar. No one more so than myself."

The dragon glanced numbly back at him, barely taking notice of his presence. His tone was ponderously, unexpectedly, somber.

"I have made a grave mistake, Comrade. A grave mistake." The dragon sighed. His attention was concentrated on the crisped, smoking remains of the Porprut as he picked and prodded at the blackened tendrils with his claws.

"What's troubling you?" asked Jon-Tom. He walked close and affectionately patted the dragon's flank.

The head swung around to gaze at him mournfully. "I have destroyed," he moaned, "an ideal communal society. A perfect communistic organism."

"You don't know that's what it was, Falameezar," Jon-Tom argued. "It might have been a normal creature with a single brain."

"I do not think so." Falameezar slowly shook his head, looking and sounding as depressed as it was possible for a dragon to be. Little puffs of smoke occasionally floated up from his nostrils.

"I have looked inside the corpse. There are many individual sections of creature inside, all twisted and intertwined together, intergrown and interdependent. All functioning in perfect, bossless harmony."

Jon-Tom stepped away from the scaly side. "I'm sorry."

He thought carefully, not daring to offend the dragon but worried about its state of mind. "Would you have rather you'd left it alone to nibble us to death?"

"No, Comrade, of course not. But I did not realize fully what it consisted of. If I had, I might have succeeded in making it shift its path around you. So I have been forced to murder a perfect natural example of what civilized society should aspire to." He sighed. "I fear now I must do penance, my comrade friend."

A little nervous, Jon-Tom gestured at the broad, endless field of the Swordsward. "There are many dangers out there, Comrade. Including the still monstrous danger we have talked so much about."

It was turning to evening. Solemn clouds promised another night of rain, and there was a chill in the air that even hinted at some snow. It was beginning to feel like real winter out on the grass-clad plain.

A cold wind sprang from the direction of the dying sun, went through Jon-Tom's filthy leathers. "We need your help, Falameezar."

"I am sorry, Comrade. I have my own troubles now. You will have to face future dangers without me. For I am truly sorrowful over what I have done here, the more so because with a little thought it might have been avoided." He turned and lumbered off into the rising night, his feet crushing down the Sward, which sprang up resiliently behind him.

"Are you sure?" Jon-Tom followed to the edge of the cleared circle, put out imploring hands. "We really need you, Comrade. We have to help each other or the great danger will overwhelm all of us. Remember the coming of the bosses of bosses!"

"You have your other friends, your other comrades to assist you, Jon-Tom," the dragon called back to him across the waves of the green sea. "I have no one but myself."

"But you're one of us!"

The dragon shook his head. "No, not yet. For a time I had willed to myself that it was so. But I have failed, or I would have seen a solution to your rescue that did not involve this murder."

"How could you? There wasn't time!" He could barely see the dark outline now.

"I'm sorry, Comrade Jon-Tom." Falameezar's voice was faint with distance and guilt. "Good-bye."

"Good-bye, Falameezar." Jon-Tom watched until the dragon had completely vanished, then looked disappointedly at the ground. "Dammit," he muttered.

He returned to the wagon. Lamps were lit now. Under their familiar, friendly glow Caz and Mudge were checking the condition of the dray team. Flor, Clothahump, and Talea were restocking their scattered supplies. The wizard's glasses were pinched neatly on his beak. He looked out and down as Jon-Tom, hands shoved into his pockets and gaze on the ground, sauntered up to him.

"Problems, my boy?"

Jon-Tom raised his eyes, nodded southward. "Falameezar's left us. He was upset at having to kill the damn Porprut. I tried my best to argue him out of it, but he'd made up his mind."

"You did well even to try," said Clothahump comfortingly. "Not many would have the courage to debate a dragon's decision. They are terribly stubborn. Well, no matter. We shall make our way without him."

"He was the strongest of us," Jon-Tom murmured disappointedly. "He did more in thirty seconds to the Porprut and the Mimpa than all the rest of us were able to do at all. No telling how much trouble just his presence prevented."

"It is true we shall miss his brute strength," said the wizard, "but intelligence and wisdom are worth far more than any amount of muscle."

"Maybe so." Jon-Tom vaulted into the back of the wagon. "But I'd still feel better with a little more brute strength on our side."

"We must not bemoan our losses," Clothahump said chidingly, "but must push ahead. At least we will no longer be troubled by the Mimpa." He let out an unwizardly chuckle. "It will be days before they cease running."

"Do we continue on tonight, then?"

"For a short while, just enough to leave this immediate area behind. Then we shall mount a guard, just in case, and continue on tomorrow in daylight. The weather looks unpleasant and we will have difficulty enough in holding to our course.

"Then too, while I don't know how you young folk are feeling, I'm not ashamed to confess that the body inside this old shell is very much in need of sleep."

Jon-Tom had no argument with that. Falameezar or no Falameezar, Mimpa or no Mimpa, he was dead tired. Which was a good deal better than what he'd earlier thought he'd be this night: plain dead.

The storm did not materialize the next day, nor the one following, though the Swordsward received its nightly dose of steady rain. Flor was taking a turn at driving the wagon. It was early evening and they would be stopping soon to make camp.

A full moon was rising behind layers of gray eastern clouds, a low orange globe crowning the horizon. It turned the rain clouds to gauze as it lifted behind them, shedding ruddy light over the darkening sward. Snowflakelike reflections danced elf steps on the residue of earlier rain.

From the four patient yoked lizards came a regular, heavy swish-swish as they pushed through the wet grasses. Easy conversation and occasional laughter punctuated by Mudge's lilting whistle drifted out from the enclosed wagon. Small things rose cautiously to study the onward trundling wooden beast before dropping down into grass or groundholes.

Jon-Tom parted the canvas rain shield and moved to sit down on the driver's seat next to Flor. She held the reins easily in one hand, as though born to the task, and glanced over at him. Her free hand rested across her thighs. Her long black hair was a darker bit of shadow, like a piece of broken black plate glass, against the night. Her eyes were luminous and huge.

He looked away from their curious stare and down at his hands. They twisted and moved uncomfortably in his lap, as though trying to find a place to hide; little five-footed creatures he could not cage.

"I think we have a problem."

"Only one?" She grinned at him, barely paying attention to the reins now. Without being told, the lizards would continue to plod onward on their present course.

"But that's what life's all about, isn't it? Solving a series of problems? When they're as varied and challenging as these," and she flicked long nails in the air, a brief gesture that casually encompassed two worlds and a shift in dimension, "why, that adds to the spice of it."

"That's not the kind of problem I'm talking about, Flor. This one is personal."

She looked concerned. "Anything I can do to help?"

"Possibly." He looked up at her. "I think I'm in love with you. I think I've always been in love with you. I . . ."

"That's enough," she told him, raising a restraining hand and speaking gently but firmly. "In the first place, you can't have always been in love with me because you haven't known me for always. Metaphysics aside, Jon-Tom, I don't think you've known me long enough.

"In the second place, I don't think you're really in love with me. I think you're in love with the image of me you've seen and added to in your imagination, *es verdad, amigo*? To be crude about it, you're in love with my looks, my body. Don't think I hold it against you. It's not your fault. Your desires and wants are a product of your environment.''

This was not going the way he'd hoped, he mused confusedly. "Don't be so sure that you know all about me either, Flor.''

"I'm not.'' She was not offended by his tone. "I mean, how have you 'seen' me, Jon-Tom? How have you 'known' me? Short skirt, tight sweater, always the perfect smile, perfectly groomed, long hair flouncing and pom-poms jouncing, isn't that about it?''

"Don't patronize me.''

"I'm not patronizing you, dammit! Use your head, *hombre*. I may look like a pinup, but I don't think like one. You can't be in love with me because you don't know me.''

" 'Ere now, wot the 'ell are you two fightin' about?'' Mudge stuck his furry face out from behind the canvas. " 'Tis too bloomin' nice a night for such witterin'.''

"Back out, Mudge,'' said Jon-Tom curtly at the interruption. "This is none of your business.''

"Oh, now let's not get our bowels in an uproar, mate. Suit yourself.'' With a last glance at them both, he obligingly retreated inside.

"I won't deny that I find you physically attractive, Flor.''

"Of course you do. You wouldn't be normal if you didn't.'' She stared out across the endless dark plain, kissed with orange by the rising moon. "Every man has, ever since I was twelve years old. I've been through this before.'' She looked back at him.

"The point is you don't know me, the real Flores Quintera. So you can't be in love with her. I'm flattered, but if we're going to have any kind of chance at a real relationship, we'd best start fresh, here and now. Without any preconceived notions about what I'm like, what you'd like me to be like, or what I represent to you. *Comprende*?''

"Flor, don't you think I've had a look at the real you these past weeks?" Try as he might, he couldn't help sounding defensive.

"Sure you have, but that's hardly long enough. And you can't be certain that's the real me, either. Maybe it's only another facet of my real personality, whose aspects are still changing."

"Wait a minute," he said hopefully. "You said, 'chance at a real relationship.' Does that mean you think we have a chance for one?"

"I've no idea." She eyed him appraisingly. "You're an interesting man, Jon-Tom. The fact that you can work magic here with your music is fascinating to me. I couldn't do it. But I don't know you any better than you know me. So why don't we start clean, huh? Pretend I'm just another girl you've just met. Let's call this our first date." She nodded skyward. "The moon's right for it."

"Kind of tough to do," he replied, "after you've just poured out a deeply felt confession of love. You took that apart like a professor dissecting a tadpole."

"I'm sorry, Jon-Tom." She shrugged. "That's part of the way I am. Part of the real me, as much as the pom-poms or my love of the adventure of this world. You have to learn to accept them all, not just the ones you like." She tried to sound encouraging. "If it's any consolation, while I may not love you, I do like you."

"That's not much."

"Why don't you get rid of that hurt puppy-dog look, too," she suggested. "It won't do you any good. Come on, now. Cheer up! You've let out what you had to let out, and I haven't rebuffed you completely." She extended an open hand. "*Buenos noches,* Jon-Tom. I'm Flores Maria Quintera. *Como 'stas?*"

He looked silently at her, then down at the proferred palm. He took it with a resigned sigh. "Jon-Tom...Jon Meriweather. Pleased to meet you."

After that, they got along a little more easily. The puncturing of Jon-Tom's romantic balloon released tension along with hopes. . . .

V

It was a very ordinary-looking river, Jon-Tom thought. Willow and cypress and live oak clustered thirstily along its sloping banks. Small scaly amphibians played in thick underbrush. Reeds claimed the quiet places of the slow-moving eddies.

The bank on the far side was equally well fringed with vegetation. From time to time they encountered groups of animals and humans occupied in various everyday tasks on the banks. They would be fishing, or washing clothes, or simply watching the sun do the work of carrying forth the daytime.

The wagon turned eastward along the southern shore of the Sloomaz-ayor-le-Weentli, heading toward the growing massif of the mountains and passing word of the coming invasion to any warmlander who would listen. But the River of Twos was a long way from Polastrindu, and the Jo-Troom Gate and the depredations of the Plated Folk only components of legend to the river dwellers.

All agreed with the travelers on one matter, however: the problem of trying to pass downstream and through the Teeth.

"Eh?" said one wizened old otter in response to their query, "ye want to go where?" In contrast to Mudge the oldster's fur was streaky-white. So were his facial whiskers. Arthritis bent him in the middle and gnarled his hands and feet.

"Ye'll never make it. Ye won't make it past the entrance and if ye do, ye'll not find yer way through the rock. Too many have tried and none have ever come back."

"We have resources others did not have," said Clothahump confidentially. "I am something of a formidable conjurer, and my associate here is a most powerful spellsinger." He gestured at the lanky form of Jon-Tom. They had stepped down from the wagon to talk with the elder. The dray lizards munched contentedly on rich riverbank growth.

The old otter put aside his fishing pole and studied them. His short whistle indicated he didn't think much of either man or turtle, unseen mental talents notwithstanding.

"Sorcerers ye may be, but the passage through the Teeth by way of the river is little but a legend. Ye can travel by legend only in dreams. Which is all that's likely to be left of ye if ye persist in this folly. Sixty years I've lived on the banks of the Sloomaz-ayor-le-Weentli." He gestured fondly at the flowing water behind him. "Never have I heard tell of anyone fool enough to try and go into the mountains by way of it."

"Sounds convincin' enough for me, 'e does." Mudge leaned out of the wagon and spoke brightly. "That settles that: time to turn about for 'ome."

Jon-Tom looked over his shoulder at the green-capped face. "That does not settle it."

Mudge shrugged cheerfully. "Can't biff a bloke for tryin', mate. I ought t' know better, I knows it, but somethin' in me insists on tryin' t' fight insanity in the ranks."

"Ya ought ta have more faith in da master." Pog fluttered above the wagon and chided the otter. "Ya oughta believe in him and his abilities and great talents." He drifted lower above Mudge and whispered. "Frankly, we all been candidates for da fertilizer pile since we started on dis half-assed trek, but if da boss tinks we gots to go on, we don't got much choice. Don't make him mad, chum."

But Jon-Tom had overheard. He walked back to stand next to the wagon. "Clothahump knows what he's doing. I'm sure if things turned suicidal he'd listen to reason."

"Ya tink dat, does ya?" Pog's small sharp teeth flashed as he hovered in front of Jon-Tom. One wing pointed toward the turtle, who was still conversing with the old otter.

"Da boss has kept Mudge from runnin' off and abandonin' dis trip wid t'reats. What makes ya tink he'd be more polite where you're concerned?"

"He owes me a debt," said Jon-Tom. "If I insisted on remaining behind, I don't think he'd try to coerce me."

Pog laughed, whirled around in black circles. "Dat's what you tink! Ya may be a spellsinger, Jon-Tom-mans, but you're as naïve as a baby's belly!' He rose and skimmed off over the river, hunting for insects and small flying lizards.

"Is that your opinion too, Mudge? Do you think Clothahump would keep me from leaving if that's what I wanted?"

"I wouldn't 'ave 'alf a notion, mate. But since you say you want to keep on with this madness, there ain't no point in arguin' it, is there?" He retreated back inside the wagon, leaving Jon-Tom to turn and walk slowly back down to the riverbank. Try as he would to shove the thought aside, it continued to nag him. He looked a little differently at Clothahump.

"There be only one way ye might get even partways through," continued the old otter, "and if yer lucky, out again alive. That's to have a damn good boatman. One who knows how to maneuver on the Second river. That's the only way ye'll even get inside the mountain."

"Can you recommend such an individual?" asked Clothahump.

"Oh, I know of several good boatfolk," the oldster boasted. He turned, spat something brown and viscous into the water, then looked from the turtle to Jon-Tom. "Trouble for ye is that ain't none of 'em idiots. And that's going to be as important a qualification as any kind of river skill, because only an idiot's going to try and take ye where ye wants to go!"

"We have no need of your sarcasm, young fellow," said Clothahump impatiently, "only of your advice. If you would rather not give us the benefit of your knowledge, then we will do our best to find it elsewhere."

"All right, all right. Hang onto ye shell, ye great stuffed diviner of catastrophes!

"There's one, just one, who might be willing to help ye out. He's just fool enough to try it and just damnblast good enough to bring it off. Whether ye can talk him into doin' so is something else again." He gestured to his left.

"Half a league farther on you'll find that the riverbank rises steeplike. Still farther you'll eventual come across several large oaks overlooking a notch or drop in the cliffs. He's got his place down there. Goes by the name of Bribbens Oxley."

"Thank you for your help," said Clothahump.

"Would it help if we mentioned your name to him?" Jon-Tom wondered.

The otter laughed, his whistles skipping across the water. "Hai, man, the only place me name would help you is in the better whorehouses in Wottletowne, and that's not where ye are going!''

Clothahump reached into one of his plastron compartments, withdrew a small silver coin, and offered it to the otter. The oldster stepped away, waving his hands.

"No, no, not for me, friend! I take no payment for assisting the doomed." He gathered up his pole and gear and ambled crookedly off upstream.

"Nice of him to give us that name," said Jon-Tom, watching the other depart. "Since he wouldn't take the money, why didn't we try to help his arthritis?"

"Arth . . . his joint-freezes, you mean, boy?" Clothahump adjusted his spectacles. "It is a long spell and requires time we do not have." He turned resolutely toward the wagon.

Jon-Tom continued to stand there, watching the crippled otter make his loping way eastward. "But he was so helpful."

"We do not know that yet," the turtle insisted. "I was willing to chance a little silver on it, but not a major medical spell. He could simply have told us his stories to impress us, and the name to get rid of us."

"Awfully cynical, aren't you?"

Clothahump gazed up at him as they both scrambled into the wagon. "My boy, the first hundred years of life teaches you that no one is inherently good. The next fifty tells you that no one is inherently bad, but is shaped by his surroundings. And after two hundred years . . . give me a hand there, that's a good boy." Jon-Tom helped lug the bulky body over the wooden rail and into the wagon.

"After two hundred years, you learn that nothing is predictable save that the universe is full of illusions. If the cosmos withholds and distorts its truths, why should we expect less of such pitifully minute components of it as that otter . . . or you, or me?"

Jon-Tom was left to ponder that as the wagon once more rolled noisily westward.

Everyone hoped the oldster's recommendation was sounder than his estimate of distance, for it took them two full days of traveling before they encountered three massive oaks dominating a low dip in the riverbank. While still a respectable width, the river had narrowed between the higher banks and ran with more power, more confidence, and occasional flecks of foam.

Still, it didn't appear particularly dangerous or hard to navigate to Jon-Tom. He wondered at the need for a guide. The river was far more gentle than the rapids they had passed (admittedly with Falameezar's muscle) on the journey to Polastrindu.

The path that wound its careful way down to the shore was narrow and steep. The lizards balked at it. They had to be whipped and cajoled downward, their claws shoving at the dirt as they tried to move backward instead of down the slope. Gravel and rocks slid over the side of the path. Once they nearly had a wheel slip over the edge, threatening to plunge wagon and lizards and all ass-over-heels into the tiny chasm. Verbally and physically, however, they succeeded in eventually getting the lizards to the bottom.

Reeds and ferns dominated the little cove in which they found themselves. To the left, hunkered up tight against the cliffs, they found a single low building. It was not much bigger than a shack. A few small circular windows winked like eyes as they approached it, peering out beneath brows of adobe and thatching. Smoke curled lazily from the brown and gray rock chimney made of rounded river stones.

What attracted their attention the most was the boat. It was moored in the shallows. Water lapped gently at its flanks. A well-turned railing ran around the deck, and there was no central cabin.

A heavy steering oar bobbed at the stern. There was also a single mast from which a fore-rigged sail hung limp and tired, loosely draped across the boom.

"I hope our guide is as tough as his boat looks to be," said Talea as they mounted the covered porch fronting the house.

"Only one way to find out." Jon-Tom ducked beneath the porch roof. The door set in the front of the building was cut from aged cypress. There was no window or peephole set into it.

Pog found a comfortable cross-beam, hung head down from it, and let out a relieved sigh. "Not fancy, maybe, but a peaceful place ta live. I've always liked rivers."

"How can you like anything?" Talea chided him as they inspected the house. "You see everything upside down."

"Lizard crap," said the bat with a grunt. "You're da ones dat sees everyting upside down."

Clothahump knocked on the door. There was no response. He rapped again, harder. Still nothing, so he tried the handle.

"Locked," he said curtly. "I could spell it open easily enough, but that would mean naught if the owner is not present." He sounded concerned. "Could he perhaps be off on business with a second boat?"

"If so," Jon-Tom started to say, "it wouldn't hurt us to have a short rest. We could wait until—"

The door opened inward abruptly. The frog that confronted them stood just over five feet tall, slightly less than Talea, a touch more than Mudge. Tight snakeskin shorts stopped just above his knees. The long fringework that lined its hem fell almost to his ankles. It swayed slightly as he stood inspecting them.

The shorts were matched by a fringed vest of similar material. Beneath it he wore a leathern shirt that ended above his elbows. Fringe reached from there to his wrists. He wore no hat, but a single necklace made from the vertebrae of some large fish formed a white collar around his green-and-yellow-spotted neck.

His ventral side was a pale blue that shaded to pink at the pulsing throat. The rest of his body was dark green marked with yellow and black spots. Compared to, say, Mudge or Clothahump, the coloration was somewhat overwhelming. He would be difficult to lose sight of, even on a dark day.

Examining them one at a time, the frog surveyed his visitors. He thoroughly sized up every member of the group, not missing Pog where he hung from the rafter. The bat's head had swiveled around to stare curiously at the boatman.

The frog blinked, spoke in a low monotone distinguished by its lack of inflection, friendly or otherwise.

"Cash or credit?"

"Cash," replied Clothahump. "Assuming that we can work out an agreement to our mutual satisfaction."

"Mutual my ass," said the frog evenly. "I'm the one who has to be satisfied." When Clothahump offered no rebuttal, the boatman expressionlessly stepped back inside. "Come on in, then. No point in standing out in the damp. Sick customers make lousy passengers."

They filed in, Jon-Tom and Flor electing to take seats on the floor rather than risk collision with the low, thick-beamed ceiling. In addition, the few chairs looked too rickety to support much weight.

The frog moved to a large iron stove set against a back wall. A large kettle simmered musically on the hot metal. He removed the cover, stirred the contents a few times, then sampled it with a large wooden ladle. The odor was foul. Taking a couple of large wooden shakers from a nearby wall shelf, he dumped some of their powdered contents into the kettle, stirred the liquid a little more, and replaced the iron cover, apparently satisfied.

Then he sauntered back to the thick wooden table in the center of the room. Boating equipment, hooks, ropes, woodworker's tools, braces and pegs and hammers lined the other two walls.

At the back was a staircase leading downward. Possibly it went to the hold, or to clammier and more suitable sleeping quarters.

Leaning forward across the table, the frog clasped wet palms together and stared across at Clothahump and Jon-Tom. His long legs were bent sideways beneath the wood so as not to kick his guests. Caz was standing near one wall inspecting some of the aquatic paraphernalia. Talea hunted for a suitable chair. She finally found one and dragged it up to the table, where she joined the other three.

"My name's Bribbens Oxley, of the sandmarsh Oxleys," the frog told them. "I'm the best boatman on this or any other river." This was stated quietly, without any particular emphasis or boastfulness.

"I know every loggerhead, every tree stump, every knot, boulder, and rapids for the six hundred leagues between the Teeth and Kreshfarm-in-the-Geegs. I know the hiding places of the mudfishers and the waterdrotes' secret holes. I can smell a storm two days before it hits and ride a wave gentle enough not to upset a full teacup. I even know the exact place where ten thousand years ago the witch Wutz tripped over the cauldron full of magic which doubled the river, and I know therefore whence comes the name Sloomaz-ayor-le-Weentli."

Jon-Tom gazed back out the still open door, past the dangling Pog, to what still appeared to be a quite ordinary stream. Somewhere, he imagined, the river had to fork, hence the nicknames River of Twos, Double River, and the others. Since the fork was not here and was unlikely to be between this spot and the mountains, it had to lie upstream.

He would soon have the chance to find out, he thought, as he returned his attention to the conversation.

"I can turn my craft circles 'round any other craft and reach my destination in half their time. I can ride out weather that puts other merchantmen and fisherfolk under their beds. I'm not afraid of anything in the river or out of it.

"I personally guarantee to deliver cargo and/or passengers to their chosen destination for the agreed-upon fee, on the date determined in advance, if not earlier, or to forfeit all of my recompense.

"I can outfight anyone, even someone twice my size," he said, glancing challengingly at Jon-Tom, who tactfully did not respond, "outeat any other intelligent amphibian or mammal, and I have twenty-two matured tadpoles who can attest to my other abilities.

"My fee is one goldpiece per league. I'm no cook, and you can provide your own fodder, or fish if you like. As to drink, river water's good enough for me, for I'm as home in it as in this house, but if you get drunk on my craft you'll soon find yourself swimming for shore. Any questions so far?"

No one said anything. "Anyone care to dispute anything I've said?" Still no comment from the visitors. Full of impatient energy, Talea left her seat and stalked to the door, stood there leaning against the jamb and staring out at the river. Bribbens watched her and nodded approvingly.

"Right." He leaned back in his chair, picked idly at the tangled fringe of his right sleeve. "Now then. How many of you are going, is there cargo, and where is it you wish to go?"

Clothahump tapped the table with short fingers. "There is no cargo save our nominal supplies and personal effects, and all of us are going." He added uncertainly, "Does our number affect the fee?"

The frog shoved out his considerable lower lip. "Makes no difference to me. Fee's the same whether one of you goes or all of you. The boat has to travel the same distance upstream and the same distance down again when I return. One goldpiece per league."

"That's part of the reason for my inquiry," said the wizard.

"The goldpiece per league?" Bribbens eyed him archly.

"No. The direction. You see, it's downstream we wish to go, not up."

The frog belched once. "Downstream. It's only three days from here to the base of the Teeth. Not much between. A couple of villages and that's all, and them only a day from here. No one lives at the base of the mountains. They're all afraid of the occasional predator who slinks down out of the Teeth, like the flying lizards, the Ginnentes who nest in the crags and crevices. I hardly ever find anyone who wants to go that way. Most everything lies upstream."

"Nevertheless, we wish to travel down," said the wizard. "Far farther, I dare say, than you are accustomed to going. Of course, if you chose not to go, we will understand. It would only be normal for you to be afraid."

Bribbens leaned forward sharply, was eye to eye with Clothahump across the table, his body stretched over the wood, webbed hands flat on the surface.

"Bribbens Oxley is afraid of nothing in or out of the river. Visitor or not, I don't like your drift, turtle."

Clothahump did not pull away from the batrachian face inches from his own. "I am a wizard and fear only that which I cannot understand, boatman. We wish to travel not to the base of the mountains but through them. Down the river as far as it will carry us and then out the other side of Zaryt's Teeth."

The frog sat back down slowly. "You realize that's just a rumor. There may not be any other side."

"That makes it interesting, doesn't it?" said Clothahump.

Fingers drummed on the table, marking time and thoughts. "One hundred goldpieces," Bribbens said at last.

"You said the fee didn't vary," Talea reminded him from the doorway. "One gold piece a league."

"That is for travel on earth, female. Hell is more expensive country."

"I thought you said you weren't afraid." Jon-Tom was careful to make it sound like a normal question, devoid of taunting.

"I'm not," countered Bribbens, "but neither am I stupid. If we survive this journey I want more in return than personal satisfaction.

"Once we enter the mountains I shall be dealing with unknown waters . . . and probably other unknowns as well. Nevertheless," he added with becoming indifference, "it should be interesting, as you say, wizard. Water is water, wherever it may be."

But Clothahump pushed away from the table, spoke grimly. "I'm sorry, Bribbens, but we can't pay you."

"A wizard who can't transmute gold?"

"I can," insisted Clothahump, looking embarrassed. "It's just that I've misplaced the damn spell, and it's too complicated to try and fake." He checked his plastron again. "I can give you a few pieces now and the rest, uh, later."

Bribbens rose, slapped the table loudly with both hands. "It's been an interesting conversation and I wish you all luck, which you are going to need even more than you do a good and willing boatman. Now if you don't mind excusing me, I think my supper's about ready." He started back toward the stove.

"Wait a minute." Clothahump frowned at Jon-Tom. Bribbens halted. "We can pay you, though I'm not sure how much."

"My boy, there is no point in lying. I don't do business that way. We will just have to—"

"No, we can, Clothahump." He grinned at Mudge. "I'm something of a beggar in wolf's clothing."

"Wot?" Then the otter's face brightened with remembrance. "I'd bloody well forgotten that night, mate."

Jon-Tom unsnapped his cape. It landed heavily on the table, and Bribbens eyed it with interest. As he and the others watched, Jon-Tom and Mudge slit the cape's lining. Coins poured from the rolled lower edge.

When the counting was concluded, the remnant of Jon-Tom's hastily salvaged gambling winnings totaled sixty-eight gold pieces and fifty-two silver.

"Not quite enough."

"Please," said Flor, "isn't it sufficient? We'll pay you the rest. . . ."

"Later. I know." The boatman would not bend. "Later is a synonym for never, female. Would you wish me to convey you 'almost' to the end of the river and then make you swim the rest of the way? By the same light, I will not accept 'almost' my determined fee."

"If you're as able as you are stubborn, you're for sure the best boatman on the river," grumbled Jon-Tom.

"There's something more." Talea was still leaning in the doorway, but now she was staring outside. "What about our wagon and team?"

"Sure!" Jon-Tom rose, almost bumped his head, and looked down at Bribbens. "We've got a wagon which any farmer or fisherman would be proud to own. It's big enough to carry all of us and more, and sturdy enough to have done it all the way across the Swordsward from Polastrindu. There are harnesses, yokes, four solid dray lizards, and spare wheels and supplies, all made from the finest materials. It was given to us by the city council of Polastrindu itself.''

Bribbens looked uncertain. "I'm not a tradesman.''

"At least have a look at it," Flor implored him.

The frog hesitated, then padded out onto the porch, ignoring Pog. The others filed out after him.

Tradesman or not, Bribbens inspected the wagon and its team intimately, from the state of the harness buckles to the lizard's teeth.

When he was finished underneath the wagon, he crawled out, stared at Clothahump. "I accept. It will make up the difference.''

"How munificent of you!" Caz had taken no part in the bargaining, but his expression revealed he was something less than pleased by the outcome. "The wagon alone is worth twenty goldpieces. You would leave us broke and destitute.''

"Perhaps," admitted Bribbens, "but I'm the only one who stands a chance of leaving you broke and destitute at your desired destination. I won't argue with you." He paused, added as an afterthought, "Dinner's about ready to boil over. Make up your minds.''

"We have little choice," said Clothahump, "and no further use for the wagon anyway." He glared at Caz, who turned away and studied the river, unrepentant. "We agree. When can we start?''

"Tomorrow morning. I have my own preparations to make and supplies to lay in. Meanwhile, I suggest you all get a good night's sleep." Bribbens looked at the cliffs which rose to the east.

"Into the Teeth." He fixed a bulbous eye on Jon-Tom. "You'll have no need for money in there, nor on the other side, if there is one. My offspring will find it here if I don't come back, and it will do them more good than the dead.''

Humming to himself, he turned and padded back toward his house.

They slept in the wagon again that night. As Bribbens formally explained, their fee included only his services and transport and did not extend to the use of his home.

But the following morning he was up before the sun and was ready to depart before they'd hardly awakened. "I like to get an early start," he explained as they gathered themselves for the journey. "I give value for money. You pay for a day's travel, you get a day's travel."

Caz adjusted his monocle. "Reasonable enough, considering that we've given a month's pay for every day we're likely to travel."

Bribbens looked unperturbed. "I once saw a rabbit who'd had all his fur shaved off. He was a mighty funny-looking critter."

"And I," countered Caz with equal aplomb, "once saw a frog whose mouth was too big for his head. He experienced a terrible accident."

"What kind of accident?" inquired Bribbens, unimpressed.

"Foot-in-mouth. Worst case I ever saw. It turned out to be fatal."

"Frogs aren't subject to hoof-in-mouth."

The rabbit smiled tolerantly. "My foot in his mouth."

The two held their stares another moment. Then Bribbens smiled, an expression particularly suited to frogs.

"I've seen it happen to creatures other than my own kind, three-eyes."

Caz grinned back. "It's common enough, I suppose. And I see better out of one eye than most people do out of two."

"See your way to moving a little faster, then. We can't sleep here all day." The boatman ambled off.

Talea was leaning out of the wagon, brushing sleepily at reluctant curls tight as steel springs.

"Since you layabouts aren't ready yet, I'm going to take the time to secure my team and wagon and lay out fodder for them," said the frog.

"Possessive little bugger, ain't 'e?" Mudge commented.

"It's his wagon and team now, Mudge." Jon-Tom carefully slipped his staff into the loops crossing his back beneath the flashing emerald cape. "They're in his care. Just like we are."

When they were all assembled on the boat and had tied down their packs and supplies, Bribbens loosed the ropes, neatly coiled them in place, and leaned on the long steering oar. The boat slid out into the river. Pog shifted his grip on the spreaders high up on the mast and watched as silver sky raced past blue ground.

Before very long the current caught them. The cove with its mud-and-thatch house vanished behind. Ahead lay a gray-brown wall of granite and ice; home to arboreal carnivores, undisciplined winds, and racing cloud-crowns.

Jon-Tom lay down on the edge of the craft and let a hand trail lazily in the water. It was difficult to think of the journey they'd embarked upon as threatening. The water was warmed from its long journey down from distant Kreshfarm-in-the-Geegs. The sun often snuck clear of obstructing clouds to lie pleasantly on one's face. And there seemed no chance of rain until the night.

"Three days to get to the base of the mountains, you said?"

"That's right, man," Bribbens replied. The boatman did not look at Jon-Tom when he spoke. His right arm was curled around the shaft of the steering oar, and his eyes were on the river ahead. He sat in a chair built onto the railing at the craft's stern. A long, thin curved pipe dangled from thick lips. River breeze carried the thin smoke from its small white bowl up into the sky.

"How far into the mountains does the river go?" Flor was on her knees, staring over the front of the boat. Her voice was full of expectation and excitement.

"Nobody knows," said Bribbens. "Leagues, maybe weeks worth. Maybe only a few hours."

"Where does it end, do you suppose? In an underground lake?"

"Helldrink," said the boatman.

"And what's Helldrink, *Señor Rana*?"

"A rumor. A story. An amalgam of all the fears of every creature that's ever navigated on the waters in times of trouble, during bad storms or on leaking ships, in foul harbors or under the lash of a drunken captain. I've spent my life on the water and in it. It would be worth the trip to me if we should find it, even should it mean my death. It's where all true sailors should end up."

"Does that mean we're likely to get a refund?" inquired Caz.

The boatman laughed. "You're a sharp fellow, aren't you, rabbit? I hope if we find it you'll still be able to joke."

"There should be no difficulty," said Clothahump. "I, too, have heard legends of Helldrink. They say that you know it is there before you encounter it. All you need do is deposit us safely clear of it and we will continue our journey on foot. You may proceed to your sailor's discovery however you wish."

"Sounds like a fine scenario, sir," the boatman agreed. "Assuming I can make a landing somewhere safe, if there is a safe landing. Otherwise you may have to accompany me on my discovery."

"So you're risking your life to learn the truth about this legend?" asked Flor.

"No, woman. I'm risking my life for a hundred pieces of gold. And a wagon and team. I'm risking my life for twenty-two offspring. I'm risking my life because I never turned down a job in my life. Without my reputation, I'm nothing. I had to take your offer, you see."

He adjusted the steering oar a little to port. The boat changed its heading slightly and moved still further into the center of the stream.

"Money and pride," she said. "That's hardly worth risking your life for."

"Can you think of any better reason, then?"

"You bet I can, *Rana*. One a hell of a lot less brazen than yours." She proceeded to explain the impetus for their journey. Bribbens was not to be recruited.

"I prefer money, thank you."

It was a good thing Falameezar was no longer with them, Jon-Tom thought. He and their boatman were at opposite ends of the political spectrum. Of course, with Falameezar, they would not have required Bribbens' services. He was surprised to discover that despite the archaic, inflexible political philosophy, he still missed the dragon.

"Young female," Bribbens said finally, "you have your romantic ideas and I've got mine. I'm helping you to satisfy your needs and that's all you'll get from me. Now shut up. I dislike noisy chatter, especially from romantic females."

"Oh you *do*, do you?" Flor started to get to her feet. "How would you like—"

The frog jerked a webbed hand toward the southern shore. "It's not too far to the bank, and you look like a pretty good swimmer, for a human. I think you can make it without any trouble."

Flor started to finish her comment, got the point, and resumed her seat near the craft's bow. She was fuming, but sensible. It was Bribbens' game and they had to play with his equipment, according to his rules. But that didn't mean she had to like it.

The boatman puffed contentedly on his pipe. "Interesting group of passengers, more so than my usual." He tapped out the dottle on the deck, locked the steering oar in position, and commenced repacking his pipe. "Wonder to me you haven't killed one another before now."

It was odd, Jon-Tom mused as they drifted onward, to be moving downstream and yet toward mountains. Rivers ran out of hills. Perhaps the Sloomaz-ayor-le-Weentli dropped into an as yet unseen canyon. If so, they would have a spectacular journey through the mountains.

Occasionally they had to set up the canvas roofing that attached to the railings to keep off the nightly rain. At such times Bribbens would fix the oar and curve them to a safe landing onshore. They would wait out the night there, raindrops pelting the low ceiling, until the sun rose and pushed aside the clouds. Then it was on once more, borne swiftly but smoothly in the gentle grip of the river.

Jon-Tom did not fully appreciate the height of Zaryt's Teeth until the third day. They entered the first foothills that morning. The river cut its way insistently through the green-cloaked, rolling mounds. Compared to the nearing mountains, the massive hillocks were merely bruises on the earth.

Here and there great lumps of granite protruded through the brush and topsoil. They reminded Jon-Tom of the fingertips of long-buried giants and brought back to him the legends of these mountains. While not degenerating into rapids, the river nonetheless increased its pace, as if anxious to carry those traveling upon it to some unexpected destination.

Several days passed during which they encountered nothing suggestive of habitation. The hills swelled around them, becoming rockier and more barren. Even wildlife hereabouts was scarce.

Once they did drift past a populated beach. A herd of unicorns was backed up there against the water. Stallions and mares formed a semicircle with the water at their backs, protecting the colts, which snorted and neighed nervously.

Pacing confusedly before the herd's defensive posture was a pack of perhaps a dozen lion-sized lizards. They were sleek as whippets and their red and white scales gleamed in the sunlight.

As the travelers cruised past, one of the lizards sprang, trying to leap over the adults and break the semicircle. Instead, he landed on the two-foot-long, gnarly horn of one of the stallions.

A horrible hissing crackled like fresh foil through the day and blood fountained in all directions, splattering colts and killer alike. Bending his neck, the unicorn used both forehooves to shove the contorted body of the dying carnivore off his head.

The boat drifted around a bend, its passengers ignorant of the eventual outcome of the war. Blood from the impaled predator flowed into the river. The red stain mindlessly stalked the retreating craft. . . .

VI

It was the following afternoon, when they rounded a bend in the river, that Jon-Tom thought would surely be their last.

The foothills had grown steadily steeper around them. They were impressive, but nonexistent compared to the sheer precipices that suddenly rose like a wall directly ahead. Clouds veiled their summits, parting only intermittently to reveal shining white caps at the higher elevations; snow and ice that never melted. The mottled stalks of conifers looked like twigs where they marched up into the mists.

It was a seamless gray cliff which rose up unbroken ahead of the raft. Solid old granite, impassable and cold.

Bribbens was neither surprised nor perturbed by this impassable barrier. Leaning hard on the sweep, he turned the boat to port. At first Jon-Tom thought they would simply ground on the rocks lining the shore, but when they rounded a massive, sharp boulder he saw the tiny beach their boatman was aiming for.

It was a dry notch cut into the fringe of the mountain. Warm water slapped against his boots as the boat's passengers scrambled to pull it onto the sand. Driftwood mixed with the blackened remnants of many camp fires. The little cove was the last landing point on the river.

On the visible river, anyway.

The wind tumbled and rolled down the sheer cliffs. It seemed to be saying, "Go back, fools! There is nothing beyond here but rock and death. Go back!" and a sudden gust would send Talea or Mudge stumbling westward as the wind tried to urge their retreat.

Jon-Tom waded out into the river until the water lapped at his boot tops. Leaning around a large, slick rock, he was able to see why Bribbens had rowed them into the protected cove.

Several hundred yards downstream, downstream was no more. An incessant crackling and grinding came from the river's end. An immense jam of logs and branches, bones, and other debris boiled like clotted pudding against the gray face of the mountain. Foam thundered on rock and wood like cold lava.

He couldn't see where the water vanished into the mountainside because of the obstructing flotsam, but from time to time a log or branch would be sucked beneath the brow of the cliff, presumably into the cavern beyond. The thickness of the jam suggested that the cave opening into the mountain couldn't be more than a few inches above the waterline. If it were higher, he would have been able to see it as a dark stain on the granite, and if lower, the river would have backed up and drowned out, among other things, the cove they were beached upon.

But the opening must be quite deep, because the river had narrowed until it was no more than thirty yards wide where it ground against the mountainside, and the current was no swifter than usual.

"What do we do now?" Flor had waded out to stand next to him. She watched as logs several yards thick spun and bounced off the rock. They must have weighed thousands of pounds and were waterlogged as well.

"There's no way we can move any of that stuff upstream against the current."

"It doesn't matter," he told her. "Even if Clothahump could magic them aside, the opening's still much too low to let the boat through."

"So it seems." Bribbens stood on the sand behind them. He was unloading supplies from the boat. "But we're not going in that way. That is, we are, but we're not."

"I don't follow you," said Jon-Tom.

"You will. You're paying to." He grinned hugely. "Why do you think the Sloomaz-ayor-le-Weentli is called also The Double River, The River of Twos?"

"I don't know." Jon-Tom was irritated at his ignorance. "I thought it forked somewhere upstream. It doesn't tell me how we're going to get through there," and he pointed at the churning, rumbling mass of jackstraw debris.

"It does, if you know."

"So what do we do first?" he said, tired of riddles.

"First we take anything that'll float off the boat," was the boatman's order.

"And then."

"And then we pole her out into the middle of the current, open her stoppers, and sink her. After we've anchored her securely, of course."

Jon-Tom started to say something, thought better of it. Since the frog's statement was absurd and since he was clearly not an idiot, then it must follow that he knew something Jon-Tom did not. When confronted by an inexplicable claim, he'd been taught, it was better not to debate until the supporting evidence was in.

"I still don't understand," said Flor confusedly.

"You will," Bribbens assured her. "By the way, can you both swim?"

"Fairly well," said Jon-Tom.

"I don't drown," was Flor's appraisal.

"Good. I hope the other human is likewise trained.

"For the moment you can't do anything except help with the unloading. Then I suggest you relax and watch."

When the last buoyant object had been removed from the boat, they took the frog at his word and settled down on the beach to observe.

Bribbens guided the little vessel out into the river. On locating a place that suited him (but that looked no different from anywhere else to Jon-Tom and Flor) he tossed over bow and stern anchors. Sunlight glistened off the boatman's now bare green and black back and off the smooth fur of the nude otter standing next to him.

Both watched as the anchors descended. The boat slowly swung around before halting about a dozen yards farther downstream. Bribbens tested the lines to make certain both anchors were fast on the bottom.

Then he vanished belowdecks for several minutes. Soon the boat began to sink. Shortly only the mast was visible above the surface. Then it too had sunk out of sight. Mudge swam above the spot where it had gone under, occasionally dipping his head beneath the surface. The amphibian Bribbens was as at home in the river's depths as he was on land. Mudge was almost as comfortable, being a faster swimmer but unable to extract oxygen from the water.

Soon the otter waved to those remaining on shore. He shouted something unintelligible. They saw his back arch as he dived. He repeated the dive-appear-dive-appear sequence several times. Then Bribbens broke the surface alongside him and they both swam in to the beach.

They silently took turns convoying the floatable supplies

(carefully packed in watertight skins) out to the center of the stream, disappearing with them, and then returning for more.

Finally Bribbens stood dripping on the beach. "Good thing the river doesn't come out of the mountain. Be too cold for this sort of thing."

"What sort of thing?" a thoroughly bemused Flor wanted to know.

"Let's go and you'll find out."

"Go? Go where?"

"Why, to the ship, of course," said Talea. "You don't know, do you?"

"No one explains things to me. They just look." She was almost angry.

"It will all be explained in a minute," said Clothahump patiently.

The boatman held out a watertight sack. "If you'll put your clothes in here."

"What for?" Flor's gaze narrowed.

Bribbens explained patiently, "So they won't get wet." He started to turn away. "It's no difference to me. If you want to spend the journey inside the probably cold mountain in wet clothing, that's your business. I'm not going to argue with you."

Jon-Tom was already removing his cape and shirt. Talea and Caz were doing likewise. Flor gave a little shrug and began to disrobe while the wizard made sure his plastron compartments were sealed tight. Physically he was the weakest of them, but like the boatman, he would have no difficulty going wherever they were going.

There was one problem, though. It took the form of a black lump hanging from a large piece of driftwood.

"Absolutely not! Not on your life, and sure as hell not on mine." Pog folded his wings adamantly around his body and looked immovable. "I'll wait for ya here."

"We may not return this way," explained Clothahump.

"You may not return at all, but dat ain't da point dat's botherin' me," grumbled the bat.

"Come now." Clothahump had elected to try reason on his famulus. "I could make you come, you know."

"You can make me do a lot of tings, boss," replied the bat, "but not you nor anyting else in dis world's going to drag me into dat river!"

"Come on, Pog." Jon-Tom felt silly standing naked on the beach arguing with the reluctant bat. "Flor, Talea, Caz, and I aren't water breathers either. But I trust Clothahump and our boatman to know what they're about. Surely we're going to reach air soon. I can't hold my breath any longer than you."

"Water's fit for drinking, not for living in," Pog continued to insist. "You ain't getting me into dat liquid grave and dat's final."

Jon-Tom's expression turned sorrowful. "If that's the way you feel about it." He'd seen Talea and Mudge sneaking around to get behind the driftwood. "You might as well wait here for us, I suppose."

"I beg your pardon?" said the wizard.

Jon-Tom put a hand on the turtle's shell, turned him toward the river. "It's no use arguing with him, sir. His mind is made up and—"

"Hey? Let me loose! Damn you, Mudge, get off my wings! I'll tear your guts out! I'll, I'll . . . ! Let me up!"

"Get his wings down! . . . Watch those teeth!" Flor and Jon-Tom rushed to help. The four of them soon had the bat neatly pinned. Talea located some strong, thin vines and began wrapping the famulus like a holiday package.

"Sorry to do this, old fellow," said Caz apologetically, "but we're wasting time. Jon-Tom's right though, you know. I'm probably the worst swimmer of this lot, but I'm willing to give it a go if Clothahump insists there's no danger."

"Of course not," said the wizard. "Well, very little, in any case. Bribbens knows precisely how far we must descend."

The boatman stood listening. He eyed the bat distastefully. "Right. Bring him along, then."

They carried the bound and trussed famulus toward the water's edge.

"Let me go!" Pog's fear of the river was genuine. "I can't do it, I tell ya! I'll drown. I'm warning ya all I'll come back and haunt ya the rest of your damn days!"

"That's your privilege." Talea led the way into the river.

"You'll drown all right," Bribbens told him, "if you don't do exactly as I say."

"Where are we going, then?" Jon-Tom asked, a little dazedly.

The frog pointed out and down. "Just swim, man. When we get to the spot I'll say so. Then you dive . . . and swim."

"Straight down?" Jon-Tom kicked, the water smooth and fresh around him. A little shiver of fear raced down his back. Clothahump and Bribbens and to a lesser extent Mudge need have no fear of the water. It was one of their environments. But what if they were wrong? What if the underwater cave (or whatever it was they were going down into) lay too deep?

A friendly pat on one shoulder reassured him. " 'Ere now, why the sunken face, mate? There ain't a bloomin' thing t' worry about." Mudge smiled around his wet whiskers. " 'Tain't far down atall, not even for a splay-toed 'uman."

Bribbens halted, bobbing in the warm current. "Ready then? Just straight down. I've allowed for the carry of the current, so no need to worry about that."

Everyone exchanged glances. Pog's protests bordered on hysteria.

"Here, give the flyer over." A disgusted Bribbens gripped one side of the bat, locking fingers tightly in the bindings.

Pog resembled a large mouse sealed in black plastic. "You take the other side."

"Righty-ho, mate." Mudge grabbed a handful of vines opposite the frog.

With the two strongest swimmers holding their reluctant, wailing burden, Bribbens instructed the others. "Count to three, then dive." The humans nodded. So did Caz, who was doing a good job of concealing his fears.

"Ready? One . . . two . . . better stop screaming and take a deep breath, bat, or you'll be ballast . . . three!"

Backs arched into the morning air. The howling ceased as Pog suddenly gulped air.

Jon-Tom felt himself sliding downward. Below the surface the water quickly turned darker and cooler. It clutched feebly at his naked body as he kicked hard.

Around him were the dim forms of his companions. A slick palm touched one fluttering foot, pushed gently. Looking back he could make out the plump shape of Clothahump. He was swimming casually around the nonaquatics. The water took a hundred years off his age, and he moved with the grace and ease of a ballet dancer.

The push was more to insure that no one lost his orientation and began swimming sideways than to speed the swimmers in their descent.

Even so, Jon-Tom was beginning to grow a mite concerned. Increasing pressure told him that they'd descended a respectable distance. Both he and Flor were in fairly good condition, but he was less sure of Pog and Caz. If they didn't reach the air pocket they had to be heading toward shortly, he'd have to turn around and swim for the surface.

The surface he broke was unexpected, however. He felt himself falling helplessly, head over heels, windmilling his arms in a desperate attempt to regain his balance.

A loud splash echoed up to him as someone else hit the

water. Then he landed with equal force, sank a few feet, and fought his way back to the surface and fresh air.

He broke through and inhaled several deep breaths. Nearby Talea's red curls hung straight and limp as paint from her head. She blinked away water, gasped, and sniffed once.

"Well, that wasn't bad at all. I'd heard it wasn't, but you can't always trust the tales people tell."

Her breasts bobbed easily in the current. Jon-Tom stared at her, more conscious now of her nudity than he'd been when they'd first removed their clothes up above.

But they were above. Weren't they?

Something shoved him firmly between the shoulders.

"Let the current carry you."

Jon-Tom turned in the water, stared into the vast eyes of Bribbens. Looking past him he saw the ship. It was neatly anchored and sat stable in the middle of the stream, perhaps ten yards away. They were drifting toward it.

Following the boatman's advice he relaxed, his body grateful for the respite after the dive, and let the current push him toward the boat. Mudge was already aboard, restocking supplies. He leaned over the side and gave Jon-Tom a hand up, then did the same for Talea.

There was a large, flopping thing on deck that Jon-Tom first thought to be an unfortunate fish. It flipped over, and he recognized the still bound and outraged body of Pog. He accepted Mudge's proferred towel, dried himself, and began to untie the famulus' bonds.

"You okay, Pog?"

"No, *I'm not okay,* dammit! I'm cold, drenched, and sore all over from that fall."

"But you made it through all right." Jon-Tom loosened another slipknot and one wing stretched across the deck. It jerked, sent water flying.

"Not much I can do about it now, I guess," he said angrily.

With the other wing unbound the bat got to his knees, then his feet. He stood there fanning both wings slowly back and forth to dry them.

Mudge joined them. His fur shed the water easily and, almost dry, he was slipping back into his clothes.

"Wot's up, mate?" he asked the bat. "Don't you 'ave no word for your old buddy?"

The large sack of clothing lay opened nearby. Jon-Tom moved to sort his own attire from the wad.

"Yeah, I got something to say ta my old buddy. You can go fuck yourself!" The bat flapped hard, lifted experimentally off the deck, and rose to grip the right spreader. He hung head down from there, his wings still extended and drying.

"Now don't be like that, mate," said the otter, fitting his cap neatly over his ears and fluffing out the feather. "It was necessary. You were 'ardly about t' come voluntarily, you know."

Pog said nothing further. The otter shrugged and left the disgruntled apprentice to his huff.

Jon-Tom buttoned his pants. While the others continued dressing around him, he took a moment to inspect their extraordinary new surroundings.

There was a dull roaring as if from a distant freight train. It sounded constantly in the ears and was a subtle vibration in his own body. His first thought was that they were in a dimly lit tunnel. In a way they were.

The ship rode easily at anchor. On either side were high, moist banks lush with mosses and fungi. That they were not normal riverbanks was proven by the peculiar habits of the higher growths clinging to them. These ferns and creepers put out roots both upward and down, into both running rivers.

Above was a silver-gray sky: the underside of the upper

river. Jon-Tom estimated the distance between the two streams at perhaps ten meters. The mast of the boat cleared the watery ceiling easily.

How the two rivers flowed without meeting, without smashing together and eliminating the air space between them, was an interesting bit of physics. More likely of magic, he reminded himself.

"Easy part's over with." Bribbens moved to wind in the bow anchor, using the small winch bolted there.

"The easy part?" Jon-Tom didn't hear the boatman too clearly. Water still sloshed in his ears.

"Yes. This much of the Sloomaz-ayor-le-Weentli is known. Little traveled in its lower portion, but still known." He pointed with a webbed hand over the bow. Ahead of them the river(s) disappeared into darkness.

"What's ahead is not."

Jon-Tom walked forward and gave the boatman a hand with the winch. "Thanks," Bribbens said when they were finished.

A strong breeze blew in Jon-Tom's face. It came from the blackness forward and chilled his face even as it dried his long hair. He shivered a little. The wind came from *inside* the mountain. That hinted at considerable emptiness beyond.

Here there was no mass of water-soaked debris to prevent their continued traveling. The mouthlike opening could easily swallow the logs and branches bunched against the mountainside above. The cliff did not descend this far.

When they had the second anchor up and secured and the boat was drifting downstream once more, Bribbens moved to a watertight locker set in the deck. It offered up oil lamps and torches. These were set in hook or hole and lit.

The wind blew the flames backward but not out. Oil light flickered comfortingly inside conical glass lamps.

"Why didn't you explain it to us?" Flor brushed at her long black mane while she chatted with the boatman.

Bribbens gestured at the squat shape of Clothahump, who rested against the railing nearby. "He suggested back at my cove that it'd be a good idea not to say anything to you."

Jon-Tom and Flor looked questioningly at Clothahump.

"That is so, youngsters." He pointed toward the flowing silver roof. "From there to here's something of a fall. I wasn't positive of the distance or of what your mental reactions to such a peculiar dive might be. I thought it best not to go into detail. I did not wish to frighten you."

"We wouldn't have been frightened," said Flor firmly.

"That may be so," agreed the wizard, "but there was no need to take the chance. As you can see we are all here safe and sound and once more on our way."

A muttered obscenity fell from the form on the right spreader.

They were interrupted by a loud multiple splashing to starboard. As they watched, several fish the size of large bass leaped skyward. Their fins and tails were unusually broad and powerful.

Two of the leapers fell back, but the third intersected the flowing sky, got his upper fins into the water, and wiggled its way out of sight overhead. Several minutes passed, and then it rained minnows. A huge school of tiny fish came shooting out of the upper river to disappear in the lower. The two unsuccessful leapers were waiting for them. They were soon joined by the descending shape of the stronger jumper.

Jon-Tom had grown dizzy watching the up-and-down pursuit. His brain was more confused than his eyes. The new optical information did not match up with stored information.

"The origin of the name's obvious," he said to the boatman, "but I still don't understand how it came to be."

Bribbens proceeded to relate the story of the Sloomaz-ayor-le-Weentli, of the great witch Wutz and her spilled cauldron of magic and the effect this had had upon the river forevermore.

When he'd finished the tale Flor shook her head in disbelief. "*Grande, fantastico*. A schizoid stream."

"What makes the world go 'round, after all, Flor?" said Jon-Tom merrily.

"Gravitation and other natural laws."

"I thought it was love."

"As a matter of fact," said Clothahump, inserting himself into the conversation, "the gravitational properties of love are well known. I suppose you believe its attractive properties wholly psychological? Well let me tell you, my boy, that there are certain formulae which . . ." and he rambled off into a learned discussion, half balderdash and half science: which is to say, fine magic. Jon-Tom and Flor tried to follow, largely in vain.

Talea leaned on the bow railing, her gaze fixed on the blackness ahead and around them. The cool wind continued, ruffling her hair and making her wonder what lay ahead, concealed by the screen of night.

For days they drifted downstream in darkness; water above, water below, floating through an aqueous tube toward an uncertain destination. Jon-Tom was reminded of a corpuscle in the bloodstream. After all the talk of Zaryt's "Teeth" and of traveling into the "belly" of the mountain, he found the analogy disquieting.

From time to time they would anchor in midstream and supplement their supplies from the river's ample piscean population. Occasionally Bribbens and Mudge would make exploratory forays into the upper river. They would climb the mast, Mudge helping the less adapted boatman. A small float attached to an arrow was shot into the underside of the current overhead. The float was inflated until it held securely. Then the cord trailing from it would be tied to the mast. Bribbens and the otter would then shinny up it, to disappear into the liquid ceiling.

With them went small sealed oil lamps fitted with handles. These provided light in the darkness, a necessity since even such agile swimmers as the two explorers could become lost in the deep waters.

On the twelfth day, when the monotony of the trip had become dangerously settled, Bribbens slid down the line in a state of uncharacteristic excitement.

"I think we're through," he announced cheerily.

"Through? Through where? Surely not the mountains." Clothahump frowned. "It could not be. The range is too massive to be so narrow. And the legends..."

"No, no, sir. Not through the mountains. But the airspace above the upper river has suddenly expanded from but a few inches to one many feet high. There is a substantial cave, far more interesting to look at than this homogeneous tunnel. We can travel above now, and there's some light as well."

"What kind of light?" Flor wanted to know.

"You'll see."

Preparations were made. Buoyant material did not have to be dragged or shoved downward this time. Instead, they simply had to raise it to the upper stream and insert it, whereupon it would instantly bob to the second surface. Mudge was waiting to slip a line on such packages and drag them to shore.

When all their stores had been transferred, the nonaquatics climbed the mast rope and pushed themselves into the upper river. It was far easier to ascend than that first uncertain dive had been.

Jon-Tom broke the surface with wind to spare. He remained there a while, treading water as he inspected the cavern into which the river emerged.

The boatman had understated its size in his usual phlegmatic fashion. The cave was enormous. Off to his left Jon-Tom could see the abrupt cessation of the solid stone wall that had formed a tight lid on the upper stream for so many days. Little debris drifted this far on the river, and what few pieces and bits of wood tumbled by were worn almost smooth from the continual buffeting against that unyielding overhang.

More amazing were the cavern walls. They appeared to be coated with millions of tiny lights. He swam lazily toward the nearby beach, crawled out and selected a towel with which to dry himself, and moved to inspect the nearest glowing rocks.

The lights were predominantly gold in hue, though a few odd bursts and patches of red, blue, green, and yellow were visible. The bioluminescents were lichens and fungi of many species, ranging from mere colored smears against the rock to elaborate mushrooms and step fungi. Individually their lumen output was insignificant, but in the millions they illuminated the cavern as thoroughly as an evening sun.

He was kneeling to examine a cluster of bright blue toadstools when a vast rush and burble sounded behind him. He turned, instinctively expecting to see some unmentionable river monster rising from the depths. It was only their boat.

The first days on board he'd wondered at the purpose of great collapsed intestines, carefully scraped and dried, that lined the little craft's hold. Now he knew. Having been inflated in turn they'd given the boat sufficient lifting power to rise like a balloon from the lower river right up to the surface of its twin.

Now it bobbed uncertainly as Bribbens rushed to open the valves sealing each inflated stomach before they could lift the ship from its second surface to the ceiling of the cavern. Water ran off the decks and out the seacocks. Mudge pumped furiously to purge the remaining water from the hold.

Dry and dressed, the passengers were soon traveling once more eastward. The scenery had improved greatly. Jon-Tom hoped the cavern would not shrink around them and force them again down to the dull surface of the understream.

He needn't have worried. Instead of compacting, the cavern grew larger. It seemed endless, stretching vast and fluorescent ahead of them.

Phosphorescent growths made the river an artist's palette, oils of many colors all run together and anarchically brilliant. Gigantic stalactites drooped like teeth from the distant ceiling. Some were far larger than the boat. They drifted past huge panels of flowstone, frozen rivers of stained calcite. Helictites curled and twisted from the walls, twitching at gravity like so many crystalline whiskers. Fungi flashed from them all.

On both sides they could see passages branching from the main cavern. Jon-Tom had a powerful urge to grab a lamp and do some casual spelunking. But Clothahump reminded him there would be ample exploring to do without deviating from their course. So long as the river continued to run eastward they would keep to the boat.

The size and magnificence of the cavern kept him from thinking about the composition of the Sloomaz-ayor-le-Weentli. It was disconcerting to sail along a river that flowed not on rock or sand but on air.

"How do you know it even has a solid bottom?" Flor once asked their boatman. "Maybe it's a triple—or quadruple—river?"

Bribbens rested in his seat at the stern, one arm draped protectively across the steering oar.

"Because I've been in and out of it many times, lady. Anyway, no matter where you are on the river the anchors always bite into the second bottom."

Here and there the warm glow of the bioluminescents would fade and then vanish. At such times they had to rely on the lamps for light until they reached another fluorescent section.

It didn't bother Pog. He'd finally recovered from his lengthy grumpiness. To him the darkness was natural, and he enjoyed the stretches of no-light. They could hear him swooping and darting beyond the range of the boat's lamps, playing dodgem with the cave formations. Sometimes he'd leave the boat for long stretches of time, much to Clothahump's displeasure and concern, only to have his internal sonar unerringly bring him back to the ship many hours later.

"Beautiful," Jon-Tom was murmuring as he watched the glowing shapes drift past. "It's absolutely beautiful."

Talea stood next to him and eyed the dark openings that branched off from the main cavern. Sometimes these gaping holes would come right down to the river's edge.

"Funny idea of beauty you have, Jon-Tom. I don't like it at all."

"Humans got no appreciation of caves," said Pog with a snort, weaving in the air above them. "Dis all wasted on ya except da spellsinger dere, an' dat's da truth!"

"Can I help it if I prefer light to dark, freedom to confinement?" she countered.

"Amen," said Flor heartily.

For both women the initial loveliness of the formations had been surrendered to the superstitious dread most people hold of deep, enclosed places. Jon-Tom was the only one with a real interest in caves, and so he was somewhat immune to such fears. To him the immense shapes, laid down patiently over the ages by dripping water and dissolved limestone, were as exquisite as anything the world of daylight had to offer.

Flor and Talea were not alone in their nervousness, however.

"I think I liked it better inside the rivers," Mudge said one morning. "Leastwise there a chap knew where 'e was, wot?"

He indicated the darkness of a large, unilluminated side passage with a sweep of one furry arm. "Don't care much for this place atall. I ain't ready t' be buried just yet."

"Superstition," Clothahump muttered. "The bane of civilization."

As for their boatman, he remained as calm as if he'd been sailing familiar waters.

"Does this place have a name?" Jon-Tom asked him, watching a clump of bright azure mushrooms on the shore.

"Only in legend." Bribbens looked away for a moment. An impossibly long tongue flicked out and snared something which Jon-Tom saw only as a ghost of glittering, transparent wings and body.

The frog smacked his lips appraisingly. "No color, but the flavor isn't bad." He nodded at the cavern. "In stories and legends of the riverfolk this is known as the Earth's Throat."

"And where does it go?" Flor asked him.

Bribbens shrugged. "Who knows? Your hard-shelled mentor believes it to travel much of the way through the mountains. Perhaps he's right. I prefer to think we'll come out there instead of, say, the earth's belly."

"That doesn't sound very nice." Nearby Talea fingered the haft of her knife as though she could intimidate the surrounding darkness with it.

Or whatever else might be out there. . . .

VII

They were beginning to think they might complete the passage through the Teeth (or at least to the end of the river) without mishap. Long days of idle drifting, the boat carried smoothly by the current, had lulled the fears they'd acquired on the Swordsward.

Pog, his hearing more acute than anyone else's, was first to note the noise.

"Off key," he explained in response to their queries, "but it's definitely somebody's idea of song. More than one of whatever it is, too."

"I'm sure of it." Caz's long ears were cocked alertly toward the northern shore. They twitched in counterpoint to his busy nose.

It was several minutes more before the humans could hear the subject of their companion's intense listening. It was a rhythmic rising and falling, light and ethereal as an all-female choir might produce. Definitely music, but nothing recognizable as words.

It was occasionally interrupted by a few moments of vivace modulation that sounded like laughter. Jon-Tom could appreciate the peculiar melodies, but he didn't care for the laughter-chords one bit.

Bribbens interrupted their listening, his tone quiet as always but unusually urgent. "Tiller's not answering properly."

Indeed, the boat was drifting steadily toward the north shore. There was a gravel beach and rocks: not much of a landing place. Muscles strained beneath the boatman's slick skin as he fought the steering, but the boat continued to incline landward.

Soon they were bumping against the first rocks. These obstacles poked damp dark heads out of the water around the boat.

Flor stumbled away from the railing on the opposite side and screamed. Jon-Tom rushed to join her. He stared over the side and recoiled instinctively.

Dozens of shapes filled the water. They had their hands on the side of the boat and were methodically pushing at it even though it was already half grounded on the rocky bottom.

"Steady now," said Talea warningly. She stood at the bow, her knife and sword naked in the glow-light, and pointed to the land.

A great number of creatures were marching toward the boat. They were identical to the persistent pushers in the water. All were approximately five feet tall and thin to the point of emaciation. They were faintly human, memories of almost-people parading in unison.

Two legs and two arms. They were nude but smooth-bodied and devoid of external sex organs. For that matter they displayed nothing in the way of differentiating characteristics. They might have been stamped from a single mold.

Their white flesh was truly white, blank-white, like milk and bordering on translucence. Two tiny coal-pit eyes sat in the puttylike heads where real eyes ought to have been. There were no pupils, no ears or nostrils, and only a flat slit of a mouth cutting the flesh below the eye-dots. Hands had short fingers, which along with the legs looked jointless as rubber.

In time to the music they marched toward the ship, waving their arms slowly and hypnotically while singing their moaning, methodical song.

Jon-Tom looked to Clothahump. The wizard looked baffled. "I don't know, my boy. None of the legends says anything about a tribe of albino chanters living in the Throat." He called to the marchers.

"What are you called? What is it you want of us?"

"What can we do for you?" Flor asked, adding something unintelligible in Spanish.

The singers did not respond. They descended the slight slope of the beach with fluid grace. The ones in the lead began reaching, clutching over the railing.

Two of them grabbed Talea's right arm. "Ease back there," she ordered them, pulling away. They did not let go and continued to tug at her insistently.

Several other pale singers were already on the deck and were pulling with similar patient determination at Jon-Tom and Mudge.

" 'Ere now, you cold buggerers, take your bloody 'ands off me!" The otter twisted free.

So did Talea and Jon-Tom. Yet the pale visitors wordlessly kept advancing, groping for the strangers.

Another sound quietly filled the cavern. It seeped across the river and dominated the rise and fall of the expressionless choir. A deep, low moaning, it was in considerable contrast to the melody of the white singers. It was not at all nice. In fact, it seemed to Jon-Tom that it embodied every overtone of

111

menace and malignance one could put into a single moan. It issued from somewhere back in the black depths, beyond where the singers had come from.

"That's about enough," said Bribbens firmly. He hefted his backup steering sweep and began swinging it at the singers stumbling about on deck. Two of them went down with unexpected lack of resistance. Their heads bounced like a pair of rubber balls across the deck. The black eyespots never twitched and they uttered not a word of pain. Their singing, however, ceased. One of the skulls bounced over the railing and landed in the water with a slight splash, to sink quickly out of sight.

A shocked Bribbens paused to stare at the decapitated corpses. There was no blood.

"Damn. They aren't alive."

"They are," Clothahump insisted, struggling awkwardly in the grasp of three singers who were trying to wrestle his heavy body off the ship, "but it is not our kind of alive."

"I'll make them our kind of dead." Talea's sword was moving like a scythe. Three singers fell neatly into six halves. They lay on the deck like so many lumps of white clay, motionless and cold.

Jon-Tom hurried to assist Clothahump. "Sir, what do you think we . . . ?"

"Fight for it, my boy, fight! You can't argue with these things, and I have a feeling that if we're taken from this boat we'll never see it again." He had retreated inside his shell, confounding his would-be abductors.

Above the shouts of the boat's defenders and the singsong of their horribly indifferent assaulters came a reprise of that ominous, basso groaning. It was definitely nearer, Jon-Tom thought, and redoubled his efforts to clear the deck.

He was swinging the club end of his staff in great arcs, indiscriminately lopping off heads, arms, legs. The singers broke like hardened clay, but the dozens dismembered were replaced by ranks of thoughtless duplicates, still droning their eerie anthem.

"Get us out in the current!" Talea was trying to keep the white bodies away from the bow.

With Mudge shielding him from clutching fingers Bribbens put down his oar and returned to the main sweep. Though he leaned on it as hard as he could, and though the current was with them, they still couldn't move away from the shore.

Jon-Tom leaned over the side. Using his reach and the long club he began clearing bodies from the waterline. White hands pulled possessively at him from behind, but Flor was soon at his side swinging her mace, cutting them down like pale shrubs. Most of them ignored her. Possibly it had something to do with her white leather clothing, he mused.

He concentrated on swinging the club in long arcs, knocking away heads or pieces of boneless skull with great rapidity. Their slight resistance barely slowed the force of his swings.

When the heads were knocked loose the bodies simply ceased their shoving and slid below the surface. A few bobbed on the current and drifted like styrofoam down the river.

The singing continued, undisturbed by the bloodless slaughter, by screams of anger or despair. Rising louder around the boat was that rich, bellowing moan. It had become loud enough now to drown out the chorus. A few fragments of rock fell from the cavern roof.

Finally enough of the bodies had been swept from the side of the boat for it to drift once more out into the river. Like so many termites supple white singers continued to march down toward the water. They walked until the water was up to their chests and began swimming slowly after the boat.

Breathing hard, Jon-Tom leaned back against the railing, holding tight to his staff for additional support. All of the original swimmers who'd forced the craft in to shore had been knocked away or decapitated. Now that they were out again in midstream, the current kept them well ahead of their lugubrious pursuers.

"I don't understand what—" He was talking to the boatman, but Bribbens wasn't listening. He'd suddenly locked the steering oar in position and was unbolting smaller ones from the deck.

"Paddle, man! Paddle for your life!"

"What?" Jon-Tom looked back at the shore, expecting to see the horde of singers clumsily stumbling after them across the rocks.

Instead his gaze fastened onto something that stifled the scream welling up in his throat and turned it into that peculiar choking noise people make at times of true horror. A vast, glowing gray mass filled the cavern shore behind them. It came near to touching the ceiling. Where large formations rose the gray substance flowed over or around it, displaying a consistency partly like cloud and then like lard. Its moans rattled the length of the cavern and echoed back from distant walls.

It looked like a fog wrapped with mucus, save for two enormous, pulsing pink eyes. They stared lidlessly down at the tiny fleeing ship and the stick figures frozen on its deck.

Bits of its flanks were in constant motion. These portions of mucus slid toward the ground. As they did so their color paled to a now familiar white. Tumbling like the eggs of some gigantic insect, they dropped off the huge slimy sides onto the rock and gravel. There they rolled over and stood upright on newly formed legs. Simultaneously a section of their smooth faces parted and a fresh voice would join intuitively in the awful mellifluous chorus of its duplicates.

Something hard and unyielding struck Jon-Tom in his midsection. Looking down he saw the hardwood oar Bribbens had shoved at him. The glaring frog face moved away, to pass additional oars to the rest of his passengers.

Then he was back at his sweep, rowing madly and yelling at his companions. "Paddle, damn you all, paddle!"

Jon-Tom's feet finally moved. He leaned over the side and ripped with the oar at the dark surface of the river. It was difficult going and the leverage was bad, but he rowed until his throat screamed with pain and a deep throbbing pounded against his chest.

Yet that horror lurching and tumbling drunkenly along the shore just behind them put strength in weakened arms. Talea, Flor, Caz, and Mudge imitated his efforts. Pog had hidden behind his wings, where he hung from the spreaders, a shivering droplet of black membrane, flesh, and fear. Clothahump stood and watched, watched and mumbled.

A thick gray pseudopod reached across the river, emerging from the slate-colored moving mountain. It slapped violently at the water only yards from the stern of the fleeing vessel. For all its nebulous horror, the substance of the monster was real enough. Water drenched those on board.

Black almost-eyes glistened wetly as white grub-things continued peeling from the pulsating bulk of the beast. Jon-Tom frowned; someone had spoken above the reverberant bellowing. He looked across at Clothahump.

"The Massawrath." The wizard noticed Jon-Tom staring at him, and he repeated the name. "I have seen it in visions, my boy, suspected it in trances, but to have located its lair . . . Is it not appalling and unique? Do you not recognize any of this?"

"Recognize . . . ? Clothahump, have you gone mad? Or have we all? Or is it just that . . . that . . ."

He hesitated. For all its utterly alien appearance, there was truly something almost familiar about the apparition.

Again the pseudopod slapped at them. There was a broken groan from the boat. The tip of the massive appendage had struck just to Clothahump's left, tearing away railing along with a bit of the deck. The turtle had instinctively withdrawn and rolled several yards bowward. There he stuck out arms and legs once more and struggled to his feet while Bribbens rowed harder than ever and quietly cursed the abomination pursuing them.

Several partly formed white shapes had fallen from the end of the pseudopod. They lay on deck, their uncompleted limbs thrashing slowly. Among them was a head that had not grown a proper body and a lower torso the chest region of which tapered to a point.

Jon-Tom pulled in his oar and began kicking the disgusting things over the side. The last one clutched and pulled at him. It had arms but no legs. He was forced to touch it. Somehow he kept down his nausea and pulled it away from his legs. The white, rubbery flesh was cold as ice. He lifted it and heaved it over the railing, its weak grip sliding along his arm. It splashed astern while the Massawrath hunched its way over boulders and stalagmites, pacing just aft of the racing ship and gibbering mindlessly.

"If the river narrows and brings us in reach, we're finished." Talea spoke in a high, nervous voice and wrestled with the long oar.

"What *is* it?" Jon-Tom wiped his hands on his pants but the clamminess he'd picked off the flesh wouldn't dry. He raised his oar and shoved it back into the water.

"The Massawrath," Clothahump repeated. His hurried tumble across the deck apparently hadn't affected him. "She is the Mother of Nightmares. This is her lair, her home."

Jon-Tom tried not to watch the loping gray slime. Bits of congealed white, animated puddings, continued to drip from those vast flanks, climb to their feet, and march for the water. They remained at least twenty yards astern though they kept up their pursuit. They did not have the muscular strength (if they had muscles, Jon-Tom thought) to overtake the boat. An army of fellow singers surged and marched around the base of the Massawrath. Some were indifferently squished beneath the vast mass, others shoved aside into the water.

"And what are the white things?" Flor forced herself to ask.

Clothahump peered over his glasses at her in evident surprise. "Why child, what would you expect the Mother of Nightmares to produce, except nightmares? I asked if you recognized them. Having no dreams to invade they are presently unformed, shapeless, incipient. Here in their place of birthing they are partly solid. When they pass out and into the minds of thinking creatures they have become thin as wind. Their lives are brief, empty, and full of torment."

"Wha-at?" Caz swallowed, tried again. "What does the blasted thing want with us?" The fur was as stiff on his neck as the nails of a yogi's board.

"Nightmares need dreams to feed on," explained the wizard. "Minds on which to fasten. What the Massawrath Mother feeds on I can only imagine, but I am not ready to offer myself to find out. I do not think it would be pleasant to be nightmared to death. Mayhap she feeds on the loose minds of the mad, carried back to her by those fragments of nightmare offspring that survive longer than a night. It is said the insane never awaken."

It continued to trail them, roaring and moaning. Pale things fell like white sweat from her back and sides. Occasionally a fresh appendage, gray and wet, would extend out toward them. It did not again come close enough to contact the boat.

Jon-Tom remembered Talea's frantic warning: if anything forced them nearer the Massawrath's shore they would be better off killing each other.

Another worry was the vibration he'd been feeling for more than a few minutes. Though it steadily intensified, it *seemed* to have no connection with the pursuing Mother of Nightmares. Soon a vast thunder filled his ears, powerful enough to reduce even the Massawrath's moan to a faint wailing.

Still it grew in volume. Now the maddened gray hulk struck out at the boat with dozens of pseudopods of many lengths. They raised water from the river and dropped dozens of slimy nightmares behind the boat.

The roaring grew louder still, until it and the vibration underfoot merged and were one. Exhausted from wrestling with the steering sweep, Bribbens leaned across it and tried to catch his breath. Then he frowned, staring over the bow. Several minutes went by and an expression of great calm came over his face.

Jon-Tom relaxed on his own oar and panted uncontrollably. "You . . . you recognize it?"

"Yes, I recognize it." The boatman looked happy, which was encouraging. He also looked resigned, which was not. "Every boatman knows the legends of the Sloomaz-ayor-le-Weentli. It could only be one thing, you know.

"At least the Massawrath will not have us. This will be a cleaner, surer death."

"What death? What are you talking about?" Talea and the others had shipped their own oars as their pursuer fell back.

Bribbens reached out with an arm and gestured across the bow. Ahead of them a thick fog was becoming visible. It boiled energetically and spread a cloud across the roof of the great cavern.

"Clothahump?" Jon-Tom turned back to the wizard. "What's he raving about?"

"He is not raving, my boy." The stocky sorcerer had also turned his attention away from the fading horror behind them. "He told you once, remember? It is why the Massawrath cannot follow and why she flails in rage at us. She cannot cross Helldrink."

Thunder deafened Jon-Tom, and he had to put his hands to his ears. He felt the noise through the deck, through his legs and entire body. It pierced his every cell.

Fog and roaring, mist and thunder drew nearer. What did that say? It's speaking to you, he told himself, announcing its presence and declaring its substance. It was familiar to Bribbens, who'd never seen it. Should it therefore also be recognizable to him?

Waterfall, he thought. He knew it instantly.

Hurrying to the storage lockers, he tried to think of a saving song. The duar was in his hands, clean and dry, waiting to be stroked to life, waiting to sing magic. He draped straps over his neck, felt the familiar weight on his shoulders.

One final time long cables of gray mucus reached out for them. The Massawrath had extended itself to the utmost, but its reach still fell short. Quivering with frustration, it hunkered down on the rocks now well behind the boat, the volcanic pits of its eyes glaring balefully at those now beyond its grasp.

Ahead fog boiled ceilingward like wet flame.

Jon-Tom stared mesmerized at the mist and hunted through his repertoire for an appropriate song. What could he sing? That they were nearing a waterfall was all too clear, but what kind of waterfall? How high, how wide, how fast or . . . ?

Desperately he belted out several choruses from half a dozen different tunes relating to water. They produced no visible result. The boat's course and speed remained unchanged. Even the gneechees seemed to have deserted him. He'd come to expect their almost-presence whenever he'd strummed magic, and their absence panicked him.

Nothing ahead now but swirling vapor. Then Talea cursed loudly. Caz gave a warning shout and locked his arms around the railing while Mudge put his head on the deck and covered

119

his eyes with his hands, as though by not seeing he might not be affected.

A faint mumbling rose behind Jon-Tom. Helpless and confused, he spared a second to look around.

Clothahump was standing by the steering sweep, next to a stoic Bribbens. The wizard's short, stubby arms were raised, the fingers spread wide on his left hand while those on the right made small circles and traced invisible patterns in the air.

With a snap the mainsail rose taut, the luff rope zipping up the mast with a whirr though no hand had touched the rigging. A terrified Pog reacted to the ascending sail by letting loose the spreader he'd been hanging from. A powerful updraft caught him, and he had to flap furiously to regain his perch. This time he clung flat to the spreader, arms and legs wrapped as tightly about the wooden cross member as his wings were around his body.

Clothahump's murmur changed to a stentorian, wizardly monotone. Now the wind blew hard in their faces, rough and threatening where the gentle on-bow breeze of previous days had been a comfortable companion.

The roar that permeated his entire body had numbed Jon-Tom's hearing completely. But his vision still functioned. They were almost upon a cauldron of spray and fog. Water particles danced in the air and became one with the river. He wanted to close his eyes, but curiosity kept them open. They no longer could see or hear the Massawrath.

A harder gray loomed immediately ahead, a definitive axis around which the mist boiled and fumed: the edge. The little boat crossed it . . . and kept going. All the while Clothahump continued his recitation. Even his charged voice was lost in the aqueous thunder, though Jon-Tom thought he could make out the part of the chant that made mention of "hydrostatic immunatic even keel please.'' The boat now eased out on the turgid air.

With the cold, distant interest of a parachutist whose chute has failed to open, Jon-Tom let the duar lie limp against him and moved to the railing. He looked over the side.

A thousand feet deep, the waterfall was. No, five thousand. It was hard to tell, since it disappeared into mist-shrouded depths. It might have dropped less than a thousand feet, or for all he could tell it might have plunged straight to the heart of the earth. Or to hell, if its legend-name was accurate.

Instead, the depths seemed to hold a fiery, red-orange glow. It arose from a distant whirlpool point.

As the boat continued to cruise smoothly across emptiness, he finally saw the source of much of the thunder. There was not just one waterfall, but four. Others crashed downward to port and starboard, and the fourth lay dead ahead. These sibling torrents were each as broad and fulsome as the one the boat had just crossed. Four immense cascades converged above the Pit and tumbled to a hidden infinity called Helldrink. They were vast enough to drain all the oceans of all the worlds.

The boat lurched, and everyone grabbed for something solid. They'd reached the middle of the Drink and had encountered the vortex of spray and upwelling air that dwelt there. The little vessel spun around twice, a third time, in that confluence of moist meterologics, and then was spun free by the vortex's centrifugal power. It continued sailing steadily across the chasm.

Ahead the far waterfall loomed closer. The bow made contact with the water, the keel slipped in. They were sailing steadily now upstream, against the current. Wind rising from the Drink now blew at them from astern instead of in their faces. The sail billowed and filled for the first time since they'd entered the Earth's Throat.

Clothahump suddenly leaned back against the railing. His hands dropped and his voice faltered. The boat slowed. For an awful moment Jon-Tom thought the wind wouldn't be enough to cancel the insistent force of the swift current. Only Bribbens' skill enabled them finally to resume their forward progress.

Gradually they picked up speed, until the awesome pounding of the falls had fallen to a gentle rumbling echo. They were traveling upstream now, the wind steady behind them. The same luminescent growths lined portions of cavern wall and ceiling. They were in a subterranean chamber no different from the one they had fled.

Emotionally wrung, Jon-Tom leaned over the side of the boat and gazed astern. By now the last mists had been swallowed by distance. No Massawrath clone waited here to challenge them.

It did not have to. Never again could it send its pale white children to haunt the sleep of at least one traveler. Having been exposed, Jon-Tom was now immune. The encounter had innoculated him against nightmare. One who has looked upon the Mother of Nightmares cannot be frightened by her mere minions of ill sleep.

Clothahump had slumped to the deck. He sat there rubbing his right wrist. "I am out of shape," he muttered to no one in particular. His attention rose to the mast. Pog was twisted around the upper spreaders like a black coil.

The bat was slowly unwrapping himself. His malaria-like shivers faded, and he spoke in a querulous whisper. "Ointments, Master? Unguents and balms for ya arm, maybe a blue pill for ya head?"

"You okay?" Jon-Tom gazed admiringly down at the exhausted wizard.

"I will be, boy." He spoke hoarsely to his famulus. "Some ointment, yes. No pill for my head, but I will have one of the green ones for my throat. Five minutes of nonstop chanting." He sighed heavily, glanced back to Jon-Tom.

"Keep in mind, my boy, that a wizard's greatest danger is not lack of knowledge nor the onset of senility nor such forgetfulness as I am now prone to. It's laryngitis."

Then everyone was swarming happily around him. Except the unperturbable, steady Bribbens. The boatman remained at his post, eyes directed calculatingly upstream. They had left the boat in his hands, and he left the congratulating in theirs.

It was later that Mudge found Jon-Tom seated near the bow and staring morosely ahead. Strong wind from behind lifted his bright green cape, and he tucked it around and between his upraised knees. The duar lay in his lap. He plucked disconsolately at it as multihued formations passed in glowing revue.

" 'Ere now, lad," said the otter concernedly, leaning over and squeak-sniffing, "wot's the matter, then? That Massawatch-oriswhatever's behind us now, not comin' down at us."

Jon-Tom drew another chord from the instrument, smiled faintly up at the otter. "I blew it, Mudge." When the otter continued to look puzzled, he added, "I could've done the same thing as Clothahump, but I couldn't come up with the right music." He looked down at the duar.

"I couldn't think of a single appropriate tune, not even a chord. If it had all been up to me," he said with a shrug, "we'd all be dead by now."

"But we ain't," Mudge pointed out cheerfully, "and that be the important thing."

"Our cheeky companion is correct, you know." Caz had come up behind them both. Now he stood opposite Mudge, looking at the seated human. His paws were behind his back and folded just above the puffball of a tail. "I doesn't matter

123

who does the saving. Just as friend Mudge says, the fact that we are saved is the important thing. Remember, it was you who tamed the great Falameezar that fiery night in Polastrindu. Not Clothahump. You want to hold all the glory for yourself?''

When he saw that the irony was lost on Jon-Tom he added, ''We all work for the same end. It matters nothing who does what so long as that end is achieved. It shall be, unless some of us put our personal feelings and desires above it.''

Mudge looked a little uncomfortable at the rabbit's bluntness. '' 'E's right, mate. We can't be thinkin' o' ourselves in this business.'' The last was said with a straight face. ''You'll 'ave plenty o' opportunity t' demonstrate your wonderfulness t' the ladies when this all be done with.'' He winked and whistled knowingly before leaving for the stern.

Caz considered giving the self-pitying human a comforting pat, decided Jon-Tom might regard it as patronizing, and left to join Mudge.

Jon-Tom, sitting by himself, muttered aloud, ''The ladies have nothing to do with it.'' He watched the cavern walls glide past. Gentle spray licked his face, kicked up from the bow as the boat made its way upstream.

They didn't, he insisted to himself, resting his chin on folded hands. He'd only been worried about the general welfare.

Then he grinned, though there was no one to see him. The trouble with studying law is that you develop a tendency to bullshit yourself as well as your counterparts. What about the theory that all great events, all the turning points of history, had in some measure or another been motivated by matters of passion? Catherine the Great, Napoleon, Hitler, Washington . . . the sexual theory of history explained a hell of a lot of things economics and social migration and such did not.

It was quite a different kind of history that balanced on the outcome of their little expedition. Jon-Tom had never accorded the theory much credit anyway. Yet though meant at least partly in jest, Mudge's words forced home to him how often emotional yearnings coupled with the basic desires of the body could overwhelm those usually thought of as rational creatures.

So he was sitting there moping about nothing except himself. That was selfish and stupid. Maybe it had affected the thinking of Napoleon and Tiberius and others, but it wouldn't affect *him*. It was a damn good thing Clothahump had found the words that had escaped his human companion.

His moroseness fading, he strummed softly on the duar. A flicker of dancing motes haunted his left elbow. When he turned to inspect them, they'd gone. Gneechees.

What still did worry him was the thought that the next time he might be called upon to sing some magic, he might be as mentally paralyzed as he'd been when nearing Helldrink. He would have to fight that.

It wasn't the thought of death or the failure of their mission that troubled him as he sat there and played. It was a fear of personal failure, a fear that had haunted him since he'd been a child. It was the fear which had driven him to pursue two different careers without being able to choose between them.

And though he didn't realize it, it was the fear which had driven more men and women to greatness than far more rational motivations. . . .

VIII

Several days later the cathedral hove into view. It was not a cathedral, of course. But it might have been. No one could say. That turned out not to be as confusing as it seemed.

To Jon-Tom it looked like a cathedral. The ceiling of the great underground chamber in which it rose was several hundred feet high. Towers and turrets nearly touched that far stone roof. At that distance massive stalactites, each weighing many tons, resembled pins hanging from a carpet.

The bioluminescents were especially dense here and the chamber and its far reaches so brightly lit that it took the travelers several minutes to adjust to that unexpectedly vibrant organic glow.

It was more like a hundred cathedrals, Jon-Tom thought, all executed in miniature and piled one atop the other. Care and fine craftsmanship were apparent in every line and curve of the labyrinthine structure. Thousands of tiny colored windows gleamed on dozens of levels. The edifice filled much of the huge chamber.

It was a measure of the distances his mind had crossed that it was only incidental to him that the building shone a rich, metallic gold. Of course, that might only be a result of extensive use of gilt paint. Still, he vowed privately to keep a close watch on their avaricious otter.

The term miniature was applicable to more than just the building. When it became clear to them that the inhabitants of the strange boat were not hostile, the builders began to show themselves.

No more than four inches tall, the little people were covered with a rich umber fur that suggested sable. This fur was quite short, and long, fine hair of the same shade grew on the heads of male and female alike. Hordes of them started emerging from tiny doors and cubbyholes. Most resumed working on the building. Acres of scaffolding bristled on battlements and turrets and towers. One group of several dozen were installing a massive window all of a yard high.

Bribbens eased the boat in toward shore. At closer range they could make out thousands of golden sculptures adorning the building, gargoyles and worm-sized snakes and things only half realized because they originated in other dimensions, from a different biological geometry. Unlike the gneechees, these wonderful creations could be viewed, if not wholly perceived.

As the boat drifted still closer the thousands of tiny workers began milling uncomfortably, clustering close by doorways and other openings. Jon-Tom hailed them from his position at the bow, trying to assuage their worries.

"We mean you no harm," he called gently. "We're only passing through your lands and admire your incredible building. What's it for?"

From the crest of a water-caressed rock a fur-covered

nymph all of three and a half inches tall shouted back at him. He had to strain to understand the tiny lady.

"It is the Building," she told him matter-of-factly, as though that should be explanation enough to satisfy anyone.

"Yes," and he lowered his voice still further when he saw that his normal tone was painfully loud to her, "but what is the building for?"

"It is the Building," the sprite reiterated. "We call it 'Heart-of-the-World.' Does it not shine brightly?"

"Very brightly," Talea said appreciatively. "It's very beautiful. But what *is* it for?"

The down-clad waif laughed delicately. "We are not sure. We have always worked on the Building. We always will work on the Building. What else is there to life but the Building?"

"You say you call it 'Heart-of-the-World.'" Jon-Tom studied the radiant walls and glistening spires. At first he thought it had been made of real gold, then stone covered with gilt paint. Now he wasn't sure. It might be metal of another kind, or plastic, or ceramic, or some unimaginable material he knew nothing of.

"Perhaps it is the very heart of the world itself," the little lady offered in suggestion. She smiled joyfully, showing perfect minuscule teeth. "We do not know. It beats with light as a heart does. If our work were to be stopped, perhaps the light would go out of the world."

Jon-Tom considered saying more but found reason and reality at odds with one another, mixed up like a dog and a cat chasing each other around a pole, getting nowhere. He looked helplessly to Clothahump for an explanation. So did his companions.

"Who can say?" The wizard shrugged. "If it is truly the architecture of the heart of the world, then at least we can tell others that the world is well and truly fashioned."

"Thank you, sir." The sprite leaped nimbly to another rock further upstream to keep pace with them. "We do our best. We have become very adept at adding to and maintaining the Building."

"Make sure," Jon-Tom called to her, "that its glow never goes out!" They were passing into a narrower section of the river cavern, leaving the unnamed little folk and their enigmatic, immense construct behind.

"Who knows," he said quietly to Flor, "if it is the heart of the world, then they'd better not be disturbed in their work. That's a hell of a responsibility. And if it's not, if it's only a building, an obsession, it's too beautiful to let die anyway."

"I never thought the heart of the world would be a building," she said.

"Aren't we all structures?" With the Massawrath and Helldrink safely far behind he was feeling alive and expansive. He'd always been that way: high ups and abyssal downs. Right now he was up.

"Each of us develops piece by piece. We're full of carefully built rooms and halls, audience chambers and windows, and we're populated with changing individualistic thoughts. I never imagined the heart of the world would be a building, though." He stared back down the tunnel. It was growing dark, the radiant growths vanishing as they were prone to at unexpected intervals.

"In fact, I never thought of the world as having a heart."

The last rich light from the distant chamber was lost to sight as they rounded a slight bend in the river. Bribbens was lighting the first lamp.

"That's a nice thought, Jon-Tom. If only having a heart meant you would be happy."

"I suppose it often means the opposite." But when the import of her last comment finally penetrated, she had left him to chat with their stolid steersman.

Jon-Tom hesitated, thought about pursuing it further by rejoining her to say, "Flor, are you trying to tell me something?" But he was as afraid of showing ignorance if he was interpreting her wrongly as he was of failure.

So he sat himself down in the flickering light and began to clean and tune his duar. As he tightened or loosened the strings, a gneechee or two would appear behind him, peering over his shoulder. He knew they were there and did his best to ignore them.

They were compelled to run on lamplight. Gradually the immense cave formations, the helictites and flowstone and such, began to grow smaller. In the narrowing confines of the river channel the rush and roar reverberated louder from the walls. The continuing absence of the familiar fluorescent fungi and their cousins was becoming unsettling.

No one liked the darkness. It reminded them too much of sleep, and that reminded them of the now distant but never to be forgotten sight of the Massawrath. More importantly, their lamp oil was running out. Bribbens had prepared well, but he hadn't expected to journey for long in total darkness. The now sorely missed bioluminescents were all that had kept them from traveling in black. Soon it appeared they might have to do so, relying on Pog's abilities to guide them, unless the light-producing vegetation reappeared.

A hand was shaking him. It was too small to be part of the Massawrath, too solid to be one of its children. Nevertheless he had an instant of terror before coming awake.

"Get up, Jon-Tom. Move your ass!" It was the urgent voice of Talea.

"What?" But before he could say anything more she'd moved on to the next sleeping form. He heard her banging on an echoing surface.

"Wake up, wizard. You lazy old wizard, wake up!" She sounded worried.

131

"I still admit to 'old' but not the other." A grumbling Clothahump clambered to his feet.

Jon-Tom blinked, fought to dig sleep from his eyes. It was hard to see anything in the reduced light from the lamps. Bribbens was trying to conserve their dwindling supply of oil.

Then he saw the cause of her anxiety. In the blackness ahead was a writhing sheet of flame, completely blocking the river. It hung in the air there, a dull, thick orange-silver that did not move. The others awoke and moved to the bow to examine it. All agreed it was a most peculiar kind of fire.

As they cruised closer no rise in temperature or indeed any heat at all could be felt. The orange-silver hue did not change.

"Can it be another structure like the Heart-of-the-World building of the little folk?" Flor licked her lower lip and stared anxiously forward.

"No, no. The color is all wrong, supple shadow, and there is no sign of separation; levels, floors, or windows." Caz faced the wizard. "What is your opinion of it, sir?"

"Just a moment, will you?" Clothahump sounded irritable. "I'm not fully awake yet. Do you children think I have your physical resiliency simply because my brain is so much more active? Now then, this surely cannot be dangerous." He called back to Bribbens. "Steady ahead, my good boatman."

"Don't have much choice." The frog snapped off his reply as he tightened his grip on the steering sweep. "Tunnel's become too narrow for us to turn 'round in. Some of the rocks hereabouts look sharp. I don't want to chance 'em, so it's steady ahead unless it turns desperate."

The boatman was forced to raise his voice to a near shout to make himself understood. The rush of air in the pipe of a cave argued noisily with the increased force of the current.

They watched silently while that cold flame came nearer. Then there was another, dimmer light haloing it, and the orange-silver no longer blocked their progress. The new light came from tiny shining points that flickered unevenly, but not like gneechees. These were both visible and motionless.

"Well, shit." Mudge put hands on hips and sounded thoroughly disgusted with himself. " 'Tis a prize pack o' idiots we be, mates."

Jon-Tom didn't understand immediately, but it didn't take long until he knew the reason for the otter's embarrassment. When he did so he felt equally ashamed of his own fear.

The orange-silvery color was familiar enough. Then they emerged from the cavern. The great rising orb of moon no longer shone directly down into the Earth's Throat.

"We made it." He hugged a startled Talea. "Damned if we didn't!"

The character of the land they had emerged into was very different from that of the Swordsward and the river country of Bribbens' home. It was evident they had climbed a considerable distance.

Behind them towering crags reached for the stars. Clouds capped them, though they were not as thick as those on the eastern flanks of the range. No open plains or low scrub bordered the river here. There was no fragrant coniferous forest or high desert.

Mountains rose all around the little river valley in which they found themselves. Despite the altitude the country displayed the aspect of more tropical climes. It was warm but not hot, nor was it particularly humid. Jon-Tom thought of a temperate-zone climax forest.

Vines and creepers leaped from tree to tree. A thick undergrowth prevented them from seeing more than a few yards inland on either shore.

It was with relief that Jon-Tom inhaled the fresh air, fragrant with the aroma of flowers and green things. Though hardly tropical, the climate was more pleasant despite the altitude than any place he'd yet been. Compared to the bone-rattling winds of the Swordsward it was positively Edenic.

"Fine country," he said enthusiastically. "I'm surprised none of the warmlanders have tried to migrate here."

"Even if they knew this land existed they could not get over the mountains," Clothahump reminded him. "Only a very few in memory have ever made that journey. Even if would-be settlers could survive the trip, kindly keep in mind that this land is already occupied. Legend says the Weavers dislike any strangers. Consider what their opinion would be of potential colonists."

"And these are the people we're trying to make allies of?" Flor wondered.

"They are not overt enemies," Clothahump told her, shaking his head slowly. "Legend says they are content enough here in their land. Yet I admit legend also insists they hold no love for any but their own kind. It is said they like most to keep to themselves and maintain their privacy.

"As near as I know we are the first folk to journey past the mountain barrier in hundreds of years. Perhaps the legends no longer hold true. It may be that in all that time the inhabitants of the Scuttleteau have mellowed."

"They sure sound charming," said Flor apprehensively. "I can't wait to meet them." Her voice rose in tone, and she mimed a sardonic greeting. "*Buenos dias*, Señor Weaver. *Como esta usted*, and please don't eat me, I'm only a tourist." She sighed and grimaced at the wizard. "I wish I were as confident of success as you are."

"I'm 'ardly an optimist, meself," Mudge commented, surveying the near shore and considering a warm swim.

"Oh well. Surely they will see the need," said Caz hopefully, "to stand together against a common threat."

"That is to be hoped," the wizard agreed. "But we cannot

be certain. We can only pray for a friendly welcome. Should we actually achieve anything more than that, it would exceed my wildest hopes."

There were some shocked looks in response to that. Jon-Tom spoke for all of them. "You mean . . . you're not sure you can persuade them?"

"My dear boy, I never made any such claim."

"But you gave me the impression . . ."

Clothahump held up a hand. "I made no promises. I merely stated that there was little we could do if we remained in Polastrindu and that we might have some chance of securing another strong ally were we to successfully complete this journey. I never said that reaching the Scuttleteau was a guarantee we could do that. Nor did I ever display any optimism about striking such an alliance. I simply declared that I thought it would be a good idea to try."

"You stiff-backed, bone-brained old fart, you led us on!" Talea was nearly too furious for words. "You cajoled us through all that," and she pointed back toward the mouth of the tunnel they'd recently emerged from, "through everything we've suffered since leaving Polastrindu, without thinking we had any chance to succeed?"

"I did not say we did not have a chance." Clothahump patiently corrected her. "I said our chances were slim. That is different from nonexistent. When I say achieving such an alliance would exceed my wildest hopes, I am merely being realistic, not fatalistic. The chance is there."

"Why the fuck couldn't you have been 'realistic' back in Polastrindu?" she growled softly. "Couldn't you have told us how slight you thought our chances of success were?"

"I could have, but no one thought to ask me. As to the first, if I had been more, shall we say, explicit in my opinions, none of you would have come with me. Those who might have would not have done so with as much confidence and determination as you have all displayed thus far.''

Since this logic was irrefutable, no one chose to argue. There was some spirited name-calling, however. The wizard ignored it as one would have the excited chatter of children. Pog found the situation unbearably amusing.

''Now ya see what I have ta deal wid, don'tcha?'' He giggled in gravely bat-barks as he swung gleefully from the spreader. ''Maybe now ya all'll sympathize wid poor Pog a little bit more!''

''Shut your ugly face.'' Talea heaved a hunk of torchwood at him. He dodged it nimbly.

''Now, now, Talea-tail. Late for recriminations, don'tcha tink?'' Again the rich laughter. ''His Bosship has ya all where he wants ya.'' A series of rapid-fire squeeks seeped out as he delightedly lapped up their discomfort.

''It does seem you've been somewhat less than truthful with us, sir,'' said Caz reprovingly.

''Not at all. I have not once lied to any of you. And the odds do not lessen the importance of our trying to conclude this alliance. The more so now that we have actually completed the arduous journey through the Earth's Throat and have reached the Scuttleteau.

''Admittedly our chances of persuading the Weavers to join with us are slight, but the chance is real so long as we are real. We must reach for every advantage and assistance we can.''

''And if we die on the failure of this slight chance?'' Flor wanted to know.

''That is a risk I have resigned myself to accepting,'' he replied blandly.

''I see.'' Talea's fingers dug into the wood of the railing. She stared at the river as she spoke. ''If we all die, that's a risk *you're* prepared to take. Well, I'm not.''

"As you wish." Clothahump gestured magnanimously at the water. "I herewith release you from any obligation to assist me further. You may commence your swim homeward."

"Like hell." She peered back at Bribbens. "Turn this deadwood around."

The boatman threw her a goggle-eyed and mournful look. "How much can you pay me?"

"I . . ."

"I see." He turned his attention back to the river ahead. "I take orders only from those who can pay me." He indicated Clothahump. "He paid me. He tells my boat where it is to go. I do not renege on my business agreements."

"Screw your business agreements, don't you care about your own life?" she asked him.

"I honor my commitments. My honor is my life." This last was uttered with such finality that Talea subsided.

"Commitments my ass." She turned to sit glumly on the deck, glaring morosely at the wooden planking.

"I repeat, I have not lied to any of you." Clothahump spoke with dignity, then added by way of an afterthought, "I should have thought that all of you were ready to take any risk necessary in this time of crisis. I see that I was mistaken."

It was quiet on the boat for several hours. Then Talea looked up irritably and said, "I'm sorry. Bribbens is right. We all made a commitment to see this business through. I'll stick to mine." She glanced back at the wizard. "My fault. I apol . . . I apologize." The unfamiliar word came hard to her. There were murmurs of agreement from the others.

"That's better," Clothahump observed. "I'm glad that you've all made up your minds. Again. It was time to do so because," and he pointed over the bow, "soon there will be no chance of turning back."

Completely spanning the river a hundred yards off the bow was a soaring network of thick cables. They made a silvery shadow on the water, a domed superstructure of glistening filaments in the intensifying morning light.

Waiting and watching with considerable interest from their resting places high up in the cables were half a dozen of the Weavers.

Clothahump knew what to expect. Caz, Mudge, Talea, Pog, and Bribbens had some idea, if through no other means than the stories passed down among generations of travelers.

But Jon-Tom and Flor possessed no such mental buffering. Primeval fear sent a shudder through both of them. It was instinctive and unreasoning and cold. Only the fact that their companions showed no sign of panic prevented the two otherworlders from doing precisely that.

The six Weavers might comprise a hunting party, an official patrol, or simply a group of interested river gazers out for a day's relaxation. Now they gathered near the leading edge of the cablework.

One of them shinnied down a single strand when the boat began to pass beneath. Under Bribbens' directions and at Clothahump's insistence, Mudge and Caz were taking down the single sail.

"No point in making a show of resistance or attempting to pass uncontested," the wizard murmured. "After all, our purpose in coming here is to meet with them."

Unable to override their instincts, Jon-Tom and Flor moved to the rear of the boat, as far away from their new visitor as they could get.

That individual secured the bottom of his cable to the bow of the little boat. The craft swung around, tethered to the overhead network, until its stern was pointing upstream.

Having detached the cable from the end of his abdomen, the Weaver rested on four legs, quietly studying the crew of the peculiar boat with unblinking, lidless multiple eyes. Four arms were folded across his cephalothorax. His body was bright yellow with concentric triangles decorating the under-side of the sternum. His head was a beautiful ocher. The slim abdomen had blue stripes running down both the dorsal and ventral sides.

Complementing this barrage of natural coloration was a swirling, airy attire of scarves and cloth. The material was readily recognizable as pure silk. It was twisted and wrapped sari-style around the neck, cephalothorax, abdomen, and upper portions of the legs and arms. Somehow it did not entangle the Weaver's limbs as he moved.

It was impossible to tell how many pieces of silk the visitor was wearing. Jon-Tom followed one feathery kelly-green scarf for several yards around legs and abdomen until it vanished among blue and pink veils near the head. A series of bright pink bows knotted several of the scarves together and decorated the spinneret area. Mandibles moved idly, and occasionally they could see the twin fangs that flanked the other mouth-parts. The Weaver was a nightmare out of a Max Ernst painting, clad in Technicolor.

The nightmare spoke. At first Jon-Tom had trouble under-standing the breathy, faint voice. Gradually curiosity over-threw his initial terror, and he joined his companions in the bow. He began to make sense of the whispery speech, which reminded him of papers blowing across stepping-stones.

As the Weaver talked, he tested the cable he'd spun himself from bridge to boat. Then he sat down, having concluded his prayer or invocation or whatever it had been, by folding his four legs beneath him. His jaw rested on the upper tarsals and claws. The body was three feet long and the legs almost doubled that.

"it has been a long time," said the veiled spider, "far beyond my lifetime, beyond i think the memory of any currently alive, since any of the warmland people have visited the scuttleteau."

Jon-Tom tried to analyze the almost nonexistent inflection. Was the Weaver irritated, or curious, or both?

"no one can cross the mountains." A pair of arms gestured toward the towering peaks that loomed above them.

"We did not come over the mountains," said Clothahump, "but through them." He nodded toward the river. "We came on this watercourse through the Earth's Throat."

The spider's head bobbed from side to side. "that is not possible."

"Then how the hell do you think we got here?" Talea said challengingly, bravery and bluster overcoming common sense.

"it may be that . . ." The spider hesitated, the whispery tones little louder than the breeze wafting across the ship. Then faint, breathy puffs came from that arachnoid throat. It was a laughter that sounded like the wind that gets lost in thick trees and idles around until it blows itself out.

"ah, sarcasm. a trait of the soft-bodied, i believe. what do you wish here on the scuttleteau?"

Jon-Tom felt himself drawn to the side by Caz while the wizard and Weaver talked. The rabbit gestured toward the sky.

The other five Weavers now hung directly above the boat from short individual cables. It was obvious they could be on the deck in seconds. They carried cleverly designed knives and bolas that could be easily manipulated by the double flexible claws tipping each limb.

"They've been quiet enough thus far," said Caz, "but should our learned leader's conversation grow less than accommodating, we should anticipate confronting more than one of them." His hand slid suggestively over the knife slung at his own hip, beneath the fine jacket.

Jon-Tom nodded acknowledgment. They separated and casually apprised the others of the quintet dangling ominously over their heads.

When Clothahump had finished, the spider moved back against the railing and regarded them intently. At least, that was the impression Jon-Tom received. It was difficult to tell not only how he was seeing them mentally, but physically as well. With four eyes, two small ones and two much larger ones mounted higher on his head, the Weaver would be hard to surprise.

"you have come a long way without being sure of the nature of your eventual reception. to what purpose? you have talked much and said little, the mark of a diplomat but not necessarily of a friend. why then are you here?"

Above, the Weaver's companions swayed gently in the breeze and caressed their weapons.

"I'm sorry, but we can't tell you that," said Clothahump boldly. Jon-Tom moved to make certain his back was against the mast. "Our information is of such vital importance to the Weavers that it can only be related to the highest local authority."

"nothing a warmlander can say is of any importance to the weavers." Again came that distant, whistling laugh, blowing arrogantly across the deck.

"*Nilonthom*!" roared Clothahump in his most impressive sorceral tone. Vibrations rattled the boat. Whitecaps snapped on the crests of sudden waves, and there was a distant rumble of thunder. The five watchers in the net overhead bounced nervously on their organic tethers while the Weaver in the boat stiffened against the rail.

Clothahump lowered his arms. One had to stare hard at the inoffensive-appearing little turtle with the absurd spectacles to believe that voice had truly issued from that hard-shelled body.

"By my annointment as Sorcerer-Majestic of the Last Circle, by the brow of Elrath-Vune now long dust, by all the oaths that bind all the practitioners of True Magic back to the

141

beginnings of divination, I swear to you that what I have to say *is* vital to the survival of Weaver as well as warmlander, and that it can be imparted only to the Grand Webmistress herself!''

That pronouncement appeared to shake their visitor as badly as had the totally unexpected demonstration of wizardly power.

''most impressive in word and action,'' the spider husked. ''that you are truly a wizard cannot be denied.'' He recovered some ''octupul'' poise and executed a short little bow, crossing all four upper limbs across his chest.

''forgive my hesitation and suspicions and accept my apologies should i have offended you. my name is ananthos.''

''Are you in charge of the river guards, then?'' Flor indicated the five remaining armed Weavers still drifting in the wind overhead.

The spider turned his head toward her, and she fought hard not to shudder. ''your meaning is obscure, female human. we do not 'guard' the bridge. there are not any who would harm it, and none until now come out of the hole into which the river dies.''

''Then why are you here at all? Why the bridge?'' Jon-Tom didn't try to conceal his puzzlement.

''this is,'' and the Weaver gestured with one limb at the network of silken cables and its watchful inhabitants, ''a lifesaving grid. it was erected here to protect those young and ignorant weavers who are fond of playing in the river lamayad and who sometimes tend to drift too close to the hole which kills the water. were they to vanish within they would be forever lost.

''did you think then we were soldiers? there is no need for soldiers on the scuttleteau. we have no enemies.''

''Then a revelation is in store,'' muttered Clothahump so low the Weaver did not hear him.

''the bridge is to help protect infants,'' ananthos finished.

"Now don't that soothe a beatin' 'eart!" Mudge whispered disbelievingly to Jon-Tom. "A fearsome lookin' lot like this and 'e says they've no soldiers. Wot a fine pack o' allies they'll make, eh?"

"They've got weapons," his companion argued, "and they look like they know how to use them." He raised his voice and addressed the Weaver. "If this is nothing more than a station for rescuing wayward children, then why do you and your companions carry weapons?"

Ananthos gestured at the surrounding forest. "to protect ourselves, of course. even great fighters may be overwhelmed by a single large and powerful foe. there are beasts on the scuttleteau that would devour all on this craft and the craft itself in a single gulp. because we do not maintain an army to confront nonexistent enemies does not mean we are fleet-limbed cowards who run instead of fight. or did you think we were all eggsuckers?" He bared his respectable fangs.

"the confident and strong have no need of an army. each weaver is an army unto itself."

"It is about armies and fighting that we come," said Clothahump, "and about such matters that we must speak to the Webmistress."

Ananthos appeared as upset as a spider could possibly be. "to bring warmlanders into the capital is a great responsibility. by rights of history and legend i should turn you around and send you back into the hole from whence you emerged. and yet"—he struggled with the conflict between prescribed duty and personal feelings and thoughts—"i cannot dismiss the fact that you have made an impossible journey for reasons i am not equipped to debate. if it is of the importance you insist, i would fail did i not escort you to the capital. but to see the grand webmistress herself . . ."

He turned away from them, whether from embarrassment or indecision or both they could not tell.

"Why don't you," said Caz helpfully, "take us into protective custody, convey us to the capital under guard, and turn us over to your superiors?"

Ananthos looked back at him, his head bobbing in that odd side-to-side motion that was half nod and half shake. He spoke in a whispery, grateful hush.

"you have some understanding of what it means to be responsible to someone placed higher than oneself, warmlander of the big ears."

"I've been in that uncomfortable situation before, yes," Caz admitted drolly, polishing his monocle.

"i bow to your excellent suggestion."

IX

He leaned back and called breathily upward. "arethos, imedshud! *intob coom*." Two of the watchful Weavers dropped to the deck, their spinnerets snipping off the cables trailing from their abdomens. They studied the warmlanders with interest.

"these will accompany us on the journey, for i can hardly claim to have you in restriction, as your tall white friend has suggested, all by myself. yet i am charged with the watchfulness on this bridge and cannot leave it deserted. so three of us will accompany you and three remain here.

"we shall proceed upstream. a day's journey from here, the river lamayad splits. several days further it splits again. against that divide, set against the breath, is our capital, my home."

He added warningly, "what happens then is no longer my responsibility. i can make no promises as to the nature of your reception, for i am low in the hierarchy, most low, for all that no weaver lies in the mud and none soars above the others. our hierarchy is a convenience and necessary to governing, and that is all.

"as to an audience with the grand webmistress..." his voice trailed away meaningfully.

"Diplomacy moves best when it moves cautiously," said Caz, "and not in dangerous leaps."

"For now it will be more than enough if you see us to the capital, Ananthos," Clothahump assured him.

The spider seemed greatly relieved. "then my thoughts are clear. i am neither helping nor hindering you, merely referring you to those in the position to do so." He turned and ceremoniously detached the cable holding the bow of the motionless boat.

Bribbens had remained by his oar during the discussion. Now he leaned gently on it as once again the wind began to fill the sail. The boat turned neatly on its axis as the cry of "ware the boom!" rang out from the steersman. Soon they had passed beneath the intricate webwork spanning the river and were once again traveling upstream.

"i've never seen a warmlander." Ananthos was standing quite close to Jon-Tom. "most interesting biology." Despite ten thousand years of primitive fears, Jon-Tom did not pull away when the spider reached out to him.

Ananthos extended a double-clawed leg. It was covered with bristly hairs. The delicate silk scarves of green and turquoise enveloping the limb mitigated its menacing appearance. The finger-sized claws touched the man's cheek, pressed lightly, and traveled down the face to the neck before withdrawing. Somehow Jon-Tom kept from flinching. He concentrated on those brightly colored eyes studying him.

"no fur at all like the short bewhiskered one, except on top. and soft...so soft!" He shuddered. "what a terrible fragility to live with."

"You get used to it," said Jon-Tom. It occurred to him that the spider found him quite repulsive.

They continued studying each other. "That's beautiful silk," the man commented. "Did you make it yourself?"

"do you mean, did i spin the silk or manufacture the scarf? in truth i did neither." He waved a leg at the others. "we differ even more in size than you seem to. some of our smaller cousins produce far finer silk than a clumsy oaf like myself is capable of. they are trained to do so, and others carefully weave and pattern their produce." He reached down and unwrapped a four-foot turquoise length and handed it to Jon-Tom.

A palmful of feathers was like lead compared to the scarf. He could have whispered at it and blown it over the side of the boat. The dye was a faint blue, as rich as the finest Persian turquoise with darker patches here and there. It was the lightest fabric he'd ever caressed. Wearing it would be as wearing nothing.

He moved to hand it back. Ananthos' head bobbed to the left. "no. it is a gift." Already he'd refastened two other long scarves to compensate for the loss of the turquoise. Jon-Tom had a glimpse of the intricate knot-and-clip arrangement that held the quasi-sari together.

"Why?"

Now the head bobbed down and to the right. He was beginning to match head movements to the spider's moods. What at first had seemed only a nervous twitching was becoming recognizable as a complex, highly stylized group of suggestive gestures. The spiders utilized their heads the way an Italian used his hands, for speech without speaking.

"why? because you have something about you, something i cannot define. and because you admired it."

"I'll say we've got something about us," Talea grumbled. "An air of chronic insanity."

Ananthos considered the comment. Again the whispery laughter floated like snowflakes across the deck. "ah, humor! humor is among the warmlander's richest qualities. perhaps the most redeeming one."

"For all the talk of hostility our legends speak of, you seem mighty friendly," she said.

"it is my duty, soft female," the Weaver replied. His gaze went back to Jon-Tom. "please me by accepting the gift."

Jon-Tom accepted the length of silk. He wrapped it muffler-like around his neck, above the indigo shirt. It didn't get tangled in his cape clasp. In fact, it didn't feel as though it was there at all. He did not consider how it might look sandwiched between the iridescent green cape and purpled shirt.

"I have nothing to offer in return," he said apologetically. "No, wait, maybe I do." He unslung his duar. "Do the Weavers like music?"

Ananthos' answer was unexpected. He extended two limbs in an unmistakable gesture. Jon-Tom carefully passed over the instrument.

The Weaver resumed his half-sit, half-squat and laid the duar across two knees. He had neither hands nor fingers, but the eight prehensile claws on the four upper limbs plucked with experimental delicacy at the two sets of strings.

The melody that rose from the duar was light and ethereal, alien, atonal, and yet full of almost familiar rhythms. It would begin to sound almost normal, then drift off on strange tangents. Very few notes contributed to a substantial tune. Ananthos' playing reminded Jon-Tom more of samisen music than guitar.

Flor leaned blissfully back against the mast, closed her eyes, and soaked up the spare melody. Mudge sprawled contentedly on the deck while Caz tried, without success, to tap time to the disjointed beat. Nothing soothes xenophobia so efficiently as music, no matter how strange its rhythms or inaudible the words.

An airy wail rose from Ananthos and his two companions. The three-part harmony was bizarre and barely strong enough to rise above the breeze. There was nothing ominous in their singing, however. The little boat made steady progress against the current. In spite of his unshakable devotion to his job, even Bribbens was affected. One flippered foot beat on the deck in a futile attempt to domesticate the mystical arachnid melody.

It might be, Jon-Tom thought, that they would find no allies here, but he was certain they'd already found some friends. He fingered the end of the exquisite scarf and allowed himself to relax and sink comfortably under the soothing spell of the spider's frugal fugue. . . .

It was early in the morning of the fourth day on the Scuttleteau that he was shaken awake. Much too early, he mused as his eyes opened confusedly on a still dark sky.

He rolled over, and for a moment memory lagged shockingly behind reality. He started violently at the sight of the furry, fanged, many-eyed countenance bending over him.

"i am sorry," said Ananthos softly. "did i waken you too sharply?"

Jon-Tom couldn't decide if the Weaver was being polite and offering a diplomatic way out or if it was an honest question. In either case, he was grateful for the understanding it allowed him.

"No. No, not too sharply, Ananthos." He squinted into the sky. A few stars were still visible. "But why so early?"

Bribbens' voice sounded behind him. As usual, the boatman was first awake and at his duties before the others had risen from beneath their warm blankets. "Because we're nearing their city, man."

Something in the frog's voice made Jon-Tom sit up fast. It

was not fear, not even worry, but a new quality usually absent from the boatman's plebian monotone.

Pushing aside his blanket, he turned to look over the bow, matching Bribbens' gaze. Then he understood the strange new quality he'd detected in the boatman's voice: wonderment.

The first rays of the sun were arriving, having mounted the mountain shield soaring ahead of the boat. In the distance lay a range of immense peaks more massive than Zaryt's Teeth. Several crags vanished into the clouds, only to reappear above them. Jon-Tom was no surveyor, but if the Teeth contained several mountains higher than twenty thousand feet then the range ahead had to average twenty-five.

More modest escarpments dominated the north and south. Swathed in glaciers and clouds, the colossal eastern range also displayed an additional quality: dark smoke and occasional liquid red flares rose from several of the peaks. The towering range was still alive, still growing.

The sparks and smoke that drifted overhead came from a massif much closer than the eastern horizon, however. Quite close a black caldera rose from surrounding foothills to a height a good ten thousand feet above the river, which banked to the south before it. Ice and snow crowned the fiery summit.

Snow gave way to conifers and hardwoods, they in turn surrendered to the climax vegetation of the variety which flanked the river, and that at last to a city which crept up and clung to the volcano's flanks. Small docks spread thin wooden fingers out into the river.

"my home," said Ananthos, "capital and ancestral settlement from which the first weavers laid claim to the scuttleteau and all the lands that abut it." He spread four forearms. "i welcome you all to gossameringue-on-the-breath."

The city was a marvel, like the scarf. The similarities did not end there, for like the scarf it was woven of fine silk.

Morning dew adhered to struts and suspensions and flying buttresses of webwork. Roofs were hung from supports strung lacily above instead of being supported by pillars from beneath. Millions of thick, silvery cables supported buildings several stories high, all agleam with jewels of dew.

Other cables as thick as a man's body, spun from the spinnerets of dozens of spiders, secured the larger structures to the ground.

On the lower, nearer levels they could discern dozens of moving forms. It was clear the city was heavily populated. Spreading as it did around the base of the huge volcano and climbing thousands of feet up its sides, it appeared capable of housing a population in the tens of thousands.

There was enough spider silk in that single city, if it could be unwrapped to its seminal strands, to cocoon the Earth.

Once Jon-Tom had spent an hour marveling at a single small web woven by one spider on an ocean coast. It had been speckled with dew from the morning fog.

Here the dew seemed almost choreographed. As the first rising rays of the sun struck the city, it suddenly turned to a labyrinth of platinum wires and diamond dust. It was too bright to look at, but the effect faded quickly as the dew evaporated. The sun rose higher, the enchanting effect dissipating as rapidly as the sting from a clash of cymbals. Left behind was a spectacle of suspended structures only slightly less impressive.

Gossameringue was all spheres and ellipses, arches and domes. Jon-Tom could not find a sharp angle anywhere in the design. Everything was smooth and rounded. It gave the city a soft feeling which its inhabitants might or might not reflect.

As the sun worked its way up into the morning sky, the little boat put in at the nearest vacant dock. A few early morning workers turned curious multiple eyes on the unique cargo of warmlanders. They did not interfere. They only stared. As befitted their historical preference for privacy, these few Weavers soon turned to their assigned tasks and ignored the arrivals. It troubled Clothahump. A people fanatic about minding its own business does not make a ready ally.

Under Ananthos' escort they left the boat and crossed the docks. Soon they had entered a silk and silver world.

"This mission had best be successful," said Caz as they began to climb. He placed his broad feet carefully. The roadway was composed of a fine checkerboard of silk cables. They were stronger than steel and did not quiver even when Jon-Tom experimentally jumped up and down on one, but if one missed a rung of the gigantic rope ladder and fell through, a broken leg was a real possibility.

After a while caution gave way to confidence and the party was able to make faster progress up the side of the mountain.

"I'll settle for just getting out of here alive," Talea whispered to the rabbit.

"Precisely my meaning," said Caz. He gestured back the way they'd come. The river and docks had long since been swallowed up by twisting, contorting bands of silk and silken buildings. "Because we'd never find our way out of here without assistance."

It was not all silk. Some of the buildings boasted sculptured stone or wood, and there was some use of metalwork. Windows were made of fine glass, and there was evidence of vegetable matter being employed in sofas and other furniture.

Though the Weavers were not arboreal creatures, their construction ignored the demands of gravity. The whole city was an exercise in the aesthetic applications of geometry. It was difficult to tell up from down.

Caz was right, Jon-Tom thought worriedly. Without Weaver help they would never find their way back to the river.

They climbed steadily. Wherever they passed, daily routines ground to a halt as the populace stared dumbfoundedly at creatures they knew only from legend. Ananthos and his two fellow guards took an aggressive attitude toward those few citizens who tried to touch the warmlanders.

The only ones who weren't shoved aside were the curious hordes of spiderlings who swarmed in fascination around the visitors' legs. Most of these infants had bodies a foot or more across. They were a riot of color underfoot; red, yellow, orange, puce, black, and more in metallic, dull, or iridescent shades. They displayed stripes and spots, intricate patterns and simple solids.

It was difficult to make sense of the extraordinary variety of colors and shapes because the predominant sensation was one of wading through a shallow pond made of legs. With remarkable agility the youngsters scrambled in and between the feet of the visitors, never once having a tiny leg kicked or stepped on.

They reserved most of their attention for Talea, Flor, and Jon-Tom. Bribbens and Clothahump they ignored completely. Nor were they in the least bit shy.

One scrambled energetically up Jon-Tom's right side, pulling thoughtlessly at his fortunately tough cape and pants. It rode like a cat on his right shoulder, chattering breathily to its less enterprising companions. Jon-Tom tried hard to think of it as a cat.

The adolescent displayed a cluster of painted lines that ran from its mandibles back between its eyes and down the back of its head. The cosmetics did not give Jon-Tom a clue as to its sex. He thought of brushing it away, but it behooves a guest to match the hospitality of his hosts. So he left it alone, resolutely ignoring the occasional reflexive flash of poisonous fangs.

The spiderling sat there securely and waved its foot-long

legs at disapproving adults and envious brethren. It whispered in a rush to its obliging mount.

"where do you come from? you are warm, not cold like the prey or the creatures of the forest. you are very tall and thin and you have hair only atop your head and there very dense." The youngster's partly clad abdomen brushed rhythmically against the back of Jon-Tom's neck. He assumed it was a friendly gesture. The fur on the spiderling's bottom was as soft as Mudge's.

"you have funny mouths and your fangs are hidden. may i see them?"

Jon-Tom patiently opened his mouth and grimaced to show his teeth. The spiderling drew back in alarm, then moved cautiously closer.

"so many. and they're white, not black or brown or gold. they are so flat, save two. how can you suck fluids with them?"

"I don't use my fangs—my teeth—to suck fluids," Jon-Tom explained. "What liquid I do ingest I swallow straight. Mostly I eat solid food and use my teeth to chew it into smaller pieces."

The youngster shuddered visibly. "how awful, how gruesome! you actually eat solid, unliquified flesh? your fangs don't look up to the task. i'd think they'd break off. ugh, ugh!"

"It can be tough sometimes," Jon-Tom confessed, recalling some less than palatable meals he'd downed. "But my teeth are stronger than yours. They're not hollow."

"i wonder," said the spiderling with the disarming honesty common to all children, "if you'd taste good."

"I'd hope so. I'd hate to think I've lived all these years just to give some friend an upset stomach. I'd probably be pizza-and-coke flavored."

"i don't know what is a pissaoke." The infant bared tiny

fangs. "i don't suppose you'd let me have a taste? your elders aren't watching." He sounded hopeful.

"I'd like to oblige," Jon-Tom said nervously, "but I haven't had anything to eat yet today and might make you sick. Understand?"

"oh well." The youngster didn't sound too disappointed. "i don't guess i'd like you sucking out one of my legs, either." He quivered at the thought. "you're a nice person, warmlander. i like you." Jon-Tom experienced the abdomen caress once again. Then the spiderling jumped down to join his fellow scamperers.

"luck to you, warmlander!"

"And to you also, child," Jon-Tom called hastily back to him. Ananthos and several responsible bystanders were finally shooing the spiderlings away. The children waved and cheered in excited whispers, like any others, their multiple, multicolored legs waving good-byes.

A greater weight pressured his left arm and he looked around uncertainly. It was no disrespectful spiderling, however. Flor's expression was ashen, and she slumped weakly against him. He quickly got an arm under her shoulders and gave her some support.

"What's wrong, Flor? You look ill."

"What's wrong?" Fresh shock replaced some of the paleness that had dominated her visage. "I've just been poked, probed, and swarmed over by a dozen of the most loathesome, disgusting creatures anyone could . . ."

Jon-Tom made urgent quieting motions. "Jesus, Flor. Keep your voice down. These are our hosts."

"I know, but to have them touch me all over like that." She was trembling uncontrollably. "*Aranas* . . . uckkkk! I hate them. I could never even stand the little ones the size of my thumb, for all that Mama used to praise them for catching the cockroaches. So you can imagine how I feel about these. I could hardly stand it on the boat." She moved unsteadily away from his arm. "I don't know how much more of this I can take, Jon-Tom," and she gestured at Ananthos, who was marching ahead of them.

They turned up another, broader web-road. "What matters isn't what they look like," Jon-Tom told her sternly, "but what's behind their looks. In this case, intelligence. We need their help or Clothahump wouldn't have herded us all this way." He eyed her firmly.

"Think you can manage by yourself now?"

She was breathing deeply. The color was returning to her face. "I hope so, *compadre*. But if they climb over me like that again..." A brief reprise of the trembling. "I feel so... so icky."

" 'Icky' is a state of mind, not a physiological condition."

"Easy for you to say, Jon-Tom."

"Look, they probably don't think much of the way we look, either. I know they don't."

"I don't care what they think," she shot back. "Santa Maria, I hope we finish with this place quickly."

"Oh, I don't know." He noted the way in which the rising sun, bright despite the intensifying cloudiness, sparkled off the millions of cables and the silken buildings and webwork walkway they were climbing. "I think it's kind of pretty."

"The fly complimenting the spider," she muttered.

"Except that the flies are here hunting for allies."

"Let's hope they are allies."

"Ahhh, you worry too much." He gave her an affectionate pat on the back. She forced a grin in response, thankful for his moral support.

Jon-Tom's attention returned forward, and to his surprise he found himself staring straight into Talea's eyes. The instant their gazes locked she turned away.

He decided she probably hadn't been looking at him.

Probably trying to memorize their path in case they had to try and flee. Such preparation and suspicion would be typical of the redhead. It did not occur to him that the glance might have been significant of anything else.

They had climbed several thousand feet by the afternoon. Ahead loomed an enormous structure. How many spiders, Jon-Tom wondered, had labored for how many years patiently spinning the silk necessary to create those massive ramparts of hardened silk and interlaced stone?

The royal palace of Gossameringue was made largely of hewn rock cemented together not with mortar or clay or concrete but layer on layer of spider silk. Turrets of silver bulged from unexpected places. The entire immense structure was suspended from a vast overhang of volcanic rock by cables a yard thick. Those cables would have supported a mountain. Though the wind was stronger here, high up the volcanic flank, the palace did not move. It might as well have been anchored in bedrock.

They entered a round, silk-lined tube and were soon walking through tunnels and hallways. It grew dark only slowly inside since the glassy silk admitted a great deal of light. Eventually torches and lamps were necessary, however, to illuminate the depths.

They confronted a portal guarded by a pair of the largest spiders yet seen. Each had a body as big as Jon-Tom's, but with their loglike legs they spanned eighteen feet from front to back.

They were a rich dark brown, without special markings or bright colors anywhere on their bodies. The multiple black eyes were small in comparison to the rest of the impressive mass. Shocking-pink and orange silks enveloped torsos and legs. There was also a set of white scarves tied around two forelegs and the nonexistent necks. Huge halberds with intricately carved wooden shafts rested between powerful forelegs.

They didn't move, but Jon-Tom knew they were closely scrutinizing the peculiar arrivals. For the first time since they'd entered Gossameringue he was frightened. Thoughts of the friendly spiderlings faded from his mind. It would have been little comfort had he realized that the pair of impressive guards before them were there precisely to intimidate visitors.

Ananthos turned to them. "you will have to wait here." After conversing briefly with the two huge tarantulas he and his two associates disappeared through the round entrance.

While they waited, the visitors occupied themselves by inspecting the now indifferent guards and the gleaming silk walls. The silk had been dyed red, orange, and white in this corridor and shone wetly in the light of the lamps. Jon-Tom wondered how far from the entrance they'd come.

Mudge sauntered over next to him. "I don't know 'ow it strikes you, mate, but seems t' me our eight-legged friends 'ave been gone a 'ell of a long time now."

Jon-Tom tried to sound secure as well as knowledgeable. "You don't just walk in on the ruler of a powerful people and announce your demands. The diplomatic niceties have to be observed. History shows that."

"More o' your studies, wot? Well, maybe it do take some time at that. Never met a lot o' bureaucrats that did move much faster than the dead. I expect they're all like that, slow movin' an' slow thinkin', no matter 'ow many legs they got."

"Here they come," Jon-Tom told him confidently.

But it was not Ananthos and his familiar comrades who emerged from the opening but instead a tall, very thin-legged arachnid with a delicate body and eyes raised high on the front of his skull. His forelegs were tied up in an intricate network of blue silk ribbons and there were matching purple ones on the rearmost limbs.

One wire-thin leg pointed at Caz, who stood nearest the

portal, while dozens of spiders of varied size and color suddenly poured from behind him.

"immobilize them and carry them down!"

"Hey, wait a minute." Jon-Tom was unable to get his staff around before he'd been seized by half a dozen hooking legs. Others thrust threatening spears and knives at his belly.

"There has been a mistake." Clothahump was already disappearing around a corner, carried on his back.

"Put me down or I'll cut your smelly heads off!" All fire and helpless frustration, Talea was being carted closely behind the wizard.

Then Jon-Tom felt himself turned on his back and borne on dozens of hairy legs, kicking and protesting with equal lack of effect.

They went down into darkness. How far he couldn't guess, but it wasn't long before they were dumped into a silk-and-stone cell under the imperious direction of the emaciated and beribboned spider in charge.

The silk lining the chamber was old and filthy. There were no windows to let in light, only a few oil lamps in the corridor beyond. Jon-Tom gathered himself up and moved to inspect the cross-hatched webwork that barred their exit.

It was not sticky to the touch, but was quite invulnerable. He leaned against it and shouted at their retreating captors.

"Stop, you can't put us in here! We're diplomatic visitors. We're here to see the Grand Webmistress and . . . !"

"Save your wind, my friend." Caz stood at the outermost corner of the cell, squinting up the silk ladder-steps. "They've gone."

"Shit!" Jon-Tom kicked at an irregular, flattened piece of shiny material. At first he thought it was a piece of broken pottery. Closer inspection revealed it was a section of chitin. It clattered off a stone set in the far wall.

"God damn that sly-voiced Ananthos. He led us all this way by making us believe he was our friend."

"He never said he was our friend." Bribbens sat against a wall, his head resting on his knees. "Merely that he was doing his duty. Get us this far, then it'd be up to us, he said." The frog chuckled throatily. "Certainly hasn't gone out of his way to make it easy for us, looks like."

Talea was sniffing the air and frowning. "I don't know if any of you have noticed it yet, but—"

There was a startled scream. Jon-Tom looked left. Flor had been standing there. Now she'd fallen forward and landed hard on the floor. Her foot had vanished through an opening in the wall and the rest of her was slowly following. . . .

X

They hadn't noticed the passageway when they'd been chucked into the cell. There was no telling where it ran to or what had hold of Flor. Blood oozed from beneath her nails as she tried to dig her fingers into the floor.

Jon-Tom was first at her side. Without thinking, he leaned over and heaved a head-sized rock at her foot. There was a breathy exclamation of surprise and pain from beyond. She stopped sliding.

Caz and Mudge half dragged, half carried her across the cell. Whatever had hold of her had missed her leg, but her boot was neatly punctured just behind the calf.

As he backed away from the opening several legs scrambled through. They were attached to a two-foot-wide bulbous body of light green with blue stripes and spots. Jon-Tom took note of the fact that it wore only one black silk scarf tied around the left rear leg at the uppermost joint.

The visitor was followed closely by a second, smaller

spider. This one was an electric maroon with a single large gray rectangle on its abdomen. A third spider squeezed into their cell, barely clearing the passageway. It was gray-brown with white circles on cephalothorax and abdomen and had shockingly red legs. All wore only the single black scarf on identical limbs.

The three spiders stood confronting the wary knot of warmlanders.

"what the hell," said the first spider who'd entered, in a tone so high and flighty it was barely intelligible, "are you?"

"Diplomatic ambassadors," Clothahump informed them, with as much dignity as he could muster under the circumstances.

The little arachnid bobbed his head in that maybe yes, maybe no movement Jon-Tom had come to recognize. "maybe you're diplomatic ambassadors to you," he said, "but you're just food to us."

"they look nice and soft," said the big one in a slightly deeper but still tenebrous voice. His body was a good three feet across, bulky, and with three foot legs. "diplomats or blasphemers, ambassador or storage-stealers, what difference does it make?" He displayed bright red fangs. "dinner is dinner."

"You think so? Touch one of us again," said Jon-Tom warningly, "and I'll shove your fangs down your throat."

The first spider cocked multiple eyes at him. "will you now, half-limbed?" The latter was an apparent reference to Jon-Tom's disproportionately fewer number of limbs. "tell you a thing. if you can do that we'll treat you as something more than dinner. if you can't"—he pointed with a leg toward the shivering Flor—"we start with that one for an appetizer."

"Why her, why not me?"

The spider could not grin, but conveyed that impression nonetheless. "almost had a taste. she smells full of fluid."

It was too much for the terrified arachniphobe, that casual talk of being sucked dry like a lemon. She turned and vomited.

"there, you see?" said the spider knowingly.

Jon-Tom quelled his own rising nausea. He ignored the gagging sounds behind him to keep his attention on the big red-legged spider. It had scuttled off to the side, away from its companions.

"you can have me if you can get me," it taunted.

"Same goes for me," said Jon-Tom grimly. "Leave the others out of this."

"we'll do that for a start." The spider was sitting back on his hind legs, waving the four front limbs ritualistically as it bobbed from side to side. Then it brought them down and rushed forward.

It had been a while since Jon-Tom had practiced any karate. Four years, in fact. But he'd become reasonably good before he'd quit. What he hadn't learned was how to attack something with eight limbs. Not that they would matter if the spider got those red fangs into him. Even if this particular arachnid's venom wasn't very toxic, the shock alone might be enough to kill.

The attacker's intent seemed to involve throwing as many legs as possible at its prey in order to distract him while the fangs bit home.

It was possible the spider wouldn't expect an attack. If the eight limbs were confusing to Jon-Tom, then perhaps his human length and long legs might equally puzzle the spider. Besides, the best defense is a good offense, he reasoned.

So he ran at his opponent instead of away from it, keeping his eyes on his target as he was supposed to and trying hard to remember. Up on the opposite foot, kick out with the right, left leg tucked under the other.

Agile claws reacted quickly, but not quickly enough. They

scraped at Jon-Tom's neck and arms. They didn't prevent his right foot from landing hard between the eight eyes (there was no chin to aim for).

The impact traveled up Jon-Tom's leg. He landed awkwardly on his left foot, stumbled, and fought desperately to regain his balance.

It wasn't necessary. The spider had stopped in its tracks. Making mewling noises horribly reminiscent of a lost kitten, it sat down, rolled over on its back, and clawed at its face. The leg movements slowed like a clock winding down. Jon-Tom waited nearby, panting hard in a defensive posture.

The leg movements finally ceased. Green goo dripped from between the eyes, which no longer shone in the lamplight. The spider who'd entered the cell first scrabbled over to its motionless, larger companion.

"damme," he breathed in disbelief, "you've killed jogand."

Jon-Tom caught his breath, frowned. "What do you mean, I've killed him? I didn't kick him hard enough to kill him."

"dead for sure, for sure," said the smaller spider, turning a respectful gaze on the man. Blood continued to seep from the wound.

Fragile exoskeleton, Jon-Tom thought in relief and astonishment. Come to think of it, he'd seen a lot of clubs here. They'd be very effective against recalcitrant arachnids. Instead of a glass jaw, the spider possessed a glass body.

Or maybe he'd just slipped in a lucky blow. Either way . . .

He glared warily at the remaining pair. "No hard feelings?"

The first spider gazed distastefully down at his dead companion. "jogand always was the impulsive type."

They were distracted by a clattering in the corridor. A spider they did not recognize approached the webwork silk bars. He was not the skinny one with all the ribbons. As they watched silently, he poured the contents of a pear-shaped bottle on a section of the bars. They began to dissolve like so much hot jelly.

Another figure emerged from the shadows to stand just behind the jailer: Ananthos.

"i am terribly sorry," he told them, waving many legs at the cell. "this was done without higher orders or good knowledge. the individual responsible has already been punished."

"Blimey but if we didn't think you'd sold us over!" said a relieved Mudge.

Ananthos looked outraged. "i would never do such a thing. i take my responsibilities seriously, as you well should know." Then he noticed the corpse on the cell floor, looked back into the cell.

"'Twere 'is wizardship there," said Mudge, indicating Jon-Tom. Ananthos bowed respectfully toward the human.

"a good piece of work. i am sorrowful for the trouble caused you."

A pathway large enough to allow egress had been made in the bars. Ananthos' companions moved aside as the prisoners exited.

The small spider tried to follow Clothahump out and was promptly clobbered behind the head by one of the guards. The spider shrank back into the cell.

"not you," muttered the guard. "warmlanders only."

"why not? aren't we part of their party now?" He hooked foreclaws over the rapidly hardening new bars two of the guards were spinning.

"you are common criminals," said Ananthos tiredly. "as you must know, common criminals are not permitted audience with the grand webmistress."

The little spider hesitated. His head cocked toward Jon-Tom. "you're going to see the grand webmistress?"

"That's what we've come all this way for."

"then we'll stay right here. you can't force us to come!" And both spiders drew back behind the bleeding corpse of their dead companion, scuttled for the tunnel leading to their own cell.

Their sudden shift sparked uncomfortable thoughts in John-Tom's mind as he followed Talea's twisting form up the stairwell they'd so recently been hustled down.

"What do you suppose he meant by that?" She looked back down at him and shrugged.

"i told you i could do nothing for you beyond bringing you to gossameringue," Ananthos explained. "it must be considered that the webmistress not only might not assist you but may condemn you to rejoin those rabble in their hole," and he gestured with a leg back down the stairs.

"So we could find ourselves right back in jail?" asked Flor.

"or worse." He continued to point downward with the waving, silk-swathed leg. "i hope you will not hold what occurred down there against me. a chamberlaine overstepped her authority."

"We know it wasn't your fault," said Clothahump reassuringly. Pog seemed about to add something but kept his mouth shut at a warning glance from the wizard.

Before long they had retraced their ignominious descent and stood before the high, arching doorway flanked by the two immense guards. A small blue spider met them there. He was full of apologies and anxiety.

When he'd finished bobbing and weaving, he beckoned them to follow.

The chamber they entered was high and dark. A few narrow windows were set in the rear wall. Only a couple of lamps burned uncertainly in their wall holders, shedding reluctant amber light on vast lounges and pillows of richly colored silk. It did not occur to anyone to wonder what they were stuffed with.

More surprising was the large quantity of decorative art. There were sculptures in metal and wood, in stone and embalmed spider silk. Gravity-defying mobiles stretched from ceiling to floor. Some were cleverly lit from within by tiny lamps or candles. Some of the sculpture was representational, but a surprising amount was abstract. Silken parallelograms vied with stress patterns for floor space. The colors of both sculptures and furniture were subdued in shade but bright of hue: orange, crimson, black and purple, deep blues and deeper greens. There were no pastels.

"the grand webmistress Oll bids you welcome, strangers from a far land," the little spider piped. "i leave you now." He turned and scurried quickly out the doorway.

"i must go also," said Ananthos. He hesitated, then added, "some of your ideas mark you almost akin to the eternal weave. perhaps we shall meet again some day."

"I hope so," said Jon-Tom, whispering without knowing why. He watched as the spider followed the tiny herald in retreat.

They walked farther into the chamber. Clothahump put hands on nonexistent hips, murmured impatiently, "Well, where are you, madam?"

"up here!" The voice was hardly stentorian, but it was a good deal richer than the breathy weaver whispers they'd had to contend with thus far; chocolate mousse compared to chocolate pudding. It seemed the voice had slight but definite feminine overtones, but Jon-Tom decided he might be anthropomorphosizing as he stood there in the near darkness.

"here," said the voice once more. The eyes of the visitors traveled up, up, and across the ceiling. High in the right-hand corner of the chamber was a vast, sparkling mass of the finest silk. It had been inlaid with jewels and bits of metal in delicate mosaic until it sucked all the light out of the two feeble lamps and threw it back in the gaze of any fortunate onlookers. The silk itself had been arranged in tiny abstract geometric forms that fit together as neatly as the pieces of a silver puzzle.

A vast black globe slid over the side of the silken bower. On a thin thread it fell slowly toward the chamber floor, like a huge drop of petroleum. It was not as large as the massive tarantulas guarding the entryway, but it was far bulkier than Ananthos and most of the other arachnid inhabitants of Gossameringue. The bulbous abdomen was nearly three feet across. Save for a brilliant and all too familiar orange-red hourglass splashed across the underside of the abdomen, the body appeared to be encased in black steel.

Multiple black eyes studied the visitors expressionlessly. The spinnerets daintily snipped the abdomen free from the trailing silk cable. Settling down on tiptoe, the eight legs folded neatly beneath the body. Then the enormous black widow was resting comfortably on a sprawling red cushion, preening one fang with a leg tip.

"i am the grand webmistress Oll," the polite horror informed them. "you must excuse the impoliteness of cleaning my mouth, but my husband was in for breakfast and we have only just now finished."

Jon-Tom knew something of the habits of black widows. He eyed the jeweled boudoir above and shuddered.

Clothahump, unfazed by the Grand Webmistress' appearance, stepped briskly to the fore. Once again he laid out the reason for their extraordinary journey. He detailed their experiences on the Swordsward, in the Earth's Throat, related the magical crossing of Helldrink. Even in his dry, mechanical voice the retelling was impressive.

The Grand Webmistress Oll listened intently, occasionally permitting herself a whispered expression of awe or appreciation. Clothahump rambled on, telling of the peculiar new evil raised by the Plated Folk and their imminent invasion of the warmlands.

Finally he finished the tale. It was silent in the chamber for several minutes.

Oll's first reaction was not expected. "you! come a little nearer." She finally had to raise a leg and point, since it was impossible to tell exactly where those lidless black eyes were looking.

She pointed at Jon-Tom.

His hesitation was understandable. After the initial shock of their appearance, he'd been able to overcome his instinctive reactions to the spiders. He'd done so to a point where he'd grown fond of Ananthos and his companions, to a point where he could allow curious spiderlings to clamber over his body. Even the three antisocial types they'd encountered in the cells below had seemed more abhorrent for their viciousness than their shape.

But the dark, swollen body before him was representative of a kind he'd been taught to fear since childhood. It brought to the surface fears that laughed at logic and reason.

A hand was nudging him from behind. He looked down, saw Clothahump staring anxiously at him.

"come, come, fellow," said the Webmistress. "i've just eaten." A feathery, thick laugh. "you look as though you'd be all bone, anyway."

Jon-Tom moved closer. He tried to see the Webmistress in a matronly cast. Still, he couldn't keep his gaze entirely away from the dark fangs barely hidden in their sheaths. Just a graze from one would kill him instantly, even if the widow's venom had been somewhat diluted by her increased size.

A black leg, different from any he'd yet encountered in Gossameringue, touched his shoulder. It traveled down his arm, then his side. He could feel it through his shirt and pants.

Close now, he was able to note the delicate and nearly transparent white silks that encompassed much of the shining black body. They had been embroidered with miniature scenes of Gossameringue life. Attire impressive and yet sober enough for a queen, he thought.

"what is your name, fellow?"

"Jon-Tom. At least, that's what my friends call me."

"i will not trouble you with my entire name," was the reply. "it would take a long time and you would not remember it anyhow. you may call me Oll." The head shifted past him. "so may you all. as you are not citizens of the scuttleteau, you need show no special deference to me."

Again the clawed, shiny leg moved down his front. He did not flinch. "do you also support the claims and statements of the small hard-shelled one?" Another leg gestured at Clothahump.

"I do."

"well, then." She rested quietly for a moment. Then she glanced up once more at Jon-Tom. "why should we care what happens to the peoples of the warmlands?"

"You have to," Clothahump began importantly, "because it is evident that if—"

"be silent." She waved a leg imperiously at the wizard. "i did not ask you."

Clothahump obediently shut up. Not because he was afraid of the large, poisonous body but because pragmatism is a virtue all true wizards share.

"now, you may answer," she said more softly to Jon-Tom.

History, he told himself, trying not to stare at those fangs so near. Try to see in this massive, deadly form the same grace and courtesy you've observed in the other arachnids you've met. To answer the question, remember your history. Because if you don't . . .

"It's quite easily explained. Are not you and the Plated Folk ancient enemies?"

"we bear no love for the inhabitants of the greendowns, nor they for us," was the ready reply.

"Isn't it clear, then? If they are successful in conquering all of the warmlands, what's to prevent them from coming for you next?"

There was dark humor lacing the reply. "if they do there will be such a mass feasting as gossameringue has never seen!"

Jon-Tom thought back to something Clothahump had told him. "Oll, in thousands of years and many, many attempts the Plated Folk have failed even to get past the Jo-Troom Gate, which blocks the Pass leading from the Greendowns to the warmlands."

"that is a name and place i have heard of, though no weaver has ever been there."

"Despite this, Clothahump, who is the greatest of wizards and whose opinion I believe in all such things, insists this new magic the Plated Folk have obtained control of may enable them to finally overthrow the peoples of the warmlands. After hundreds of previous failures.

"If they can do that after thousands of years of failure, why should they not do so to you as well? A thousand swords can't fight a single magic."

"we have our own wizards to defend us," Oll replied, but she was clearly troubled by Jon-Tom's words. She looked past him. "how do i know you are all the wizard this fellow says you are?"

Clothahump looked distressed. "Oh ye gods of blindness that cloud the vision of disbelieving mortals, not another demonstration!"

171

"it will be painless." She turned and called to the shadows. "ogalugh!"

A frail longlegs came tottering out from behind a high pile of cushions. Jon-Tom wondered if he'd been listening back there all along or if he'd just recently arrived. He barely had the strength to carry the thin silks that enveloped his upper body and ran in spirals down his legs.

He looked at Clothahump. "what is the highest level of the plenum?"

"Thought."

"by what force may one fly through the airs atop a broom?"

"Antigravity."

"what is the way of turning common base metals into gold?"

Clothahump's contemptuous and slightly bored expression suddenly paled.

"Well, uh, that is of course no easy matter. You require the entire formula, of course, and not merely the descriptive term applied to the methodology."

"of course," agreed the swaying inquisitor.

"Base metal into gold, my . . . it has been a while since I've had occasion to think on that."

Quit stalling, Jon-Tom urged the wizard silently. Give them an answer, any answer. Then the truth will come out in the arguing. But say *something*.

"You need four lengths of sea grass, a pentagram with the number six carefully set in each point, the words for shifting electron valences, and . . . and . . ."

The Grand Webmistress, the sorcerer Ogalugh, and the other inhabitants of the chamber waited anxiously.

"And you need . . . you need," and the wizard looked up so assuredly it seemed impossible he'd forgotten something so basic for even a moment, "a pinch of pitchblende."

Ogalugh turned to face the expectant Oll, spoke while bobbing and weaving his head. "our visitor is in truth, a wizard webmistress. how great i cannot say from three questions, but he is of at least the third order." Clothahump harrumphed but confined his protest to that.

"none but the most experienced and knowledgeable among the weavers of magic would know the last formula." He tottered over to rest a feathery leg on the turtle's shoulder.

"i welcome you to gossameringue as a colleague."

"Thank you." Clothahump nodded importantly, began to look pleased with himself.

The longlegs addressed Oll. "it may be that these visitors are all that they claim, webmistress. the fact that they have made so perilous a journey without assurance of finding at its end so much as a friendly welcome is proof alone of high purpose. i fear therefore that the words of my fellow wizard are truth."

"a troublesome thing if true," said the webmistress, "a most troublesome thing if true." She eyed Jon-Tom. "there has been hatred and emnity between the plated folk and the people of the scuttleteau for generations untold. if they can conquer the inhabitants of the warmlands then it may be, as you say, that they can also threaten us." She paused in thought, then climbed lithely to her feet.

"it will be as it must be, though heretofore it has never been." She stood close by Jon-Tom, the hump of her abdomen nearly reaching his shoulder. "the weavers will join the people of the warmlands. we will do so not to help you but to help ourselves. better the children of the scuttleteau have company in dying." She turned to face Clothahump.

"bearer of bad truths, how much time do we have?"

"Very little, I would suspect."

"then i will order the calling put out everywhere on the scuttleteau this very day. it will take time to assemble the best fighters from the far reaches. yet that is not the foremost of our problems. it is one perhaps you might best solve, since the proof of your abilities as travelers is not to be denied.'' She studied the little group of visitors.

''how in the name of the eternal weave are we to get *to* the jo-troom gate? we know only that it lies south to southwest of the scuttleteau. we cannot go back through the earth's throat, the way you've come to us. even if so large a group could cross helldrink, my people will not chance the chanters.''

''Offspring of the Massawrath,'' Caz murmured to Mudge. ''Can't say as I blame them. I'm still not sure it wasn't blind luck that got us through there, not sensible actions.''

''I don't want to go back myself,'' said Talea.

''Nor me, Master,'' said Pog, hanging from a strand of dry silk overhead.

''Then it follows that if we cannot return by our first route we must make a new one southward.''

''through the mountains?'' Ogalugh did not sound enthusiastic.

''Are they so impassable then?'' Clothahump asked him.

''no one knows. we are familiar with the mountains of the scuttleteau and to some small extent those surrounding us, but we are not fond of sharp peaks and unmelting snows. many would perish on such a journey, unless a good route exists. if one does, we do not know of it.''

''so it will be up to you, experienced travelers, to seek out such a path,'' stated the queen.

''your pardon, webmistress,'' said the spindly sorcerer, ''but there are a people who might know such a way, though they would have no need or use of it themselves.''

''why must wizards always talk in riddles? whom do you speak of, ogalugh?''

''the people of the iron cloud.''

Rich, whispery laughter filled the chamber. ''the people of

the iron cloud indeed! they will have nothing to do with *anyone*."

"that is so, webmistress, but our visitors are experienced travelers of the mind as well as the land, for have they not this very instant convinced us to join with them?"

"we are but independent," Oll replied. "the people of the iron cloud are paranoid."

"rumor and innuendo spread by unsuccessful traders who have returned from their land empty-clawed. it is true they are less than social, but that does not mean they will not listen." He turned to face Jon-Tom.

"they are much like some of you, friend. like yourself, and those two there," he pointed to Mudge and Caz, "and that one above," and he pointed now at Pog.

"They sound most interesting," said Clothahump. "I confess I know nothing of them."

"Are they good fighters?" Flor wondered. "Maybe we can get more out of them than directions."

"they are great warriors," admitted Ogalugh readily. "but you speak so facilely of making allies of them. you do not understand. they are interested in nothing save themselves, will support no causes but their own."

"That's just what we were told to expect of the Weavers," Jon-Tom said with becoming boldness.

"but we are sensible enough to see advantage and necessity where they occur," Oll argued back. "the people of the iron cloud, i am told, are unaffected by events elsewhere. they are protected by their indifference and their isolation."

"Nothing is safe from the evil the Plated Folk build," said Clothahump somberly.

"i am already convinced, wizard," she said. "convince the ironclouders: not me. it will be enough if they can show our fighters the way through the southern peaks."

"I have some small diplomatic skill," said Clothahump

immodestly. "I believe we can persuade them to do that, at least."

"perhaps. you must, or we can be of no help to you and your peoples, no matter what the plated ones decide to do. we will march when ready, but if we cannot find a way, we will be forced to turn back.

"i will send from among the weavers a personal representative. perhaps the proof that we have joined with you will help to convince the people of the iron cloud. in any case, someone will be necessary to come back to report on the results of your mission, be it successful or not."

"Not to preempt your prerogatives, Oll," said Caz carefully. "but if we might be permitted to choose the representative . . . ?"

"Sure," said Jon-Tom quickly, turning to face the Webmistress. "Would it be okay if a river guard named Ananthos served as your representative?"

"ananthos . . . i do not know the name. a common river guard, you say?"

"Yes. He's the one who brought us here."

"a common river guard of uncommon discernment, then. but still, it should be someone of higher rank."

"Please, Oll," Jon-Tom said, "rank will mean nothing to these Ironclouders if what you say of their nature is correct. And Ananthos is familiar with us. We know we can get along with one another."

"a sound recommendation, i suppose." She sighed and that whole globular black mass quivered. "it is the common soldiers who will decide this battle to come, as they do all such battles. perhaps it is fitting that one of their rank be our ambassador. as you say, it will likely not matter to the ironclouders.

"very well. you may have this ananthos. he will go with you as would one of my own children. uzmentap!"

"yes my lady, yes my lady?" A tiny adult spider scurried into the chamber, the same one who had admitted them a little while earlier.

"put out the word to all the ends of the scuttleteau, to the uppermost flanks of the mountains and the bottoms of the rivers, to all the believers in the weave and to all who would defend their webs against the plated folk, that a *temporary* alliance has been struck with the people of the warmlands to help them drive the plated beasts back into their putrid hole of a homeland once and for all!"

"it shall be done, my lady," said the herald quickly. She dismissed him with a wave of one leg and he hurried away to do the bidding.

"we will move as soon as we have word from your messenger ananthos," she told them. "we will go hopefully with a known route and will try our best if none such is available. but i will not send the best of the weave over the high snows to a cold death."

"We know that," said Clothahump gratefully. "You can't be expected to sacrifice yourselves to no purpose. But don't worry. We'll convince these people to show us a way."

Jon-Tom did not think it a judicial time to mention the possibility that such a path might not exist.

"it is in your claws now. i will have this ananthos found and will give him my personal instructions and the scarf of ambassadorial rank. will you require an escort?"

"We've gotten this far on our own," Talea pointed out. "From what you say these Ironclouders aren't hostile, just stubborn." She patted the sword at her hip. "We can take care of ourselves."

"i did not mean to imply otherwise. i will see that you are well supplied with food and—" She broke off at the twisted expression on Flor's face, one that was sufficiently intense and abrupt to transcend interspecies differences. "perhaps

177

you had best see to your own provisioning, at that. list what you wish and i will see it is provided. i had forgotten for a moment that you partake of nourishment in a fashion somewhat different from ours.''

''Our marital habits are a little different, too.'' Jon-Tom glanced significantly toward the bejeweled boudoir.

''so i have heard. honor is a strange thing. sometimes it is better to die happy and honored than to live miserably and unrespected. and you do not consider the effects such repeated matings have on my own mind. a burdensome thing. i am not permitted a lifetime of happiness but instead short periods followed by regretful melancholy. tradition must be upheld, however.'' She waved a leg magnanimously.

''all that is required will be provided. i only hope that we have sufficient time to prepare and that we are granted a path by which to proceed.''

''We are most grateful,'' said Clothahump, bowing slightly. ''You are a Grand Webmistress indeed.''

''it is no compliment to say that one can see the truth.'' She waved several legs. ''good fortune to you, newfound friends.''

The visitors began to file out of the chamber. Jon-Tom got halfway to the portal, then turned and walked back to her.

''the audience is at an end,'' Oll told him somewhat less than politely.

''I'm sorry. But I have to know something. Then I'll leave you to your privacy.''

Fathomless eyes regarded him quietly. ''ask then.''

''Why did you single me out to talk with, instead of Clothahump or Caz or one of the others?''

''why? oh, because of your delightful and inspiring selection of garb. it marks you clearly as a superior being to your companions, wizardly talents notwithstanding.''

Turning, she walked rhythmically back to stand below the

royal bower. Reattaching fresh silk to the dangling cable, she promptly climbed up and disappeared behind the barrier of gems and silken embroidery.

Jon-Tom was left to consider his bright black leathern pants, the matching boots and dark shirt.

It was only much later, as they were departing Gossameringue with Ananthos in the lead, that Jon-Tom had the startling and unsettling thought that the Grand Webmistress might have been considering him as material for something besides conversation. . . .

XI

It was terrible in the mountains.

Higher peaks towered to east and west, but as they moved south they were traversing the windswept flanks of Zaryt's Teeth, where they merged with the lower but still impressive mountains from which the greater heights sprang. It was bitingly cold. Soon they were walking not on rock or earth but on snow so dry and fresh it crunched like sugar underfoot.

On the third day after leaving the Scuttleteau and its gentle rivers and warm forests they encountered snow flurries. The day after that they were stumbling through a modest blizzard. Oll's fears that the southern range might prove unnegotiable seemed well founded.

Mudge and Caz suffered least of all, in contrast to their companions who did not enjoy the benefits of a personal fur coat.

Everyone profited from the example set by the stoic Bribbens. Though highly susceptible to the cold he trudged patiently along, silent and uncomplaining. Oftentimes his bulbous eyes were all that could be seen outside the thick clothing the Weavers had provided. He kept his discomforts to himself, and so his companions were shamed into doing the same.

Working with only rumor and supposition, the least reliable of guides, Ananthos somehow managed to pick a path southward.

They had made little progress in five days of hard marching when Jon-Tom had his idea. A temporary camp was established in the shelter of a small cave. Jon-Tom and Flor led the others in the hunt for suitable saplings and green vines. These were then woven together with spider silk dispensed by Ananthos.

With the aid of the new snowshoes their pace improved considerably. So did their spirits, boosted not only by their improved method of travel but by the hysterical image Ananthos presented as he shuffled along on six of the carefully wrought shoes, picking his way as uncertainly and carefully as a water strider trying to cross a pool of mud.

They also improved Bribbens' morale. While they kept him no warmer, the enormous shoes on his webbed feet gave him tremendous stability.

Jon-Tom moved up to march alongside Ananthos. It was the morning of their eighth day in the mountains.

"Could we have missed it?" His breath made a cloud in front of his face. The cold fought implacably for a route through his clothes. The crude parka hastily fashioned by the Weavers was no substitute for a goose-down jacket. There was a real danger of freezing to death if they didn't find warmer country soon.

"i don't think so." Ananthos indicated the precious scroll

he kept in a protective, watertight tube strapped to his rear left leg. "i can only rely on the chart the court historians made for us. no weaver has been this far south in many years. there was no reason for doing so and, for obvious reasons, no desire to do so."

"Then how can you be so sure we haven't passed it?"

"i can be only as sure as the charts. but the tales say if one but continues south, as we have, following the lowest route through the mountains, he will come upon the iron cloud. that is, if the tales are true."

"And if there is an iron cloud at all," Jon-Tom mumbled.

A leg touched his waist, but Ananthos' reassurances were stolen by the wind.

Despair is sometimes the preface to hope. On the ninth day the weather took pity on them. The snow ceased, the storm clouds betook themselves elsewhere, and the temperature warmed considerably, though it did not rise above freezing.

As if to compensate they were confronted with another danger: snow blindness. The brilliant Alpine sun ricochetted off snowbanks and glacier fronts, turning everything to shocking, adamantine white.

They managed to fashion crude shades from Ananthos' supply of scarves. Even so they were forced to keep their gaze to the ground and their senses at highest alert, lest the next snowbank turn out to be just the fatal side of some nearly hidden chasm.

Another day and they started downward.

Two weeks after departing Gossameringue they found the iron cloud.

They were climbing a slight rise, bisecting a saddle between two slopes. For days they had seen little color but varying shades of white, so the highly reflective black that suddenly confronted them was physically shocking.

Across a rocky slope of crumbled granite patched with snow was a mountainside that appeared to have been deluged with frozen tar. It was encrusted with ice and snow in occasional crevices.

Clearly the immense, smooth masses of black which jutted like an oily waterfall from the flank of the mountainside were composed of material much tougher than tar. They resembled a succession of monstrous bubbles piled one atop another without bursting. Holes pockmarked the blackness.

It was the metallic luster that led Flor to exclaim in surprise, "*Por dios, es* hematite."

"What?" Jon-Tom turned a puzzled expression on her.

"Hematite, Jon-Tom. It's an iron ore that occurs naturally in formations like that," and she pointed to the mountainside, "though I never learned of any approaching such size. The formation is called mammary, or reniform, I think."

"What is she saying?" asked Clothahump with interest.

"That the 'iron' part of the name Ironcloud is taken from reality and not poetry. Come on!"

They descended the gentle slope on the other side of the saddle and made their way across the stony plateau. The huge black extrusion hung above them, millions of tons of near-iron as secure as the mountain itself. Viewed against the surrounding snow and sky, it did indeed look much like a cloud.

But where were the fabled inhabitants, he wondered? What could they be like? The holes which pierced the masses overhead hinted at their possible abode, but though the party surveyed them intently there was no hint of motion from within.

"It looks abandoned," said Talea, staring upward.

"Don't see a soul," Pog commented from nearby.

They slid their burdensome backpacks off while examining

the inaccessible caves above. Climbing the granite wall was out of the question. Not only did the massive formation overhang but the smooth iron offered little purchase. Without sophisticated mountaineering gear there was no way they could reach even the lowest of the caves.

It was clear enough how the invisible inhabitants managed the feat, however. From the rim of each cave opening hung a long vine. Knots were tied in each roughly six inches apart. The profusion of dangling vines, swaying gently in the mountain breeze, gave the formation the look of a dark man with a beard.

The problem arose from the fact that the shortest cable-vine was a good two hundred feet long. No one thought themself capable of the combination of strength and dexterity necessary to make the climb. Talea considered it, but the thinness of the vine precluded the attempt. Whoever used the vines weighed a good deal less than any in the frustrated party of visitors.

Mudge was agile, but he wasn't fond of climbing. Ananthos was clearly too large to enter the hole, though he stood the best chance of rising to the height.

"We waste time on peripheral argument," Clothahump finally snorted at them, when he was at last able to get a word in. "Pog!"

Everyone looked around, but the bat was nowhere to be seen.

"'Ere 'e is!" Mudge pointed toward a large boulder.

They ran to the spot to find the bat squatting resolutely on the gravel behind the rock. He looked up at them with determined bat eyes.

"No way am I going up dere and sticking my nose in one of dose black pits. No telling what might take a notion to bite it off."

"Come now, mate," said Mudge reasonably, adjusting his

parka top, "be sensible. You're the only arboreal among us. If I didn't think that vine'd bust under me weight, I'd give a climb a good try. But why the 'ell should one o' us 'ave t' risk that, when you could be up there and back in a bloody minute or two without so much as strainin' your wings?"

"An accurate evaluation of our situation." Caz positioned his monocle tighter over his left eye. He'd steadfastly refused to surrender the affectation, even at the risk of losing the monocle in the snow. "You know, you really should have been up there and back already, on your own initiative."

"Initiative, hell!" Pog flapped his wings angrily. "One more display of 'initiative' from dis crazy bunch and we'll find ourselves meat on somebody's table."

"Now Pog," Clothahump began warningly.

"Yeah, I know, I know, boss. Go to it or ya'll turn me into a human or worse." He sighed, unfurled his wings experimentally.

"perhaps i could get up there—at least if i can't fit inside, i could attach to a hole above and hang down to look in." Ananthos sounded awkward, wanting to contribute.

"You know that surface is too slick for you to get a hold on, and if you could you probably couldn't get in and move around in there. Your leg span is too wide. Besides, I think Pog should have a chance at this." Clothahump was firm.

"A chance at what? Meeting my maker in a cold hole in da sky?"

Ananthos looked pained, but Jon-Tom gave Pog encouragement with his eyes.

"If you're all determined den to see poor Pog get his throat laid open, I expect I'll have ta be about da business. I warn ya, dough, if I don't come back alive I'll come back dead and haunt ya all to an early grave."

"Don't take any chances, Pog," Jon-Tom advised him. "Probably you won't find anything, or anyone. Just fly up and check out one or two caves, see if this place is really as deserted as it looks. If it is, maybe you'll learn the reason why.''

"Maybe one of da reasons is hiding in one of dose caves!" snapped the worried bat, gesturing upward with a wing thumb.

"If so then don't hang around to argue with it," said Talea. "You're going up to look, not to fight. Get your butt back down here as fast as you can."

Pog hovered just above the ground, lit on top of the boulder he'd been hiding behind. "No need ta worry 'bout that, Talea lady." He pulled his knife from its back sheath and slipped it between his jaws.

"Wish me luck," he mumbled around the blade.

"There is no need for luck when intelligence and good judgment are exercised," said Clothahump.

Pog made a rude noise, flapped his wings, and launched himself from the crest of the rock. He dropped, skimmed inches above sharp gravel, and then began to climb, using the warm currents rising from the bare plateau to ascend in a steady spiral.

"You think he'll be okay?" Flor shielded her eyes from the glare and squinted at the sky where a black shape was growing gradually smaller. Pog now looked like a toy kite against the pure blue curtain overhead.

"Instinct is a powerful aid to self-preservation."

"Oh?" she said with just a hint of sarcasm. "What book did that come out of?"

Jon-Tom was also leaning back and looking toward the lip of the iron cloud. He just swallowed Flor's remark.

Hemarist, da tall human lady had called it. No, dat wasn't right. Hema . . . Hema*tite*. Like in a tight spot, which is what you gots yourself into, Pog thought to himself. He was high above the rocky plain now. The figures of his companions were sharp and distinct against the gray gravel. He could tell they were watching him.

Waiting ta see how I get it, he thought miserably.

He circled before the lowest of the globular projections. His personal sonar told him nothing moved inside any of the several caves he'd flown past. That at least was a promising sign. Maybe the place *was* deserted.

Black iron, huh? It looked like a vast black face to him, with no eyes but lots of little mouths ready to swallow you, swallow you whole. Pretty soon he was going to have to stick his head into one of 'em.

Why couldn't ya have listened ta your mudder, he berated himself, and gone inta da mail soivice, or crafts transport, or aerial cop work?

But nah, ya had ta fall hard for a pretty piece o' fluff who won't give ya da time o' night, den get stinking drunk and apprentice yourself ta a half senile, sadistic, hard-shelled, hard-headed old fart of a wizard in da faint hope he'll eventually turn ya inta something more presentable ta you lady love.

He thought of her again, of the smoothly elegant blend of feathers from back to tail, of the slightly cruel yet delicate curve of beak, and of those magnificent, piercing yellow eyes which turned his guts to paste when they passed over him. Ah, Uleimee, if ya only knew what I'm suffering for ya!

He caught himself, broke the thought like a ceramic cup. If she knew what you was suffering she wouldn't give a flyin' fuck about it. She's the type who appreciates results, not well-meaning failures.

So gather what's left of your small store of courage, bat, and be about your job. And don't think about whether when your time's up, old Clothamuck will have forgotten da formula for transforming ya.

But, oh my, dat cave mouth looming just ahead is dark!

Empty, dough. His eyes as well as his sonar told him that. He fluttered next to the opening for a while, wrestling with the knowledge that if he didn't explore at least one of the caves his mentor would simply force him to return and try again.

He drifted cautiously inside. He sensed the echo of his wing beats pushing air off the tunnel walls. Then he settled down to walk.

The floor of the cave was carpeted with clean straw, carefully braided into intricately patterned mats. They appeared to be in good repair. If this iron warren was abandoned, it hadn't been so for long.

The tunnel soon expanded into a larger, roughly oval-shaped chamber. It was filled with a peculiar assortment of furniture. There were lounges but no chairs, and high-backed perches. The lounges suggested creatures that walked, as did the climbing vines dangling outside each cave opening, but the high-backs pointed to arboreals like himself. He shook his head. Deductive thinking was not his strong suit.

The utensils were also confusing rather than enlightening. A little light reached the chamber from the cave opening, but his sonar was still searching the surroundings as though it were pitch dark. His heart beat almost as rapidly. Finish dis, he told himself frantically. Finish it, and get out.

Several additional chambers branched from the back of the one he was studying. He would begin with the one immediately on his right and work his way through them. Then Clothahump couldn't say he'd made only a superficial inspection and order him to return.

It turned out to be a pantry-kitchen arrangement. It was discouraging to find that whoever had lived in the cave was omnivorous. In addition to instruments for preparing meat and fruit there was also a surprising garbage pile of small insect carcasses and empty nuts.

It was an eclectic and indiscriminate diet. Perhaps it also

included bats. He shuddered, drew his wings tighter around his small body. One more room, he told himself. One more, and den if da boss wants more info he can damn well climb up and look for himself.

He entered the next chamber, found more furniture and little else. He was ready to leave when something tickled his sonar. He turned.

A pair of huge, glowing yellow eyes stared down at him. Their owner was at least seven feet tall and each of those luminous orbs was as big around as a human face. Pog stuttered but couldn't squeeze out word or shout.

"Hooooooo," said the voice beneath those fathomless eyes in a long, querulous, and slightly irritated tone, "the hell are yoooooo?"

Pog was backing toward the chamber exit. Something sharp and unyielding pricked his back.

"Tolafay asked you a question, interloper! Better answer him." The new voice was completely different from the first, high and almost human.

Pog glanced over his shoulder, saw eyes not as large as the first pair he'd encountered but larger still in proportion to the body of their owner. Four yellow eyes, four malevolent little angry suns, swam in a dizzying circle around his head. He started to slump.

The sharp thing moved, poked him firmly in the side. "And don't faint on us, interloper, or I'll see your body leaves your gizzard behind. . . ."

"What the devil's keeping him?" Jon-Tom stared with concern up at the cave where Pog had vanished.

"Maybe they go very deep into the mountainside," Talea suggested hopefully. "It may take him a while to get all the way in and all the way out again."

"Perhaps." Bribbens stared longingly at a small creek that

flowed from the base of an icefall across the barren little plateau. "How I long for a boat again." He lifted one of his enormous, snowshoed feet.

"Walking's beginning to get to me. No fit occupation for a riverman."

"If it's any consolation I'd rather be on a boat myself just now," said Jon-Tom.

Then Mudge was gesturing excitedly upward. "Ease off it, mates! 'Ere 'e comes!"

"And damned if he hasn't got company." Talea unsheathed her sword, stood ready and waiting for whatever might drop out of the sky.

Pog drifted down toward them, a black crepe-paper cutout against the bright sky. He was paced by a similar silhouette several times more massive, with a distinctly animate lump attached to its back.

Dozens of other fliers poured from the perforated cloud-cliff like water from a sieve. They did not descend but instead blended together to create a massive, threatening spiral above the plateau.

Talea reluctantly placed her sword back in its holder. "Doesn't look like they've hurt Pog. We might as well assume they're friendly, considering how badly we're outnumbered."

"Characteristic understatement, flame-fur." Caz's monocle waltzed with the sun as he craned his neck to inspect the soaring whirlpool overhead. "I make out at least two hundred of them. Size varies, but the shape is roughly the same. I think they're all owls. I've never heard of such a concentrated community of them as this, not even in Polastrindu, which has a respectable population of nocturnal arboreals."

"It is odd," Clothahump agreed. "They are antisocial and zealously guard their privacy, which fits with what the Weavers told us about the psychology of Ironcloud's inhabitants. Yet they appear to have established a community here."

Pog touched down on the high boulder he'd so recently tried to hide behind. The flier shadowing him braked ten-foot wings. The force of the backed air nearly knocked Flor off her feet.

The creature took a couple of dainty steps, ruffled its feathers, and stood staring at them. The high tufts atop the head identified this particular individual as a Great Horned Owl. Jon-Tom found himself more impressed with those great eyes, like pools of speculative sulfur, than by the creature's size.

The lump attached to its back, which even Caz had not been able to identify, now detached itself from the light, high-backed saddle it had been straddling. It slid decorative earmuffs down to its neck, unsnapped its poncho, and leaned against its companion's left wing.

Now the spiral high above started to break up. Most of the fliers returned to their respective caves in the hematite. A few assumed watchful positions.

Jon-Tom eyed the lemur standing close to the owl. It was no longer a mystery who made use of the thin, knotted vines fringing the cave mouths. With their diminutive bodies and powerful prehensile fingers and toes, the lemurs could travel up and down the cables as easily as Jon-Tom could circle an oval track.

Pog glided down from the crest of his boulder and sauntered over to rejoin his friends. "Dis guy's called Tolafay." He gestured with a wingtip at the glowering owl. "His skymate's named Malu."

The lemur stepped forward. He was barely three feet tall. "Your friend explained much to us."

"Yes. Quite a story it was, tooooo." The owl smoothed the

folds of its white, green, and black kilt. "I'm not sure how much of it I believe," he added gruffly.

"We have managed to convince half a world," replied Clothahump impatiently. "Time grows short. Civilization teeters on the edge of the abyss. Surely I need not repeat our whole tale again?"

"I don't think you have to," said Malu. He indicated the watchful Ananthos. "The mere fact that a Weaver, citizen of a notoriously xenophobic state, is traveling as ally with you is proof enough that something truly extraordinary is going on."

"look who is calling another 'xenophobic,'" whispered Ananthos surlily.

"It had better be extraordinary," the owl grumbled. He used a flexible wing tip to wipe one saucer-sized eye. "You've awakened all of Ironcloud from its daily rest. The populace will require a reasonable explanation." He blinked, shielding his face as the sun emerged from behind a stray cloud.

"How you can live with that horrid light burning your eyes is something I'll never understand."

"Oh very well," said Clothahump with a sigh. "You will convey details of our situation to your leader or mayor or—"

"We have no single leader," said the owl, mildly outraged. "We have neither council nor congress. We coexist in peace, without the burdens imposed by noisome government."

"Then how do you make communal decisions?" Jon-Tom asked curiously.

The owl eyed him as though he represented a lower species. "We respect one another."

"There will be a feasting tonight," said Malu, trying to lighten the atmosphere. "We can discuss your request then."

"That's not necessary," said Flor.

"But it is," the lemur argued. "You see, we can welcome you either as enemies or as guests. There will be a feasting either way."

"I believe I follow your meaning." Caz spoke drily, eyeing Tolafay's razor-sharp beak, which was quite capable of snapping him in half. "I sincerely hope, then, that we can look forward to being greeted as guests. . . ."

They gathered that evening in a chamber far larger than any of the others. Jon-Tom wondered at the force, technological or natural, which could have hollowed such a space in the almost solid iron.

It was dimly lit by lamp but more brightly than usual in deference to the Ironclouders' vision-poor visitors. Trophy feathers and lizard skins decorated the curving walls. Nearly a hundred of the great owls of all species and sizes reveled in music and dance along with their lemur companions.

Their guests observed the spectacle of feathers and fur with pleasure. It was comfortably warm in the cave, the first time since departing Gossameringue any of them had been really warm.

The music was strange, though not as strange as its sources. Nearby a great white barn owl stood in pink-green kilt playing a cross between a tuba and a flute. It held the instrument firmly with flexible wing tips and one clawed foot, balancing neatly on the other while pecking out the melody with a precision no mere pair of lips could match.

Owls and lemurs spilled out on the great circular iron floor, dancing and spinning while their companions at the huge curved tables ate and drank their fill. It was wonderful to watch those great wings spinning and flaying at the air as the owls executed jigs and reels with their comparatively tiny but incredibly agile primate companions. Claws and tiny padded feet slipped and hopped in and around each other without missing a beat.

The night was half dead when Jon-Tom leaned over to ask Flor, "Where's Clothahump?"

"I don't know." She stopped sipping from the narrow-mouthed drinking utensil she'd been given. "Isn't he magnificent?" Her eyes were glowing almost as brightly as those of an acrobat performing incredible leaps before their table, his long middle fingers tracing patterns in the air. A beautiful female sifaka joined him, and the dance-gymnastics continued without a pause.

Jon-Tom put the question to the furry white host on his other side.

"I don't know either, my friend," said Malu. "I have not seen the hard-shelled oldster all evening."

"Don't worry yourself, Jon-Tom." Caz looked at him from another seat down. "Our wizard is rich in knowledge, but not rich in the ability to enjoy himself. Leave him to his private meditations. Who knows when again we will have an opportunity for such rare entertainment as this?" He gestured grandly toward the dancers.

But the concern took hold of Jon-Tom's thoughts and would not let go. As he surveyed the room, he saw no sign of Pog, either. That was still more unusual, familiar as he was with the bat's preferences. He should have been out on the floor, teasing and flirting with some lithesome screech owl. Yet he was nowhere about.

Jon-Tom's companions were having too good a time to notice his departure from the table. In response to his questions a potted tarsier with incredibly bloodshot eyes pointed toward a tunnel leading deeper into the mountainside. Jon-Tom hurried down it. Noise and music faded behind him.

He almost ran past the room when he heard a familiar moaning: the wizard's voice. He threw aside the curtain barring the entryway.

Lying on a delicate bunk that sagged beneath his weight was the wizard's bulky body. He'd withdrawn arms and legs into his shell so that only his head protruded. It bobbed and twisted in an unnerving parody of the head movements of the

195

Weavers. Only the whites of his eyes showed. His glasses lay clean and folded on a nearby stool.

"Hush!" a voice warned him. Looking upward Jon-Tom saw Pog dangling from a lamp holder. The flickering wick behind him made his wings translucent.

"What is it?" Jon-Tom whispered, his attention on the lightly moaning wizard. "What's the matter?" The echoes of revelry reached them faintly. He no longer found the music invigorating. Something important was happening in this little room.

Pog gestured with a finger. "Da master lies in a trance I've seen only a few times before. He can't, musn't be disturbed."

So the two waited, watching the quivering, groaning shape in fascination. Pog occasionally fluttered down to wipe moisture from the wizard's open eyes, while Jon-Tom guarded the doorway against interruptions.

It is a terrible thing to hear an old person, human or otherwise, moan like that. It was the helpless, weak sound a sick child might make. From time to time there were snatches and fragments of nearly recognizable words. Mostly, though, the high singsong that filled the room was unintelligible nonsense.

It faded gradually. Clothahump settled like a fallen cake. His quivering and head-bobbing eased away.

Pog flapped his wings a couple of times, stretched, and drifted down to examine the wizard. "Da master sleeps now," he told the exhausted Jon-Tom. "He's worn out."

"But what was it all about?" the man asked. "What was the purpose of the trance?"

"Won't know till he wakes up. Got ta do it naturally. Dere's nothin' ta do but wait."

Jon-Tom eyed the comatose form uncertainly. "Are you sure he'll come out of it?"

Pog shrugged. "Always has before. He better. He owes me. . . ."

XII

Once there were inquiring words at the curtain and Jon-Tom had to go outside to explain them away. Time passed, the distant music faded. He slept.

A great armored spider was treading ponderously after him, all weaving palps and dripping fangs. Run as he might he could not outdistance it. Gradually his legs gave out, his wind failed him. The monster was upon him, leering down at his helpless, pinioned body. The fangs descended but not into his chest. Instead, they were picking off his fingers, one at a time.

"Now you can't play music anymore," it rumbled at him. "Now you'll have to go to law school . . . aha ha ha!"

A hand was shaking him. "Da master's awake, Jon-Tom friend."

Jon-Tom straightened himself. He'd been asleep on the floor, leaning back against the chamber wall. Clothahump was sitting up on the creaking wicker bed, rubbing his lower jaw. He donned his spectacles, then noticed Jon-Tom. His gaze went from the man to his assistant and back again.

"I now know the source," he told them brightly, "of the new evil obtained by the Plated Folk. I know now from whence comes the threat!"

Jon-Tom got to his feet, dusted at himself, and looked anxiously at the wizard. "Well, what is it?"

"I do not know."

"But you just said . . . ?"

"Yes, yes, but I do know and yet I don't." The wizard sounded very tired. "It is a mind. A wonderfully wise mind. An intelligence of a reach and depth I have never before encountered, filled with knowledge I cannot fathom. It contains mysteries I do not pretend to understand, but that it is dangerous and powerful is self-evident."

"That seems clear enough," said Jon-Tom. "What kind of creature is it? Whose head is it inside?"

"Ah, that is the part I do not know." There was worry and amazement in Clothahump's voice. "I've never run across a mind like it. One thing I was able to tell, I think." He glanced up at the tall human. "It's dead."

Pog hesitated, then said, "But if it's dead, how can it help da Plated Folk?"

"I know, I know," Clothahump grumbled sullenly, "it makes no sense. Am I expected to be instantly conversant with all the mysteries of the Universe!"

"Sorry," said Jon-Tom. "Pog and I only hoped that—"

"Forget it, my boy." The wizard leaned back against the black wall and waved a weary hand at him. "I learned no more than I'd hoped to, and hope remains where knowledge is scarce." He shook his head sadly.

"A mind of such power and ability, yet nonetheless as dead as the rock of this chamber. Of that I am certain. And yet

Eejakrat of the Plated Folk has found a means by which he can make use of that power."

"A zombie," muttered Jon-Tom.

"I do not know the term," said Clothahump, "but I accept it. I will accept anything that explains this awful contradiction. Sometimes, my boy, knowledge can be more confusing than mere ignorance. Surely the universe holds still greater though no more dangerous contradictions than this inventive, cold mind." He reached a decision.

"Now that I am sensitized to this mind, I am confident we can locate it. We must find out whose it is and destroy him or her, for I had no sense of whether the possessor is male or female."

"But we can't do dat, Master," Pog argued, "because as you say dis brain is under da control of da great sorcerer Eejakrat, and Eejakrat stays in Cugluch."

"Capital city of the Plated Folk," Clothahump reminded Jon-Tom.

"Dat's right enough. So it's obvious dat we can't . . . we can't . . ." The words came to a halt as Pog's eyes grew wide as a lemur's. "No, Master!" he muttered, his voice filled with dread. "We can't. We can't possibly!"

"On the contrary, famulus, it is quite possible that we can. Of course, I shall first discuss it with the rest of our companions."

"Discuss what?" Jon-Tom was afraid he already knew the answer.

"Why, traveling into Cugluch to find this evil and obliterate it, my boy. What else could a civilized being do?"

"What else indeed." Jon-Tom had resigned himself to going. Could this Cugluch be worse than the Earth's Throat? Pog seemed to think so, but then Pog was terrified of his own shadow.

Clothahump's strength had returned. He slid off the bed,

started for the doorway. "We must consult the rest of our party."

"They may not all be in a condition to understand," Jon-Tom warned him. "We have generous hosts, you know."

"A night of harmless pleasure is good for the soul now and then, my boy. Though it should never descend to unconsciousness. I am pleased to see that you have retained control of yourself."

"So far," said Jon-Tom fervently, "but after what you've just proposed, I may change my mind."

"It will not be so bad," said the wizard, clapping him on the waist as they swung aside the concealing curtain and moved out into the tunnel. "There will be some danger, but we have survived that several times over."

"Yeah, but it's not like an innoculation," Jon-Tom muttered. "We haven't become immune. We keep taking risks and sooner or later they've got to catch up with us." He ducked to avoid a low section of iron ceiling.

"We shall do our best, my boy, to see that it is later."

Pog remained behind, hanging quietly from the oil lamp in the now empty room. He considered remaining behind permanently. The Ironclouders would shelter him, he was sure.

That would mean no transformation, of course. All that he'd suffered at the wizard's hands, and mouth, would have been for naught. Also, as the only arboreal of the group, he knew how they depended on him for reconnaisance and such.

Besides, better death than life cursed by unrequited love.

He let free of the lamp, dipped in the air, and soared out into the tunnel after the two wizards.

There was the anticipated debate and argument the next morning. One by one, as before, the various members of the little group were won over by Clothahump's assurances, obstinacy, and veiled threats.

Their course decided, it was time to ascertain the position taken during the night by the inhabitants of Ironcloud. Five of the great owls faced the travelers on the plateau below the cave city. Two were horned, two pale barn, and one a tiny hoot, who was smaller than Pog but equal in dignity to his massive feathered brothers. With them were five lemurs. The sun was not yet up.

"We do not doubt your seriousness nor the truth you tell," Tolafay was saying, "nor the worth of your mission, but still we doubted whether it was worth breaking a rule of hundreds of years of noninvolvement in the arguments of others." He gestured at Ananthos.

"Yet we share such feelings with the inhabitants of the Scuttleteau and they have nonetheless agreed to help you. So we will help, too." Murmurs of agreement came from his companions.

"That's settled, then," said a satisfied Clothahump. "You will be valuable allies in the coming war and—"

"A moment, please." One of the lemurs stepped forward. He had a high, stiff collar and light vest above billowing pantaloons of bright yellow. "We did not say that we'd be your allies. We said we'd help.

"You asked us to give the Weavers permission to travel through our country and to provide a route southward through the mountains so they can reach the Swordsward and then make their way to the Jo-Troom Gate you speak of. That's what we'll do. We'll also try and find you a way to the Greendowns. But we won't fight."

"But I thought—" Jon-Tom began.

"No!" snapped one of the other owls. "Absolutely no. We simply can't do any more for yooooo. Don't ask it of us."

"But surely—" A restraining hand touched Talea and she quieted.

"It is more than we'd hoped for, friends. It will suffice." Clothahump turned to face Ananthos. "We have the allies we came to find."

"so you do," said the spider at last, "provided the army can be assembled in time to make the march."

"I can only hope that it does," the wizard told him solemnly, "because the fate of several worlds may depend on it."

"Not Ironcloud," said another of the owls smugly. "Ironcloud is impregnable to assault by land or air."

"So it is," agreed Caz casually, "but not by magic."

"We'll take our chances," said Tolafay firmly.

"Then there's nothing more to be said." Clothahump nodded.

Wordlessly the Ironclouders departed, owl and primate soaring to join their brethren high in the night sky. Great wings and glowing eyes shone as the night hunters returned in twos and threes to their black home. They filled the air between earth and moon.

Another pair lifted from the plateau, heading for interior darkness and a good, warm day's sleep. Jon-Tom could only hope those homes would be as invulnerable as their inhabitants believed from the eventual attacks of the Plated Folk.

The last of the lemurs stared at them curiously while her companion owl kicked impatiently at the ground. The sun had peeked over the eastern crags and those great eyes were three-quarters closed in half sleep.

"There's one thing I'd like to know. How do you warmlanders expect to penetrate Cugluch?"

"Disguise," Clothahump told her confidently.

"You do not look much like Plated Folk," replied the lemur doubtfully.

Clothahump shook a finger at her, spoke knowingly. "The greatest disguise is assurance. We will be protected because no Plated One would believe our presence. And where assurance operates, magic is not far behind."

The lemur shrugged. "I think you are all fools, brave fools, and soon-to-be-dead fools. But we will show the Weavers the path they require and you the path to your deaths." She looked upward. "Your guides come."

Two owls descended to join them. One motioned to the waiting Ananthos. The Weaver trembled slightly as he made his farewells.

"we shall meet at the gate," he told them. "that is, if I survive this journey. i am not afraid of heights, but I have never been in a high place where i could not break a fall by attaching silk to some solid object. you cannot spin from a cloud."

He climbed on the owl's back, waved legs at them. The owl took a few steps, flapping mighty wings, and then soared into the air of morning. He wore dark shades to protect him from the sunlight.

They watched until the wings became a black line on the horizon. Then the pair faded even from Caz's view.

The small hoot owl stood muttering to herself nearby. Her kilt was black, purple, and yellow. "I'm Imanooo," she informed them brusquely. "Let's get on with this. I'll point you the way for two days, but that's all. Then you're on your own."

The remaining lemur mounted his saddle. "I still think you're all fools, but," he smiled broadly, "many a brave fool has succeeded where a cautious genius has failed. Fly well." He saluted with an arm wave as he and his friend rose skyward.

Alone in their cold-weather garb, the travelers watched until the last pairing vanished into the hematite. Then Imanooo rose and started off to the south, and they followed.

The path where there was no path carried them steadily lower. The unvarying downhill hike was a welcome change from the tortuous march to Ironcloud. The day after Imanooo left them they began to discard their heavy clothing. Soon they were down among trees and bushes, and snow was only a fading memory.

Jon-Tom slowed his pace to stay alongside Clothahump. The wizard was in excellent spirits and showed no ill effects from the past weeks of marching.

"Sir?"

"Yes, my boy?" Eyes looked up at him through the thick glasses. Abruptly Jon-Tom felt uncomfortable. It had seemed so simple a while ago when he'd thought of it, a mere question. Now it fought to hide in his throat.

"Well, sir," he finally got out, "among my people there's a certain mental condition."

"Go on, boy."

"It has a common name. It's called a death wish."

"That's interesting," said Clothahump thoughtfully. "I presume it refers to someone who wishes to die."

Jon-Tom nodded. "Sometimes the person isn't aware of it himself and it has to be pointed out to him by another. Even then he may not believe it."

They walked on a while longer before he added, "Sir, no disrespect intended, but do you think you might have a death wish?"

"On the contrary, my boy," replied the wizard, apparently not offended in the least, "I have a life wish. I'm only putting myself into danger to preserve life for others. That hardly means I want to relinquish my own."

"I know, sir, but it seems to me that you've taken us from

one danger to another only to take successively bigger risks. In other words, the more we survive, the more you seem to want to chance death.''

"A valid contention based solely on the evidence and your personal interpretation of it," said Clothahump. "You ignore one thing: I wish to survive and live as much as any of you."

"Can you be certain of that, sir? After all, you've already lived more than twice a normal human lifetime, a much fuller life than any of the rest of us." He gestured at the others.

"Would it pain you so much to die?"

"I follow your reasoning, my boy. You're saying that I am willing to risk death because I've already had a reasonable life and therefore have less than you to lose."

Jon-Tom didn't reply.

"My boy, you haven't lived long enough to understand life. Believe me, it is more precious to me now because I have less of it. I guard every day jealously because I know it may be my last. I don't have less to lose than you: I have more to lose."

"I just wanted to be sure, sir."

"Of what? The reasons for my decisions? You can be, boy. They are founded upon a single motivation: the need to prevent the Plated Masses from annihilating civilization. Even if I did want to die, I would not do so until I had expended every bit of energy in my body to prevent that conflagration from destroying the warmlands. I might kill myself if I suffered from the aberration you suggest, but only after I'd saved everyone else."

"That's good to hear, sir." Jon-Tom felt considerably relieved.

"There is one thing that has been troubling me a little, however."

"What's that, sir?"

"Well, it's most peculiar." The wizard looked up at him.

"But you see, I'm not at all certain that I remember the formula for preparing our disguises."

Jon-Tom hesitated, frowned. "Surely we can't enter Cugluch without them, sir?"

"Of course not," agreed Clothahump cheerfully. "I suggest therefore that you consider some appropriate spellsongs. You have seen one of the Plated Folk. That is what we must endeavor to look like."

"I don't know if . . ."

"Try, my boy," said the wizard in a more serious tone, "for if you cannot think of anything and I cannot remember the formula, then I fear we will be forced to give up this attempt."

Though he worked at it for the next several days, Jon-Tom was unable to think of a single appropriate tune. Insects were not a favorite subject for groups whose music he knew by heart, such as Zepplin or Tull, Queen or the Stones or even the Beatles, who, he felt sure, had written at least one song about everything. He searched his memory, went through the few classical pieces he knew, jumped from Furry Lewis to Ferlin Husky to Foreigner without success.

The dearth of material was understandable, though. Love and sex and money and fame were far more attractive song subjects than bugs. The thinking helped to kill the time and made the march more tolerable.

Never once did it occur to him that Clothahump might have invented the request simply in order to keep Jon-Tom's mind on harmless matters.

Three more days passed before they reached the outskirts of the vast, festering lowlands that formed the Greendowns. They rested on a slope and munched nuts, berries, and lizard jerky while studying the fog and mist that enshrouded the lands of the Plated Folk.

Conifers had surrendered the soil to hardwoods. These now

fought to assert their dominance over palms and baobabs, succulents and creepers. Occasionally a strange cry or whistle would rise from the mist.

Jon-Tom finished his meal and stood, his leathern pants sticking to his legs from the humidity. To the west towered the snow-crowned crags of Zaryt's Teeth. It was difficult to believe that a pass broke that towering rampart. It lay somewhere to the southwest of their present position. At its far end was the Jo-Troom Gate and beyond that, a section of Swordsward and bustling, friendly Polastrindu.

His own home was somewhat more distant, a trillion miles away on the other side of time, turn right at the rip in the fabric of space and take the fourth-dimensional offramp.

He turned. Clothahump was busy with wizard's business. Pog assisted him.

"We'd better come up with something." Talea had moved to stand next to him, stood looking down into the mist. "We go down there looking like ourselves and we'll be somebody's supper before the day's out."

"Aye, that's the truth, lass," agreed Mudge. " 'E'll 'ave t' make us look like a choice slice o' 'ell."

"He already has, I think," was Caz's comment. "You'd better straighten your antenna. The left one is pointing backward instead of forward."

"I'll do that." Mudge reached up and was in the middle of straightening the errant sensor when he suddenly realized what had happened. " 'Cor, but that was quick!"

Clothahump rejoined them. Rather, they were joined by a squat, pudgy beetle that sounded something like Clothahump. Pale red compound eyes inspected them each in turn. Four arms crossed over the striated abdomen.

"What do you think, my friends? Have I solved the problem and allayed your fears, or not?"

When the initial shock finally wore off, they were able to

take more careful stock of themselves. The disguises seemed foolproof. Talea, Flor, Mudge, and the rest now resembled giant versions of things Jon-Tom usually smashed underfoot. The middle set of arms moved in tandem with their owners actual ones. Pog had turned into a giant flying beetle.

"Is that really you in there, Jon-Tom?" The thing with Flor's voice ran a clawed hand over the pale blue chitin encasing him.

"I think so." He looked down at himself, noted with astonishment the multijointed legs, the smooth undercurve of abdomen, the peculiar wave-shaped sword at his hip.

"Not too uncomfortable, my boy?"

Jon-Tom looked admiringly at the squat beetle. "It's a wonderful job, sir. I feel like I'm inside a suit of armor, yet I'm cooler than I was a few moments ago without it."

"Part of the spell, my boy," said the wizard with pride. "Attention to detail makes all the difference."

"Speakin' o' attention t' detail, Your Masterness," Mudge said, "'ow do I go about takin' a leak?"

"There are detachable sections of chitin in the appropriate places, otter. You must take care to conceal bodily functions of any kind from those we will be among. I could not imagine Plated Folk jaws through which we might eat, for example. Hopefully we can finish our business in Cugluch and be out of it and these suits before very long."

"You remembered the formula well," Jon-Tom told the wizard.

"Well enough, my boy." They left their packs and started down the slope into the steaming lowlands. "One key phrase eluded me for a time.

> "Multioptics, eyes of glass,
> sextupal reach in fiberglass,

hot outside but cool within,
suit of polymers I'll spin."

He proceeded to detail the formula that had provided such perfectly fitted disguises.

"So these are foolproof, then?" Talea asked hopefully from just ahead of them. It was difficult to think of the black-and-brown-spotted creature as the beautiful, feisty Talea, Jon-Tom mused.

"My dear, no disguise is foolproof," Clothahump replied somberly.

"Dat's for damn sure." Pog fluttered awkwardly overhead on false beetle wings.

"We are entering the Greendowns from the northern ranges," the wizard reminded them. "The Plated Folk cannot imagine someone intentionally entering their lands. The only section of their territories which might be even lightly watched is that near the Pass. We should be able to mingle freely with whoever we chance to encounter."

"That'll be the true test of these suits, won't it?" said Caz. "Not whether we look believable to each other, but whether we can fool them."

"The formula was as all-encompassing as I could fashion it," said Clothahump confidently. "In any case, we shall know in a moment."

They turned a bend in the animal path they'd been following and came face to face with a dozen workers of that benighted land. The Plated Folk were cutting hardwood and loading the logs on a lizard-drawn sled. Unable to retreat, the travelers marched doggedly ahead.

They were nearly past when one of the cutters, a foreman perhaps, walked over on short spindly legs and gestured with two of his four limbs. Jon-Tom marked the gesture for future use.

"Hail, citizens! Whence come you, and wither go?"

There was an uncomfortably long silence until Caz thought to say, "We've been out on patrol."

"Patrol . . . in the mountains?" The foreman looked askance at the snows beyond the forest's edge. He made a clicking sound that might have passed for laughter. "What were you patrolling for? Nothing comes from the north."

"We do not," said Caz, thinking furiously, "have to provide such information to hewers of wood. However, there is no harm in your knowing." His disguise gave his voice a raspy tone.

"In her wisdom the Empress has decreed that every possible approach be inspected at least once in a while. Surely you do not question her wisdom?" Caz put his hand on his scimitar, and two limbs gripped the strange weapon.

"No, no!" said the insect foreman hastily, "of course not. Now, of all times, the greatest secrecy must be preserved." He still sounded doubtful. "Even so, nothing has come out of these mountains in years and years."

"Of course not," said Caz haughtily. "Does that not prove the effectiveness of these secret patrols?"

"That is sensible, citizen," agreed the foreman, his confusion overcome thanks to Caz's inexorable logic.

The others had continued past while the rabbit had been conversing with the foreman. That worthy snapped to attention and offered an interesting salute with both arms on his left side. Caz mimicked it in return, his false middle arm functioning smoothly in tandem with the real one.

"The Empress!" said the foreman with praiseworthy enthusiasm.

"The Empress," Caz replied. "Now then, be on about your business, citizen. The Empire needs that wood." The foreman executed a sign of acknowledgment and returned to his work. Caz tried not to move too hastily down the slope after his companions.

The foreman returned to his cutters. One of the laborers glanced up and asked curiously, "What was that all about, citizen foreman?"

"Nothing. A patrol."

"A patrol, up here?"

"I know it is odd to find one in the mountains."

"More than odd, I should think." His antennae pointed downhill toward the retreating travelers. "That is a peculiar grouping for a patrol of any kind."

"I thought so also." The foreman's tone stiffened. "But it is not our place to question the directives of the High Command."

"Of course not, citizen foreman." The laborer returned quickly to his work.

Wooded hillsides soon gave way to extensive cultivated fields cleared from bog and jungle. Most were planted with a tall, flexible growth about an inch in diameter that looked like jaundiced sugar cane. Swampy plantings alternated with herds of small six-legged reptiles who foraged noisily through the soft vegetation.

They also encountered troops on maneuver, always marching in perfect time and stride. Once they were forced off the raised roadway by a column twelve abreast. It took an hour to pass, trudging from east to west.

They passed unchallenged among dozens of Plated Folk. No one questioned their disguises. But Clothahump grew uneasy at their progress.

"Too slow," he muttered. "Surely there is a better way than this, and one that will have the extra advantage of concealing us from close inspection."

"What've you got in mind, guv'nor?" Mudge wanted to know.

"A substitute for feet. Excuse me, citizen." The wizard stepped out into the road.

The wagon bearing down on him pulled to a halt. It was filled with transparent barrels of some aromatic green liquid. The driver, a rather bucolic beetle of medium height, leaned over the side impatiently as Clothahump approached.

"Trouble, citizen? Be quick now, I've a schedule to keep."

"Are you by chance heading for the capital?"

"I am, and I've no time for riders. Sorry." He lifted his reins preparatory to chucking the wagon team into motion again.

"It is not that we wish a ride, citizen," said Clothahump, staring hard at the driver, "but only that we wish a ride."

"Oh. I misunderstood. Naturally. Make space for yourselves in the back, please."

As they climbed into the wagon, Jon-Tom passed close by the driver. He was sitting stiffly in his seat, eyes staring straight ahead yet seeing very little. Seeing only what Clothahump wanted them to see, in fact.

Under the wizard's urging, the rustic whipped the team forward. The mesmerization had taken only a moment, and no one else had observed it.

"Damnsight better than walking." Talea reached awkwardly down to draw one foot toward her, wishing she could massage the aching sole but not daring to remove even that small section of the disguise.

"Sure is," agreed Jon-Tom. He balanced himself in the swaying, rocking wagon as he made his way forward. Clothahump sat next to the driver. The insect ignored his arrival.

"A great deal happening these days," Jon-Tom said by way of opening conversation.

The driver's gaze did not stray from the road. His voice was oddly stilted, as though a second mind were choosing the words to answer with.

"Yes, a great deal."

"When is it to begin, do you think, the invasion of the warmlands?" Jon-Tom made the question sound as casual as he could.

A movement signifying ignorance from the driver. "Who is to know? They do not permit wagon masters to know the inner workings of the High Military. But it will be a great day when it comes. I myself have four nestmates in the invasion force. I wish I could be among them, but my district logistician insists that food supplies will be as important as fighting to the success of the invasion.

"So I remain where I am, though it is against my desires. It will be a memorable time. There will be a magnificent slaughter."

"So they claim," Jon-Tom murmured, "but can we be so certain of success?"

For a moment, the shocked disbelief the driver felt nearly overcame the mental haze into which he'd been immersed. "How can anyone doubt it? Never in thousands of years has the Empire assembled so massive a force. Never before have we been as well prepared as now.

"Also," he added conspiratorially, "there is rumor abundant that the Great Wizard Eejakrat, Advisor to the Empress herself, has brought forth from the realms of darkness an invincible magic which will sweep all opposition before it." He adjusted the reins running to the third lizard in right line.

"No, citizens, of course we cannot lose."

"My feelings are the same, citizen." Jon-Tom returned to the rear of the wagon. Clothahump joined him a moment later, as he was chatting softly to the others.

"If confidence is any indication of battleworthiness, we're liable to be in for a bad time."

"You see?" said Clothahump knowingly as he leaned up against a pair of green-filled barrels, "that is why we must find and destroy this dead mind that Eejakrat somehow draws knowledge from, or die in the attempt.''

"Speak for yourself, guv'," said Mudge. " 'E wot fights an' runs away lives t' fight another day."

"Unfortunately," Clothahump reminded the otter quietly, "if we fail, like as not there will not be another day."

XIII

Several days passed. Farms and livestock pastures began to give way to the outskirts of a vast metropolis. Fronted with stone or black cement, tunnels led down into the earth. On the surface row upon row of identical gray buildings filled the horizon, a vast stone curve that formed the outer wheel of the capital city of Cugluch.

As they entered the first gate of many, they encountered larger structures and greater variety. Faint pulses of light from within cast ambivalent shadows on the travelers while the echoes of hammerings resounded above the babble of the chitinesque crowd. Once they passed a wagon emerging from a large, cubical building. It was piled high with long spears and pikes and halberds bound together like sheaves of grain. The weapon-laden vehicle moved westward. Westward like the troops they'd passed. Westward toward the Jo-Troom Gate.

It had rained gently every day, but was far warmer than in

the so-called warmlands. Fat, limpid drops slid off their hard-shelled disguises, only occasionally penetrating the well-fashioned false chitin. Cooled by spell, those inside the insect suits remained comfortable in spite of the humidity. Clothahump, as a good wizard should, had foreseen everything except the need to scratch the occasional itch.

Only an isolated clump of struggling trees here and there brought color to the monotonous construction of the city. It was an immense warren, much of it out of sight beneath the surface of the earth.

They pushed their way through heavier and heavier traffic, increasingly military in nature. Clothahump guided the driver smoothly, directing them deeper into the city.

Wagonloads of troops, ant- and beetle-shapes predominant, shoved civilian traffic aside as they made their way westward. Enormous beetles eight and nine feet long displayed sharpened horns to the travelers. Three or four armed soldiers rode on the backs of these armored behemoths.

Once a dull *thump* sounded from behind a large oval structure. Jon-Tom swore it sounded like an exploding shell. For an awful moment he thought it was the result of Eejakrat's unknown magic and that the Plated Folk had learned the use of gunpowder. His companions, however, assured him it was only a distant rumble of thunder.

Buildings rose still higher around them. They were matched by roads that widened to accommodate the increased traffic. Weaving ribbons of densely populated concrete and rock rose six and seven stories above the streets, hives of frenetic activity devoted now to destruction and death.

Sleep was in snatches and seconds that night. Clothahump woke them to a soggy sunrise.

Ahead in the morning mist-light lay a great open square paved with triangular slabs of gray, black, purple, and blue stone. Across this expansive parade ground, populated now only by early risers, rose a circular pyramid. It consisted of concentric ring shapes like enormous tires. These tapered to a smooth spire hundreds of feet high that pierced the mist like a gray needle.

Half a dozen smaller copies of the central structure ringed it at points equidistant from one another. There was no wall around any of them, nor for that matter around the main square itself.

Despite this the driver refused to go any further. His determination was so strong even Clothahump's hypnotic urgings failed to force him and his wagon onto the triangular paving.

"I have no permit," he said raspily, "to enter the palace grounds. It would be my death to be found on the sacred square without one."

"This is where we walk again, my friends. Perhaps it is best. I see only one or two wagons on the square. We do not want to attract attention."

Mudge let himself over the back of the wagon. "Cor, ain't that the bloody ugliest buildin' you ever saw in your life?"

They abandoned the wagon. Clothahump was last off. He whispered a few words to the driver. The beetle moved the reins and the wagon swung around to vanish up the street down which they'd come. Jon-Tom wondered at the excuse the unfortunate driver would offer when he suddenly returned to full consciousness at his delivery point after nearly a week of amnesia.

"It seems we need a permit to cross," said Caz appraisingly. "How do we go about obtaining one?"

Clothahump sounded disapproving. "We need no permit. I have been observing the pedestrians traversing the square, and none has been stopped or questioned. It seems that the threat is sufficient to secure the palace's exclusiveness. The permit may be required within, but it does not seem vital for walking the square.''

"I hope you're right, sir." The rabbit stepped out onto the paving, a gangling, thoroughly insectoid shape. Together they moved at an easy pace toward the massive pyramidal palace.

As Clothahump had surmised, they were not accosted. If anything, they found the square larger than it first appeared, like a lake that looks small until one is swimming in its center.

From this central nexus the spokes of Cugluch radiated outward toward farmland and swamp. The city was far larger than Polastrindu, especially when one considered that much of it was hidden underground.

Thick mist clung to the crests of the seven towers and completely obscured the central one. Nowhere did they see a flag, a banner, any splash of color or gaiety. It was a somber capital, dedicated to a somber purpose.

And the massive palace was especially dark and foreboding. Here at least Jon-Tom had expected some hint of brightness. Militaristic cultures were historically fond of pomp and flash. The palace of the Empress, however, was as dull as the warrens of the citizen-workers. Different in design but not demeanor, he decided.

The lowest level of the circular pyramid was several stories high. It was fashioned, as the entire palace complex no doubt was, of close-fitting stone mortared over with a gray cement or plaster. Water dripped down its curves to vanish into gutters and drains lining the base. There was a minimum of windows.

The triangular paving of the square ceased some fifteen yards from the base of the palace. In its place was a smooth surface of black cement. That was all; no fence, no hidden alarms, no hedgerows or ditches. But on that black fifteen yards, which encircled the entire palace, nothing moved save the stiffly pacing guards.

They formed a solid ring, ten yards from the palace wall, five yards apart. They marched in slow tread from left to right, keeping the same distance between them like so many wind-up toys. As near as Jon-Tom could tell they ringed the entire palace, a moving chain of guards that never stopped.

At Clothahump's urging they turned southward. The guards never looked in their direction, though Jon-Tom was willing to wager that if so much as a foot touched that black cement, the trespasser would suddenly find himself the object of considerable hostile attention.

Eventually they stood opposite an arched triangular portal cut from the flank of the palace. The entryway was three stories high. At present its massive iron gates were thrown wide. A line of armed beetles extended from either open gate out across the cement to the edge of the paving. The unbroken ring of encircling guards passed through this intercepting line with precision. The moving guards never touched any of the stationary ones.

"Now wot, guv'nor?" Mudge whispered to the wizard. "Do we just walk up t' the nearest bugger an' ask 'im polite-like if the Empress be at 'ome an' might we 'ave 'is leave t' skip on in t' see the old dear?"

"I have no desire to see *her*," Clothahump replied. "It is Eejakrat we are after. Rules survive by relying on the brains of their advisors. Remove Eejakrat, or at least his magic, and we leave the Empress without the most important part of her collective mind."

He gazed thoughtfully at Caz. "You have laid claim to a working knowledge of diplomacy, my boy, and have shown an aptitude for such in the past. I am reluctant to perform a spell among so many onlookers and so near to Eejakrat's influence. I've no doubt he has placed alarm spells all about the palace.

221

They would react to my magicking, but not to your words. We must get inside. I suggest you employ your talent for extemporaneous and convincing conversation.''

"I don't know, sir," replied the rabbit uncertainly. "It's easy to convince people you're familiar with. I don't know how to talk to these."

"Nonsense. You did well with that curious woodcutter whom we encountered during our descent. If anything, the minds you are about to deal with are simpler than those you are more familiar with. Consider their society, which rewards conformity while condemning individuality."

"If you want me to, sir, I'll give it a try."

"Good. The rest of you form behind us. Pog, you stay airborne and warn us if there is sudden movement from armed troops in our direction."

"What does it matter?" said the sorrowful bat from inside his disguise. "We'll all be dead inside an hour anyway." But he spiraled higher and did as he was told, keeping a watchful eye on the guards and any group of pedestrians who came near.

Following Caz and Clothahump, the travelers made their way toward the entrance. There was an anxious moment when they stepped from paving to cement, but no one challenged them. The guards flanking the approach kept their attention on a point a few inches in front of their mandibles.

Then it was through the encircling ring, which likewise did not react. They were a couple of yards from the entrance.

Jon-Tom had the wild notion that they might simply be able to march on into the palace when a massive beetle slightly taller but much broader than Caz lumbered out of the shadows to confront them. He was flanked by a pair of pale, three-foot-high attendants of the mutated mayfly persuasion. One of them carried a large scroll and a marking instrument. The other simply stood and listened.

"State your business, citizens," demanded the glowering hulk in the middle. He reminded Jon-Tom of a gladiator ready to enter the arena, and pity be on the lions. The extra set of arms ruined the illusion.

With the facility of an established survivor, Caz replied without hesitation. "Hail, citizen! We have special, urgently requested information for the sorcerer Eejakrat, information that is vital to our coming success." Not knowing how to properly conclude the request he added blandly, "Where can we find him?"

Their interrogator did not reply immediately. Jon-Tom wondered if his nervousness showed.

After a brief conversation with the burdenless mayfly the beetle gestured backward with two hands. "Third level, Chamber Three Fifty-Five and adjuncts."

Politely, he stepped aside.

Caz led them in. They walked down a short hallway. It opened into a hall that seemed to run parallel to the circular shape of the building. Another, similar hall could be seen further ahead. Evidently there was a single point from which the palace and thence the entire city of Cugluch radiated in concentric circles, with hallways or streets forming intersecting spokes.

Jon-Tom leaned over and whispered to Clothahump. "I don't know how you feel, sir, but to me that was much too easy."

"Why shouldn't it have been?" said Talea, feeling cocky at their success thus far. "It was just like crossing the square outside."

"Precisely, my dear," said Clothahump proudly. "You see, Jon-Tom, they are so well ordered they cannot imagine anyone stepping out of class or position. They cannot conceive, as that threatening individual who confronted us outside cannot, that any of their fellows would have the presumption to lie to gain an audience with so feared a personality as Eejakrat. If we did not deserve such a meeting, we would not be asking for it.

"Furthermore, spies are unknown in Cugluch. They have no reason to suspect any, and traitorous actions are as alien to the Plated Folk as snow. This may be possible after all, my friends. We need only maintain the pretext that we know what we are doing and have a right to be doing it."

"I'd imagine," said Caz, "that if the spoke-and-circle layout of the city and palace is followed throughout, the center would be the best place to locate stairways. Third level, the fellow said."

"I agree," Clothahump replied, "but we do not wish to find Eejakrat except as a last resort, remember. It is the dead mind he controls that must remain our primary goal."

"That's simple enough, then," said Mudge cheerfully. "All we 'ave t' do now is ask where t' find a particularly well-attended corpse."

"For once, my fuzzy fuzz-brained friend, you are correct. It will likely be placed close by Eejakrat's chambers. Let us proceed quickly to the level indicated, but not to him."

They did so. By now they were used to being ignored by the Plated Folk. Busy palace staff moved silently around them, intent on their own tasks. The narrow hallways and low ceilings combined with the slightly acidic odor of the inhabitants made Jon-Tom and Flor feel a little claustrophobic.

They reached the third level and began to follow the numbers engraved above each sealed portal. Only four chambers from the stairway they'd ascended was a surprise: the corridor was blocked. Also guarded.

Instead of the lumbering beetle they'd encountered at the entrance to the palace they found a slim, almost effeminate-looking insect seated behind a desk. Other armed Plated Folk stood before the temporary barrier sealing off the hall beyond.

Unlike their drilling brothers marching single-mindedly outside, these guards seemed alert and active. They regarded the new arrivals with unconcealed interest. There was no suspicion in their unyielding faces, however. Only curiosity.

It was Clothahump who spoke to the individual behind the desk, and not Caz.

"We have come to make adjustments to the mind," he told the individual behind the desk, hoping he had gauged the source correctly and hadn't said anything fatally contradictory.

The fixed-faced officer preened one red eye. He could not frown but succeeded in conveying an impression of puzzlement nonetheless.

"An adjustment to the mind?"

"To Eejakrat's Materialization."

"Ah, of course, citizen. But what kind of adjustment?" He peered hard at the encased wizard. "Who are you, to be entrusted with access to so secret a thing?"

Clothahump was growing worried. The more questions asked, the more the chance of saying something dangerously out of sync with the facts.

"We are Eejakrat's own special assistants. How else could we know of the mind?"

"That is sensible," agreed the officer. "Yet no mention was made to me of any forthcoming adjustments."

"I have just mentioned it to you."

The officer turned that one over in his mind, got thoroughly confused, and finally said, "I am sorry for the delay, citizen. I mean no insult by my questions, but we are under extraordinary orders. Your master's fears are well known."

Clothahump leaned close, spoke confidentially. "An attribute of all who must daily deal with dark forces."

The officer nodded somberly. "I am glad it is you who must deal with the wizard and not myself." He waved aside the guards blocking the doorway in the portable barrier. "Stand aside and let them pass."

Caz and Talea were the first through the portal when the officer suddenly put out an arm and touched Clothahump. "Surely you can satisfy the curiosity of a fellow citizen. What kind of 'adjustment' must you make to the mind? We all understand so little about it and you can sympathize with my desire to know."

"Of course, of course." Clothahump's mind was working frantically. How much did the officer actually know? He'd just confessed his ignorance, but mightn't it be a ploy? Better to say anything fast than nothing at all. His only real worry was that the officer might have some sorceral training.

"Please do not repeat this," he finally said, with as much assurance as he could muster. "It is necessary to apfrangle the overscan."

"Naturally," said the officer after a pause.

"And we may," the wizard added for good measure, "additionally have to lower the level of cratastone, just in case."

"I can understand the necessity for that." The officer grandly waved them through, enjoying the looks of respect on the faces of his subordinates while praying this visitor wouldn't ask him any questions in return.

They proceeded through the portal one by one. Jon-Tom was last through and hesitated. The officer seemed willing enough.

"It's still in the same chamber, of course."

"Number Twelve, yes," said the officer blandly.

Clothahump fell back to match stride with Jon-Tom. "That was clever of you, my boy! I was so preoccupied with trying to get us in that I'd forgotten how difficult it would be to sense past Eejakrat's spell guards. Now that is no longer a constraint. You cannot teach deviousness," he finished pridefully. "That is instinctive."

"Thank you, sir. I think. What kind of corpse do you think it is?"

"I cannot imagine. I cannot imagine a dead brain functioning, either. We shall know soon enough." He was deciphering the symbols engraved above each circular doorway. The guarded barrier had long since disappeared around the continuous curve of the hallway.

"There is number ten...and there eleven," he said excitedly, pointing to the door on their right.

"Then this must be twelve." Talea stopped before the closed door.

It was no larger than any of the others they'd passed. The corridor nearby was deserted. Clothahump stepped forward and studied the wooden door. There were four tiny circular insets midway up the left side. He inserted his four insect arms into them and pushed.

The spring mechanism that controlled the door clicked home. The wood split apart and inward like two halves of an apple.

There was no light in the chamber beyond. Even Caz could see nothing. But Pog saw without eyes.

"Master, it's not very large, but I think dat dere's someting..." He fluttered near a wall, struck his sparker.

A lamp suddenly burst into light. It revealed a bent and very aged beetle surrounded by writhing white larval forms. Startled, it glared back at them and muttered an oath.

"What is it now? I've told Skrritch I'm not to be disturbed unless...unless..." His words trailed away as he stared fixedly at Clothahump.

"By the Primordial Arm! A warmlander wizard!" He turned to a siphon speaker set in the wall nearby. "Guards,

guards!'' The maggots formed a protective, loathesome semi-circle in front of him.

''Quick now,'' Caz yelled, ''where is it?'' They fanned out into the chamber, hunting for anything that might fit Clothahump's description.

One insectoid, one mammalian, the two wizards faced each other in silent summing up. Neither moved, but they were battling as ferociously as any two warriors armed with sword and spear.

''We've got to find it fast,'' Flor was muttering, searching a corner. ''Before . . .''

But hard feet were already clattering noisily in the corridor outside. Distant cries of alarm sounded in the chamber. Then the soldiers were pouring through the doorway, and there was no more time.

Jon-Tom saw something lying near the back wall that might have been a long, low corpse. An insect shape stepped up behind him and raised a cast-iron bottle high. Just before the bottle came down on his head it occurred to him that the shape wielding it was familiar. It wasn't one of the insect guards who'd just arrived. Before he blacked out under the impact he was positive the insectoid visage was that concealing Talea's. The realization stunned him almost as badly as the bottle, which cracked his own false forehead and bounced off the skull beneath. Darkness returned to the chamber.

When he regained consciousness, he found he was lying in a dimly lit, spherical cell. There was a drain in the center, at the bottom of the sphere. The light came from a single lamp hanging directly over the drain. It was windowless and humid. Moss and fungi grew from the damp stones, and it was difficult to keep from sliding down the sloping floor. Compared to this, the cell they'd been temporarily incarcerated in back in Gossameringue had been positively palatial.

No friendly Ananthos would be appearing here to rectify a mistaken imprisonment, however.

"Welcome back to the world of the living," said Bribbens. Good times or bad, the boatman's expression never seemed to change. The moisture in the cell did not bother him, of course.

"I should've stayed on my boat," he added with a sigh.

"Maybe we all ought to 'ave stayed on your boat, mate," said a disconsolate Mudge.

It occurred to Jon-Tom that Bribbens looked like himself. So did Mudge, and the other occupants of the cell.

"What happened to our disguises?"

"Stripped away as neatly as you'd peel an onion," Pog told him. He lay morosely on the damp stones, unwilling to hang from the fragile lamp.

Clothahump was not in the cell. "Where's your master?"

"I don't know, I don't know," the bat moaned helplessly. "Taken away from us during da fight. We ain't seen him since, da old fart." There was no malice in the bat's words.

"It was Eejakrat," Caz said from across the cell. His clothing was torn and clumps of fur were missing from his right cheek, but he still somehow had retained his monocle. "He knew us for what we were. I presume he has taken special care with Clothahump. One sorcerer would not place another in an ordinary cell where he might dissolve the bars or mesmerize the jailers."

"But what he doesn't know is that we still have the services of a wizard." Flor was looking hopefully at Jon-Tom.

"I can't do anything, Flor." He dug his boot heels into a crack in the floor. It kept him from sliding down toward the central drain. "I need my duar, and it was strapped to the inside back of my insect suit."

"Try," she urged him. "We've nothing to lose, *verdad?* You don't need instrumental accompaniment to sing."

"No, but I can't make magic without it."

"Give 'er a shot anyway, guv'nor," said Mudge. "It can't make us any worse than we are, wot?"

"All right." He thought a moment, then sang. It had to be something to fit his mood. Something somber and yet hopeful.

He was fonder of rock than country-western, but there was a certain song about another prison, a place called Folsom, where blues of a different kind had also been vanquished through music. It was full of hope, anticipation, whistles, and thoughts of freedom.

Mudge obligingly let out a piercing whistle. It faded to freedom through the bars of their cell, but whistler and singer did not. No train appeared to carry them away. Not even a solitary, curious gneechee.

"You see?" He smiled helplessly, and spread his hands. "I need the duar. I sing and it spells. Can't have one without the other." The question he'd managed to suppress until now could no longer rest unsatisfied.

"We know what probably happened to Clothahump." He looked at the floor, remembering the descending iron bottle. "Where's Talea?"

"That *puta*!" Flor spit on the moss. "If we get a chance before we die I'll disembowel her with my own hands." She held up sharp nailed fingers.

"I couldn't believe it meself, mate." Mudge sounded more tired than Jon-Tom had ever heard him. Something had finally smashed his unquenchable spirit. "It don't make no bloomin' *sense*, dam it! I've known that bird off an' on for years. For 'er t' do somethin' like this t' save 'er own skin, t' go over t' the likes o' these . . . I can't believe it, mate. I can't!"

Jon-Tom tried to erase the memory. That would be easier than forgetting the pain. It wasn't his head that was hurting.

"I can't believe it either, Mudge."

"Why not, friend?" Bribbens crossed one slick green leg over the other. "Allegiance is a temporary thing, and expediency the hallmark of survival."

"Probably what happened," said Caz more gently, "was that she saw what was going to happen, that we were going to be overwhelmed, and decided to cast her lot with the Plated Folk. We know from firsthand experience, do we not, that there are human allies among them. I can't condemn her for choosing life over death. You shouldn't either."

Jon-Tom sat quietly, still not believing it despite the sense in Caz's words. Talea had been combative, even contemptuous at times, but for her to turn on companions she'd been through so much with . . . Yet she'd apparently done just that. Better face up to facts, Jon boy. "Poor boy, you're goin' t' die," as the song lamented.

"What do you suppose they'll do with us?" he asked Mudge. "Or maybe I'd be better just asking 'how'?"

"I over'eard the soldiers talkin'. I was 'alf conscious when they carried us down 'ere." Mudge smiled slightly. "Seems we're t' be the bloody centerpiece at the Empress' evenin' supper, the old dear. 'Eard the ranks wagerin' on 'ow we was goin' t' be cooked."

"I sincerely hope they do cook us," Caz said. "I've heard tales that the Plated Folk prefer their food alive." Flor shuddered, and Jon-Tom felt sick.

It had all been such a grand adventure, marching off to save civilization, overcoming horrendous obstacles and terrible difficulties. All to end up not as part of an enduring legend but a brief meal. He missed the steady confidence of Clothahump. Even if unable to save them through wizardly

231

means, he wished the turtle were present to raise their spirits with his calm, knowledgeable words.

"Any idea what time it's to be?" The windowless walls shut out time as well as space.

"No idea." Caz grinned ruefully at him. "You're the spellsinger. You tell me."

"I've already explained that I can't do anything without the duar."

"Then you ought to have it, Jon-Tom." The voice came from the corridor outside the cell. Everyone faced the bars.

Talea stood there, panting heavily. Flor made an inarticulate sound and rushed the barrier. Talea stepped back out of reach.

"Calm yourself, woman. You're acting like a hysterical cub."

Flor smiled, showing white teeth. "Come a little closer, sweet friend, and I'll show you how hysterical I can be."

Talea shook her head, looked disgusted. "Save your strength, and what brains you've got left. We haven't got much time." She held up a twisted length of wrought iron: the key.

Caz had left his sitting position to move up behind Flor. He put furry arms around her and wrestled her away from the bars.

"Use your head, giantess! Can't you see she's come to let us out?"

"But I thought . . ." Flor finally took notice of the key and relaxed.

"You knocked me out." Jon-Tom gripped the bars with both hands as Talea fumbled with the key and the awkward lock. "You hit me with a metal bottle."

"I sure did," she snapped. "Somebody had to keep her wits about her."

"Then you haven't gone over to the Plated Folk?"

"Of course I did. You're not thinking it through. I forgive you, though."

She was whispering angrily at them, glancing from time to time back up the corridor. "We know that some humans have joined them, right? But how could the locals know which humans in the warmlands are their allies and which are not? They can't possibly, not without checking with their spies in Polastrindu and elsewhere.

"When the fighting began I saw we didn't have a chance. So I grabbed a hunk of iron and started attacking you alongside the guards. When it was finished they accepted my story about being sent along to spy on you and keep track of the expedition. That Eejakrat was suspicious, but he was willing to accept me for now, until he can check with those warmland sources. He figured I couldn't do any harm here." She grinned wickedly.

"His own thoughts are elsewhere. He's too concerned with how much Clothahump knows to worry about me." She nodded up the corridor. "This guard's dead, but I don't know how often they change 'em."

There was a groan and a metallic *snap*. She pushed and the door swung inward. "Come on, then."

They rushed out into the corridor. It was narrow and only slightly better lit than the cell. Several strides further brought them up before a familiar silhouette.

"Clothahump!" shouted Jon-Tom.

"Master, Master!" Pog fluttered excitedly around the wizard's head. Clothahump waved irritably at the famulus. His own attention was fixed on the hall behind him.

"Not now, Pog. We've no time for it."

"Where've they been holding you, sir?" Jon-Tom asked.

Clothahump pointed. "Two cells up from you."

Jon-Tom gaped at him. "You mean you were that close and we could've . . ."

"Could have what, my boy? Dug through the rocks with your bare hands and untied and ungagged me? I think not. It was frustrating, however, to hear you all so close and not be able to reassure you." His expression darkened. "I am going to turn that Eejakrat into mousefood!"

"Not today," Talea reminded him.

"Yes, you're quite right, young lady."

Talea led them to a nearby room. In addition to the expected oil lamps the walls held spears and shields. The furnishings were Spartan and minimal. A broken insect body lay sprawled beneath the table. Neatly piled against the far wall were their possessions: weapons, supplies, and disguises, including Jon-Tom's duar.

They hurriedly helped one another into the insect suits.

"I'm surprised these weren't shattered beyond repair in the fight," Jon-Tom muttered, watching while Clothahump fixed his cracked headpiece.

The wizard finished the polymer spell-repair. "Eejakrat was fascinated by them. I'm sure he wanted me to go into the details of the spell. He has similar interests, you know. Remember the disguised ambassador who talked with you in Polastrindu."

They stepped quietly back out into the corridor. "Where are we?" Mudge asked Talea.

"Beneath the palace. Where else?" It was strange to hear that sharp voice coming from behind the gargoylish face once again.

"How can we get out?" Pog murmured worriedly.

"We walked in," said Caz thoughtfully. "Why should we not also walk out?"

"Indeed," said Clothahump. "If we can get out into the square we should be safe."

XIV

They were several levels below the surface, but under Talea's guidance they made rapid progress upward.

Once they had to pause to let an enormous beetle pass. He waddled down the stairs without seeing them. A huge ax was slung across his back and heavy keys dangled from his belts.

"I don't know if he's the relief for our level or not," Talea said huskily, "but we'd better hurry."

They increased their pace. Then Talea warned them to silence. They were nearing the last gate.

Three guards squatted around a desk on the other side of the barred door. A steady babble of conversation filtered into the corridor from the open door on the far side of the guard room as busy workers came and went. Jon-Tom wondered at the absence of a heavier guard until it came to him that escape would be against orders, an action foreign to all but deranged Plated Folk.

But there was still the barred doorway and the three administrators beyond.

"How did you get past them?" Caz asked Talea.

"I haven't been past them. Eejakrat believed my story, but only to a point. He wasn't about to give me the run of the city. I had a room, not a cell, on the level below this one. If I wanted out, I had to send word to him. We haven't got time for that now. Pretty soon they'll be finding the body I left."

Mudge located a small fragment of loose black cement. He tossed it down the stairs they'd ascended. It made a gratifyingly loud clatter.

"Nesthek, is that you?" one of the administrators called toward the doorway. When there was no immediate reply he rose from his position at the desk and left the game to his companions.

The excapees concealed themselves as best they could. The administrator sounded perplexed as he approached the doorway.

"Nesthek? Don't play games with me. I'm losing badly as it is."

"Bugger it," Mudge said tensely. "I thought at least two of them would come to check."

"You take this one," said Clothahump. "The rest of us will *quietly* rush the others."

"Nesthek, what are you . . . ?" Mudge stabbed upward with his sword. He'd been lying nearly hidden by the lowest bar of the doorway. The sword went right into the startled guard's abdomen. At the same instant Caz leaped out of the shadows to bring his knife down into one of the great compound eyes. The guard-administrator slumped against the bars. Talea fumbled for the keys at his waist.

"Partewx?" Then the other querulous guard was half out of his seat as his companion ran to give the alarm. He didn't make it to the far door. Pog landed on his neck and began stabbing rapidly with his stiletto at the guard's head and face.

The creature swung its four arms wildly, trying to dislodge the flapping dervish that clung relentlessly to neck and head. Flor swung low with her sword and cut through both legs.

The other who had turned and drawn his own scimitar swung at Bribbens. The boatman hopped halfway to the ceiling, and the deadly arc passed feet below their intended target.

As the guard was bringing back his sword for another cut, Jon-Tom swung at him with his staff. The guard ducked the whistling club-head and brought his curved blade around. As he'd been taught to, Jon-Tom spun the long shaft in his hands as if it were an oversized baton. The guard jumped out of range. Jon-Tom thumbed one of the hidden studs, and a foot of steel slid directly into the startled guard's thorax. Caz's sword decapitated him before he hit the floor.

"Hold!"

Everyone looked to the right. There was a waste room recessed into that wall. It had produced a fourth administrator guard. He was taller than Jon-Tom, and the insect shape struggling in the three-armed grasp looked small in comparison.

The insect head of Talea's disguise had been ripped off. Her red hair cascaded down to her shoulders. Two arms held her firmly around neck and waist while the third held a knife over the hollow of her throat.

"Move and she dies," said the guard. He began to edge toward the open doorway leading outside, keeping his back hard against the wall.

"If he gives the alarm we're finished, mates," Mudge whispered.

"Let's rush them," said Caz.

"No!" Jon-Tom put an arm in front of the rabbit. "We can't. He'll—"

Talea continued to struggle in the unrelenting grip. "Do something, you idiots!"

Seeing that no one was going to act and that she and her captor were only a few yards from the doorway, she put both feet on the floor and thrust convulsively upward. The knife slid through her throat, emerging from the back of her neck. Claret spurted across the stones.

Everyone was too stunned to scream. The guard cursed, let the limp body fall as he bolted for the exit. Pog was waiting for him with a knife that went straight between the compound eyes. The guard never saw him. He'd had eyes only for his grounded opponents and hadn't noticed the bat hanging above the portal.

Caz and Mudge finished the giant quickly. Jon-Tom bent over the tiny, curled shape of Talea. The blood flowed freely but was already beginning to slow. Major arteries and veins had been severed.

He looked back at Clothahump but the wizard could only shake his head. "No time, no time, my boy. It's a long spell. Not enough time."

Weak life looked out from those sea-green eyes. Her mouth twisted into a grimace and her voice was faint. "One of...these days you're going to have to make ... the important decisions without help, Jon-Tom." She smiled faintly. "You know ... I think I love you. ..."

The tears came in a flood, uncontrollable. "It's not fair, Talea. Damn! It's not fair! You can't tell me something like that and then leave me! You can't!"

But she died anyway.

He found he was shaking. Caz grabbed his shoulders, shook him until it stopped.

"No time for that now, my friend. I'm sorry, too, but this isn't the place·for being sorry."

"No, it is not." Clothahump was examining the body. "She'll stop bleeding soon. When she does, clean her chitin and put her head back on. It's over in the corner there, where the guard threw it.''

Jon-Tom stood, looked dazedly down at the wizard. "You can't . . . ?"

"I'll explain later, Jon-Tom. But all may not be lost."

"What the hell do you mean, 'all may not be lost'?" His voice rose angrily. "She's *dead*, you senile old . . ."

Clothahump let him finish, then said, "I forgive the names because I understand the motivation and the source. Know only that sometimes even death can be forgiven, Jon-Tom."

"Are you saying you can bring her back?"

"I don't know. But if we don't get out of here quickly we'll never have the chance to find out."

Flor and Bribbens slipped the insect head back into place over the pale face and flowing hair. Jon-Tom wouldn't help.

"Now everyone look and act official," Clothahump urged them. "We're taking a dead prisoner out for burial."

Bribbens, Mudge, Caz, and Flor supported Talea's body while Pog flew formation overhead and Jon-Tom and Clothahump marched importantly in front. A few passing Plated Folk glanced at them when they emerged from the doorway, but no one dared question them.

One of the benefits of infiltrating a totalitarian society, Jon-Tom thought bitterly. Everyone's afraid to ask anything of anyone who looks important.

They were on the main floor of the palace. It took them a while to find an exit (they dared not ask directions), but before long they were outside in the mist of the palace square.

The sky was as gray and silent as ever and the humidity as bad, but for all except the disconsolate Jon-Tom it was as though they'd suddenly stepped out onto a warm beach fronting the southern ocean.

"We have to find transport again," Clothahump was

murmuring as they made their way with enforced slowness across the square. "Soon someone will note either our absence or that of our belongings." He allowed himself a grim chuckle.

"I would not care to be the prison commandant when Eejakrat learns of our escape. They'll be after us soon enough, but they should have a hell of a time locating us. We blend in perfectly, and only a few have seen us. Nevertheless, Eejakrat will do everything in his power to recapture us."

"Where can we go?" Mudge asked, shifting slightly under the weight of the body. "To the north, back for Ironcloud?"

"No. That is where Eejakrat will expect us to go."

"Why would he suspect that?" asked Jon-Tom.

"Because I made it a point to give him sufficient hints to that effect during our conversations," the wizard replied, "in case the opportunity to flee arose."

"If he's as sly as you say, won't he suspect we're heading in another direction?"

"Perhaps. But I do not believe he will think that we might attempt to return home through the entire assembled army of the Greendowns."

"Won't they be given the alarm about us also?"

"Of course. But militia do not display initiative. I think we shall be able to slip through them."

That satisfied Jon-Tom, but Clothahump was left to muse over what might have been. So close, they'd been so close! And still they did not know what the dead mind was, or how Eejakrat manipulated it. But while willing to take chances, he was not quite as mad as Jon-Tom might have thought. I have no death wish, young spellsinger, he thought as he regarded the tall insect shape marching next to him. We tried as no other mortals could try, and we failed. If fate wills that we are to perish soon, it will be on the ramparts of the Jo-Troom Gate confronting the foe, not in the jaws of Cugluch.

Once among the milling, festering mob of city dwellers they could relax a little. It took a while to locate an alley with a delivery wagon and no curious onlookers. Clothahump could not work the spell under the gaze of kibbitzers.

The long, narrow wagon was pulled by a single large lizard. They waited. No one else entered the alley. Eventually the driver emerged from the back entrance of a warren. Clothahump confronted him and while the others kept watch, hastily spelled the unfortunate driver under.

"Climb aboard then, citizens," the driver said obligingly when the wizard had finished. They did so, carefully laying Talea's body on the wagon bed between them.

They were two-thirds of the way to the Pass, the hustle of Cugluch now largely behind them, when the watchful Jon-Tom said cautiously to the driver, "You're not hypnotized, are you? You never were under the spell."

The worker looked back down at him with unreadable compound eyes as hands moved toward weapons. "No, citizen. I have not been magicked, if that is what you mean. Stay your hands." He gestured at the roadway they were traveling. "It would do you only ill, for you are surrounded by my people." Swords and knives remained reluctantly sheathed.

"Where are you taking us, then?" Flor asked nervously. "Why haven't you given the alarm already?"

"As to the first, stranger, I am taking you where you wish to go, to the head of the Troom Pass. I can understand why you wish to go there, though I do not think you will end your journey alive. Yet perhaps you will be fortunate and make it successfully back to your own lands."

"You know what we are, then?" asked a puzzled Jon-Tom.

The driver nodded. "I know that beneath those skins of chitin there are others softer and differently colored."

"But how?"

241

The driver pointed to the back of the wagon. Mudge looked uncomfortable. "Well now wot the bloody 'ell were I supposed to do? I thought 'is mind had been turned to mush and I 'ad to pee. Didn't think 'e saw anyway, the 'ard-shelled pervert!"

"It does not matter," the driver said.

"Listen, if you're not magicked and you know who and what we are, why are you taking us quietly where we wish to go instead of turning us over to the authorities?" Jon-Tom wanted to know.

"I just told you: it does not matter." The driver made a two-armed gesture indicative of great indifference. "Soon all will die anyway."

"I take it you don't approve of the coming war."

"No, I do not." His antennae quivered with emotion as he spoke. "It is so foolish, the millenia-old expenditure of life and time in hopes of conquest."

"I must say you are the most peculiar Plated person I have ever encountered," said Clothahump.

"My opinions are not widely shared among my own people," the driver admitted. He chucked the reins, and the wagon edged around a line of motionless carts burdened with military supplies. Their wagon continued onward, one set of wheels still on the roadway, the other bouncing over the rocks and mud of the swampy earth.

"But perhaps things will change, given time and sensible thought."

"Not if your armies achieve victory they won't," said Bribbens coldly. "Wouldn't you be happy as the rest if your soldiers win their conquest?"

"No, I would not," the driver replied firmly. "Death and killing never build anything, for all that it may appear otherwise."

"A most enlightened outlook, sir," said Clothahump. "See here, why don't you come with us back to the warmlands?"

"Would I be welcomed?" asked the insect. "Would the other warmlanders understand and sympathize the way you do? Would they greet me as a friend?"

"They would probably, I am distressed to confess," said a somber Caz, "slice you into small chitinous bits."

"You see? I am doomed whichever way I chose. If I went with you I would suffer physically. If I stay, it is my mind that suffers constant agony."

"I can understand your feelings against the war," said Flor, "but that still doesn't explain why you're risking your own neck to help us."

The driver made a shruglike gesture. "I help those who need help. That is my nature. Now I help you. Soon, when the fighting starts, there will be many to help. I do not take sides among the needy. I wish only that such idiocies could be stopped. It seems though that they can only be waited out."

The driver, an ordinary citizen of the Greendowns, was full of surprises. Clothahump had been convinced that there was no divergence of opinion among the Plated Folk. Here was loquacious proof of a crack in that supposed unity of totalitarian thought, a crack that might be exploited later. Assuming, of course, that the forthcoming invasion could be stopped.

Several days later they found themselves leaving the last of the cultivated lowlands. Mist faded behind them, and the friendly silhouettes of the mountains of Zaryt's Teeth became solid.

No wagons plied their trader's wares here, no farmers waded patiently through knee-deep muck. There was only military traffic. According to Clothahump they were already within the outskirts of the Pass.

Military bivouacs extended from hillside to hillside and for miles to east and west. Tens of thousands of insect troops milled quietly, expectantly, on the gravelly plain, waiting for the word to march. From the back of the wagon Jon-Tom and his companions could look out upon an ocean of antennae and eyes and multiple legs. And sharp iron, flashing like a million mirrors in the diffuse light of a winter day.

No one questioned them or eyed the wagon with suspicion until they reached the last lines of troops. Ahead lay only the ancient riverbed of the Troom Pass, a dry chasm of sand and rock which in the previous ten millenia had run more with blood than ever it had with water.

The officer was winged but flightless, slim, limber of body and thought. He noted the wagon and its path, stopped filling out the scroll in his charge, and hurried to pace the vehicle. Its occupants gave every indication of being engaged in reasonable business, but they ought not to have been where they were. The quality of initiative, so lacking in Plated Folk troops, was present in some small amount in this particular individual officer.

He glanced up at the driver, his tone casual and not hostile. "Where are you going, citizen?"

"Delivering supplies to the forward scouts," said Caz quickly.

The officer slackened his pace, walked now behind the wagon as he inspected its occupants. "That is understandable, but I see no supplies. And who is the dead one?" He gestured with claws and antennae at the limp shape of Talea, still encased in her disguise.

"An accident, a most unforgivable brawl in the ranks," Caz informed him.

"Ranks? What ranks? I see no insignia on the body. Nor on any of you."

"We're not regular army," said the driver, much to the relief of the frantic Caz.

"Ah. But such a fatal disturbance should be reported. We cannot tolerate fighting among ourselves, not now, with final victory so soon to come."

Jon-Tom tried to look indifferent as he turned his head to look past the front of the wagon. They were not quite past the front-line troops. Leave us alone, he thought furiously at the persistent officer. Go back to your work and leave this one wagon to itself!

"We already have reported it," said Caz worriedly. "To our own commandant."

"And who might that be?" came the unrelenting, infuriating question.

"Colonel Puxolix," said the driver.

"I know of no such officer."

"How can one know every officer in the army?"

"Nevertheless, perhaps you had best report the incident to my own command. It never hurts one to be thorough, citizen. And I would still like to see the supplies you are to deliver." He turned as if to signal to several chattering soldiers standing nearby.

"Here's one of 'em!" said Flor. Her sword lopped off the officer's head in the midst of a never-to-be-answered query.

For an instant they froze in readiness, hands on weapons, eyes on the troops nearest the wagon. Yet there was no immediate reaction, no cry of alarm. Flor's move had been so swift and the body had fallen so rapidly that no one had yet noticed.

While their driver did not believe in divine intervention, he had the sense to make the decision his passengers withheld.

"Hiiii-criiickk!" he shouted softly, simultaneously snapping his odd whip over the lizard's eyes. The animal surged forward in a galloping waddle. Now soldiers did turn from conversation or eating to stare uncertainly at the fleeing wagon.

The last few troops scrambled out of the wagon's path. There was nothing ahead save rock and promise.

Someone stumbled over the body of the unfortunately curious officer, noted that the head was no longer attached, connected the perfidy with the rapidly shrinking outline of the racing wagon, and finally thought to raise the alarm.

"Here they come, friends." Caz knelt in the wagon, staring back the way they'd come. His eyes picked out individual pursuers where Jon-Tom could detect only a faint rising of dust. "They must have found the body."

"Not enough of a start," said Bribbens tightly. "I'll never see my beloved Sloomaz-ayor-le-Weentli and its cool green banks again. I regret only not having the opportunity to perish in water."

"Woe unto us," murmured a disconsolate Mudge.

"Woe unto ya, maybe," said the lithe black shape perched on the back of the driver's seat. Pog lifted into the air and sped ahead of the lumbering wagon.

"Send back help!" Jon-Tom yelled to the retreating dot.

"He will do so," Clothahump said patiently, "if his panic does not overwhelm his good sense. I am more concerned that our pursuit may catch us before any such assistance has a chance to be mobilized."

"Can't you make this go any faster?" asked Flor.

"The lanteth is built for pulling heavy loads, not for springing like a zealth over poor ground such as this," said the driver, raising his voice in order to be heard above the rumble of the wheels.

"They're gaining on us," said Jon-Tom. Now the mounted riders coming up behind were close enough so that even he could make out individual shapes. Many of the insects he didn't recognize, but the long, lanky, helmeted Plated Folk resembling giant walking sticks were clear enough. Their huge strides ate up long sections of Pass as they closed on the escapees. Two riders on each long back began to notch arrows into bows.

"The Gate, there's the Gate, by Rerelia's pink purse it is!" Mudge shouted gleefully.

His shout was cut off as he was thrown off his feet. The wagon lurched around a huge boulder in the sand, rose momentarily onto two wheels, but did not turn over. It slammed back down onto the riverbed with a wooden crunch. Somehow the axles held. The spokes bent but did not snap.

Ahead was the still distant rampart of a massive stone wall. Arrows began to zip like wasps past the wagon. The passengers huddled low on the bed, listening to the occasional *thuck* as an arrow stuck into the wooden sides.

A moan sounded above them, a silent whisper of departure, and another body joined Talea. It was their iconoclastic, brave driver. He lay limply in the wagon bed, arms trailing and the color already beginning to fade from his ommatidia. Two arrows protruded from his head.

Jon-Tom scrambled desperately into the driver's seat, trying to stay low while arrows whistled nastily around him. The reins lay draped across the front bars of the seat. He reached for them.

They receded. So did the seat. The rolling wagon had struck another boulder and had bounced, sending its occupants flying. It landed ahead of Jon-Tom, on its side. The panicky lizard continued pulling it toward freedom.

Spitting sand and blood, Jon-Tom struggled to his feet. He'd landed on his belly. Duar and staff were still intact. So was he, thanks to the now shattered hard-shelled disguise. As he tried to walk, a loose piece of legging slid down onto his foot. He kicked it aside, began pulling off the other sections of chitin and throwing them away. Deception was no longer of any use.

"Come on, it isn't far!" he yelled to his companions. Caz

247

ran past, then Mudge and Bribbens. The boatman was assisting Clothahump as best he could.

Flor, almost past him, halted when she saw he was running toward the wagon. "Jon-Tom, *muerte es muerte*. Let it be."

"I'm not leaving without her."

Flor caught up with him, grabbed his arm. "She's dead, Jon-Tom. Be a man. Leave it alone."

He did not stop to answer her. Ignoring the shafts falling around them, he located the spraddled corpse. In an instant he had Talea's body in a fireman's carry across his shoulders. She was so small, hardly seemed to have any weight at all. A surge of strength ran through him, and he ran light-headed toward the wall. It was someone else running, someone else breathing hard.

Only Mudge had a bow, but he couldn't run and use it. It wouldn't matter much in a minute anyway, because their grotesque pursuit was almost on top of them. It would be a matter of swords then, a delaying of the inevitable dying.

A furry shape raced past him. Another followed, and two more. He slowed to a trot, tried to wipe the sweat from his eyes. What he saw renewed his strength more than any vitamins.

A fuzzy wave was funneling out of a narrow crack in the hundred-foot-high Gate ahead. Squirrels and muskrats, otters and possums, an isolated skunk, and a platoon of vixens charged down the Pass.

The insect riders saw the rush coming and hesitated just long enough to allow the exhausted escapees to blend in with their saviors. There was a brief, intense fight. Then the pursuers, who had counted on no more than overtaking and slaughtering a few renegades, turned and ran for the safety of the Greendowns. Many did not make it, their mounts cut out from under them. The butchery was neat and quick.

Soft paws helped the limping, panting refugees the rest of

the way in. A thousand questions were thrown at them, not a few centering on their identity. Some of the rescuers had seen the discarded chitin disguises, and knowledge of that prompted another hundred queries at least.

Clothahump adjusted his filthy spectacles, shook sand from the inside of his shell, and confronted a minor officer who had taken roost on the wizard's obliging shoulders.

"Is Wuckle Three-Stripe of Polastrindu here?"

"Aye, but he's with the Fourth and Fifth Corps," said the raven. His kilt was yellow, black, and azure, and he wore a thin helmet. Two throwing knives were strapped to his sides beneath his wings, and his claws had been sharpened for war.

"What about a general named Aveticus?"

"Closer, in the headquarters tent," said the raven. He brushed at the yellow scarf around his neck, the insignia of an arboreal noncommissioned officer. "You'd like to go there, I take it?"

Clothahump nodded. "Immediately. Tell him it's the mad doomsayers. He'll see us."

The raven nodded. "Will do, sir." He lifted from the wizard's shell and soared over the crest of the Gate.

They marched on through the barely open doorway. Jon-Tom had turned his burden over to a pair of helpful ocelots. The Gate itself, he saw, was at least a yard deep and formed of massive timbers. The stonework of the wall was thirty times as thick, solid rock. The Gate gleamed with fresh sap, a substance Caz identified as a fire-retardant.

The Plated Folk might somehow pierce the Gate, but picks and hatchets would never breech the wall. His confidence rose.

It lifted to near assurance when they emerged from the Pass. Spread out on the ancient river plain that sloped down from the mountains were thousands of camp fires. The warmlanders had taken Clothahump's warning to heart. They would be ready.

He repositioned his own special burden, taking it back from the helpful soldiers. With a grimace he unsnapped the insect head and kicked it aside. Red hair hung limply across his shoulder. He stroked the face, hurriedly pulled his hand away. The skin was numbingly cold.

There were two arrows in her back. Even in death, she had protected him again. But it would be all right, he told himself angrily. Clothahump would revive her, as he'd promised he would. Hadn't he promised? Hadn't he?

They were directed to a large three-cornered tent. The banners of a hundred cities flew above it. Squadrons of brightly kilted birds and bats flew in formation overhead, arrowhead outlines full of the flash and silver of weapons. They had their own bivouacs, he noted absently, on the flanks of the mountains or in the forest that rose to the west.

Wuckle Three-Stripe was there, still panting from having ridden through the waiting army to meet them. So was Aveticus, his attitude and eyes as alert and ready as they'd been that day so long ago in the council chambers of Polastrindu. He was heavily armored, and a crimson sash hung from his long neck. Jon-Tom could read his expression well enough: the marten was eager to be at the business of killing.

There were half a dozen other officers. Before the visitors could say anything a massive wolverine resplendent in gold chain mail stepped forward and asked in a voice full of disbelief, "Have ye then truly been to Cugluch?" Rumor then had preceded presence.

"To Cugluch an' back, mate," Mudge admitted pridefully. " 'Twas an epic journey. One that'll long be spoken of. The bards will not 'ave words enough t' do 'er justice."

"Perhaps," said Aveticus quietly. "I hope there will be bards left to sing of it."

"We bring great news." Clothahump took a seat near the central table. "I am sorry to say that the great magic of the Plated Folk remains as threatening as ever, though not quite as enigmatic.

"However, for the first time in recorded history, we have powerful allies who are not of the warmlands." He did not try to keep the pleasure from his voice. "The Weavers have agreed to fight alongside us!"

Considerable muttering rose from the assembled leadership. Not all of it was pleased.

"I have the word of the Grand Webmistress Oll herself, given to us in person," Clothahump added, dissatisfied with the reaction his announcement produced.

When the import finally penetrated, there were astonished murmurs of delight.

"The Weavers . . . We canna lose now. . . . Won't be a one of the Plated Bastards left! . . . Drive them all the way to the end of the Greendowns!"

"That is," said Clothahump cautioningly, "they will fight alongside us if they can get here in time. They have to come across the Teeth."

"Then they will never reach here," said a skeptical officer. "There is no other pass across the Teeth save the Troom."

"Perhaps not a Pass, but a path. The Ironclouders will show them the way."

Now derision filled the tent. "There is no such place as Ironcloud," said the dubious Wuckle Three-Stripe. "It is a myth inhabited by ghosts."

"We climbed inside the myth and supped with the ghosts," said Clothahump calmly. "It exists."

"I believe this wizard's word is proof enough of anything," said Aveticus softly, dominating the discussion by sheer strength of presence.

"They have promised to guide the Weaver army here,"

Clothahump continued to his suddenly respectful audience. "But we cannot count on their assistance. I believe the Plated Folk will begin their attack any day. We confronted and escaped from the wizard Eejakrat. While he does not know that we know little about his Manifestation, he will not assume ignorance on our part, and thus will urge the assembled horde to march. They appeared ready in any case."

That stimulated a barrage of questions from the officers. They wanted estimates of troop strength, of arboreals, weapons and provisioning, of disposition and heavy troops and bowmen and more.

Clothahump impatiently waved the questions off. "I can't answer any of your queries in detail. I am not a soldier and my observations are attuned to other matters. I can tell you that this is by far the greatest army the Plated Folk have ever sent against the warmlands."

"They will be met by more warmlanders than ever they imagined!" snorted Wuckle Three-Stripe. "We will reduce the populating of the Greendowns to nothing. The Troom Pass shall be paved with chitin!" Cries of support and determination came from those behind him.

The badger's expression softened. "I must say we are pleased, if utterly amazed, to find you once again safely among your kind. The world owes you all a great debt."

"How great, mate?" asked Mudge.

Three-Stripe eyed the otter distastefully. "In this time of crisis, how can you think of mere material things?"

"Mate, I can always th—" Flor put a hand over the otter's muzzle.

The mayor turned to a subordinate. "See that these people have anything they want, and that they are provided with food and the best of shelter." The weasel officer nodded.

"It will be done, sir." He moved forward, saluted crisply

His gaze fell on the form lying limply across Jon-Tom's back. "Shall the she be requiring medical care, sir?"

Red hair tickled Jon-Tom's ear. He jerked his head to one side, replied almost imperceptibly.

"No. She's dead."

"I am sorry, sir."

Jon-Tom's gaze traveled across the tent. Clothahump was conversing intently with a cluster of officers including the wolverine, Aveticus, and Wuckle Three-Stripe. He glanced up for an instant and locked eyes with the spellsinger. The instant passed.

The relief Jon-Tom had sought in the wizard's eyes was not there, nor had there been hope.

Only truth.

XV

The meeting did not take long. As they left the tent the
tension of the past weeks, of living constantly on the edge of
death and disappointment, began to let go of them all.

"Me for a 'ot bath!" said Mudge expectantly.

"And I for a cold one," countered Bribbens.

"I think I'd prefer a shower, myself," said Flor.

"I'd enjoy that myself, I believe." Jon-Tom did not notice
the look that passed between Caz and Flor. He noticed
nothing except the wizard's retreating oval.

"Just a minute, sir. Where are you going now?"

Clothahump glanced back at him. "First to locate Pog.
Then to the Council of Wizards, Warlocks, and Witches so
that we may coordinate our magicking in preparation for the
coming attack. Only one may magic at a time, you know.
Contradiction destroys the effectiveness of spells."

"Wait. What about . . . you know. You promised."

Clothahump looked evasive. "She's dead, my boy. Like

love, life is a transitory thing. Both linger as long as they're able and fade quickly.''

"I don't want any of your fucking wizardly platitudes!" He towered over the turtle. "You said you could bring her back."

"I said I might. You were despondent. You needed hope, something to sustain you. I gave you that. By pretending I might help the dead I helped the living to survive. I have no regrets.''

When Jon-Tom did not respond the wizard continued, "My boy, your magic is of an unpredictable quality and considerable power. Many times that unpredictability could be a drawback. But the magic we face is equally unpredictable. You may be of great assistance . . . if you choose to.

"But I feel responsibility for you, if not for your present hurt. If you elect to do nothing, no one will blame you for it and I will not try to coerce you. I can only wish for your assistance.

"I am trying to tell you, my boy, that there is no formula I know for raising the dead. I said I would try, and I shall, when the time is right and other matters press less urgently on my knowledge. I must now try my best to preserve many. I cannot turn away from that to experiment in hopes of saving one." His voice was flat and unemotional.

"I wish it were otherwise, boy. Even magic has its limits, however. Death is one of them."

Jon-Tom stood numbly, still balancing the dead weight on his shoulders. "But you said, you told me . . ."

"What I told you I did in order to save you. Despondency does not encourage quick thinking and survival. You have survived. Talea, bless her mercurial, flinty little heart, would be cursing your self-pity this very moment if she were able."

"You lying little hard-shelled—"

Clothahump took a cautious step backward. "Don't force

me to stop you, Jon-Tom. Yes, I lied to you. It wasn't the first time, as Mudge is so quick to point out. A lie in the service of right is a kind of truth."

Jon-Tom let out an inarticulate yell and rushed forward, blinded as much by the cold finality of his loss as by the wizard's duplicity. No longer a personality or even a memory, the body on his shoulders tumbled to the earth. He reached blindly for the impassive sorcerer.

Clothahump had seen the rage building, had taken note of the signs in Jon-Tom's face, in the way he stood, in the tension of his skin. The wizard's hands moved rapidly and he whispered to unseen things words like "fix" and "anesthesia."

Jon-Tom sent down as neatly as if clubbed by his own staff. Several soldiers noted the activity and wandered over.

"Is he dead, sir?" one asked curiously.

"No. For the moment he wishes it were so." The wizard pointed toward the limp form of Talea. "The first casualty of the war."

"And this one?" The squirrel gestured down at Jon-Tom.

"Love is always the second casualty. He will be all right in a while. He needs to rest and not remember. There is a tent behind the headquarters. Take him and put him in there."

The noncom's tail switched the air. "Will he be dangerous when he regains consciousness?"

Clothahump regarded the softly breathing body. "I do not think so, not even to himself."

The squirrel saluted. "It will be done, sir."

There are few drugs, Clothahump mused, that can numb both the heart and the mind. Among them grief is the most powerful. He watched while the soldiers bore the lanky, youthful Jon-Tom away, then forced himself to turn to more serious matters. Talea was gone and Jon-Tom damaged. Well, he was sorry as sorry could be for the boy, but they would do without his erratic talents if they had to. He could not cool the boy's hate.

Let him hate me, then, if he wishes. It will focus his thoughts away from his loss. He will be forever suspicious of me hereafter, but in that he will have the company of most creatures. People always fear what they cannot understand.

Makes it lonely though, old fellow. Very lonely. You knew that when you took the vows and made the oaths. He sighed, waddled off to locate Aveticus. Now there was a rational mind, he thought pleasantly. Unimaginative, but sound. He will accept my advice and act upon it. I can help him.

Perhaps in return he can help me. Two hundred and how many years, old fellow?

Tired, dammit. I'm so tired. Pity I took an oath of responsibility along with the others. But this evil of Eejakrat's has got to be stopped.

Clothahump was wise in many things, but even he would not admit that what really kept him going wasn't his oath of responsibility. It was curiosity. . . .

Red fog filled Jon-Tom's vision. Blood mist. It faded to gray when he blinked. It was not the ever present mist of the awful Greendowns, but instead a dull glaze that faded rapidly.

Looking up, he discovered multicolored fabric in place of blue sky. As he lay on his back he heard a familiar voice say, "I'll watch him now."

He pushed himself up on his elbows, his head still swimming from the effects of Clothahump's incantation. Several armed warmlanders were exiting the tent.

"Ya feeling better now?"

He raised his sight once more. An upside-down face stared anxiously into his own. Pog was hanging from one of the crosspoles, wrapped in his wings. He spread them, stretching, and yawned.

"How long have I been out?"

" 'Bout since dis time yesterday."

"Where's everyone else?"

The bat grinned. "Relaxing, trying ta enjoy themselves. Orgy before da storm."

"Talea?" He tried to sit all the way up. A squat, hairy form fluttered down from the ceiling to land on his chest.

"Talea's as dead as she was yesterday when you tried ta attack da master. As dead as she was when dat knife went into her t'roat back in Cugluch, an dat's a fact ya'd better get used ta, man!"

Jon-Tom winced, looked away from the little gargoyle face confronting him. "I'll never accept it. Never."

Pog hopped off his chest, landed on a chair nearby, and leaned against the back. It was designed for a small mammalian body, but it still fit him uncomfortably. He always preferred hanging to sitting but given Jon-Tom's present disorientation, he knew it would be better if he didn't have to stare at a topsy-turvy face just now.

"Ya slay me, ya know?" Pog said disgustedly. "Ya really think you're something special."

"What?" Confused, Jon-Tom frowned at the bat.

"You heard me. I said dat ya tink you're something special, don't ya? Ya tink you're da only one wid problems? At least you've got da satisfaction of knowing dat someone loved ya. I ain't even got dat.

"How would ya like it if Talea were alive and every time ya looked at her, so much as smiled in her direction, she turned away from ya in disgust?"

"I don't—"

The bat cut him off, raised a wing. "No, hear me out. Dat's what I have ta go trough every day of my life. Dat's what I've been going trough for years. 'It don't make sense,' da boss keeps tellin' me." Pog sniffed disdainfully. "But he don't have ta experience it, ta live it. 'Least ya know ya was loved, Jon-Tom. I may never have dat simple ting. I may have ta go trough da rest of my life knowin' dat da one I love gets the heaves every time I come near her. How would you like ta live wid dat? I'm goin' ta suffer until I die, or until she does.

"And what's worse," he looked away momentarily, sounding so miserable that Jon-Tom forgot his own agony, "she's here!"

"Who's here?"

"Da falcon. Uleimee. She's wid da aerial forces. I tried ta see her once, just one time. She wouldn't even do dat for me."

"She can't be much if she acts like that toward you," said Jon-Tom gently.

"Why not? Because she's reactin' to my looks instead of my wondaful personality? Looks are important. Don't let anybody tell ya otherwise. And I got a real problem. And dere's smell, and other factors, and I can't do a damn ting about 'em. Maybe da boss can, eventually. But promises don't do nuthin' for me now." His expression twisted.

"So don't let me hear any more of your bemoanings. You're alive an' healthy, you're an interesting curiosity to da females around ya, an you've got plenty of loving ahead of ya. But not me. I'm cursed because I love only one."

"It's kind of funny," Jon-Tom said softly, tracing a pattern on the blanket covering his cot. "I thought it was Flor I was in love with. She tried to show me otherwise, but I couldn't . . . wouldn't, see."

"Dat wouldn't matter anyhow." Pog fluttered off the chair and headed for the doorway.

"Why not?"

"Blind an' dumb," the bat grumbled. "Don't ya see anyting? She's had da hots for dat Caz fellow ever since we fished him outa da river Tailaroam.'' He was gone before Jon-Tom could comment.

Caz and Flor? That was impossible, he thought wildly. Or was it? What was impossible in a world of impossibilities?

Bringing back Talea, he told himself.

Well, if Clothahump could do nothing, there was still another manipulator of magic who would try: himself.

Troops gave the tent a wide berth during the following days. Inside a tall, strange human sat singing broken love songs to a corpse. The soldiers muttered nervously to themselves and made signs of protection when they were forced to pass near the tent. Its interior glowed at night with a veritable swarm of gneechees.

Jon-Tom's efforts were finally halted not by personal choice but by outside events. He had succeeded in keeping the body from decomposing, but it remained still as the rock beneath the tent. Then on the tenth day after their hasty retreat from Cugluch, word came down from aerial scouts that the army of the Plated Folk was on the march.

So he slung his duar across his back and went out with staff in hand. Behind he left the body of one who had loved him and whom he could love in return only too late. He strode resolutely through the camp, determined to take a position on the wall. If he could not give life, then by God he would deal out death with equal enthusiasm.

Aveticus met him on the wall.

"It comes, as it must to all creatures," the general said to him. "The time of choosing." He peered hard into Jon-Tom's face. "In your anger, remember that one who fights blindly usually dies quickly."

Jon-Tom blinked, looked down at him. "Thanks, Aveticus. I'll keep control of myself."

"Good." The general walked away, stood chatting with a couple of subordinates as they looked down the Pass.

A ripple of expectancy passed through the soldiers assembled on the wall. Weapons were raised as their wielders leaned forward. No one spoke. The only noise now came from down the Pass, and it was growing steadily louder.

As a wave they came, a single dark wave of chitin and iron. They filled the Pass from one side to the other, a flood of murder that extended unbroken into the distance.

A last few hundred warmlander troops scrambled higher into the few notches cut into the precipitous canyon. From there they could prevent any Plated Folk from scaling the rocks to either side of the wall. They readied spears and arrows. A rich, musky odor filled the morning air, exuded from the glands of thousands of warmlanders. An aroma of anticipation.

The great wooden gates were slowly parted. There came a shout followed by a thunderous cheer from the soldiers on the ramparts that shook gravel from the mountainsides. Led by a phalanx of a hundred heavily armored wolverines, the warmlander army sallied out into the Pass.

Jon-Tom moved to leave his position on the wall so he could join the main body of troops pouring from the Gate. He was confronted by a pair of familiar faces. Caz and Mudge still disdained the use of armor.

"What's wrong?" he asked them. "Aren't you going to join the fight?"

"Eventually," said Caz.

"If it proves absolutely necessary, mate," added Mudge. "Right now we've a more important task assigned to us, we do."

"And what's that?"

"Keepin' an eye on yourself."

Jon-Tom looked past them, saw Clothahump watching him speculatively.

"What's the idea?" He no longer addressed the wizard as "sir."

The sorcerer walked over to join them. His left hand was holding a thick scroll half open. It was filled with words and symbols.

"In the end your peculiar magic, spellsinger, may be of far more use to us than another sword arm."

"I'm not interested in fighting with magic," Jon-Tom countered angrily. "I want to spill some blood."

Clothahump shook his head, smiled ruefully. "How the passions of youth do alter its nature, if not necessarily maturing it. I seem to recall a somewhat different personality once brought confused and gentle to my Tree."

"I remember him also," Jon-Tom replied humorlessly. "He's dead too."

"Pity. He was a nice boy. Ah well. You are potentially much more valuable to us here, Jon-Tom. Do not be so anxious. I promise you that as you grow older you will be presented with ample opportunities for participating in self-satisfying slaughter."

"I'm not interested in—"

Sounding less understanding, Clothahump cut him off testily. "Consider something besides yourself, boy. You are upset because Talea is dead, because her death personally affects *you*. You're upset because I deceived *you*. Now you want to waste a potentially helpful talent to satisfy *your* personal blood lust." He regarded the tall youth sternly.

"My boy, I am fond of you. I think that with a little maturation and a little tempering, as with a good sword, you will make a fine person. But for a little while at least, try thinking of something besides *you*."

The ready retort died on Jon-Tom's lips. Nothing penetrates the mind or acts on it so effectively as does truth, that most efficient but foul-tasting of all medicines. Clothahump had only one thing in his favor: he was right. That canceled out anything else Jon-Tom could think of to say.

He leaned back against the rampart, saw Caz and Mudge, friends both, watching him warily. Hesitantly, he smiled.

"It's okay. The old bastard's right. I'll stay." He turned from them to study the Pass. After a pause and a qualifying nod from Clothahump, Mudge and Caz moved to join him.

The wolverine wedge struck the center of the Plated Folk wave like a knife, leaving contorted, multilated insect bodies in their wake. The rest of the warmlander soldiers followed close behind.

It was a terrible place for a battle. The majority of both armies could only seethe and shift nervously. They were packed so tightly in the narrow Pass that only a small portion of each force could actually confront one another. It was another advantage for the outnumbered warmlanders.

After an hour or so of combat the battle appeared to be going the way of all such conflicts down through the millenia. Led by the wolverines the warmlanders were literally cutting their way up the Pass. The Plated Folk fought bravely but mechanically, showing no more initiative in individual combat than they did collectively. Also, though they possessed an extra set of limbs, they were stiff-jointed and no match for the more supple, agile enemies they faced. Most of the Plated Folk were no more than three and a half feet tall, while certain of the warmlanders, such as the wolverines and the felines, were considerably more massive and powerful. And none of the insects could match the otters and weasels for sheer speed.

The battle raged all that morning and on into the afternoon. All at once, it seemed to be over. The Plated Folk suddenly threw away their weapons, broke, and ran. This induced considerable chaos in the packed ranks behind the front. The panic spread rapidly, an insidious infection as damaging as any fatal disease.

Soon it appeared that the entire Plated Folk army was in retreat, pursued by yelling, howling warmlanders. The soldiers at the Gate broke out in whoops of joy. A few expressed disappointment at not having been in on the fight.

Only Clothahump stood quietly on his side of the Gate, Aveticus on the other. The wizard was staring with aged eyes at the field of battle, squinting through his glasses and shaking his head slowly.

"Too quick, too easy," he was murmuring.

Jon-Tom overheard. "What's wrong . . . sir?"

Clothahump spoke without looking over at him. "I see no evidence of the power Eejakrat commands. Not a sign of it at work."

"Maybe he can't manipulate it properly. Maybe it's beyond his control."

" 'Maybes' kill more individuals than swords, my boy."

"What kind of magic are you looking for?"

"I don't know." The wizard gazed skyward. "The clouds are innocent of storm. Nothing hints at lightning. The earth is silent, and we've naught to fear from tremorings. The ether flows silently. I feel no discord in any of the levels of magic. It worries me. I fear what I cannot sense."

"There's a possible storm cloud," said Jon-Tom, pointing. "Boiling over the far southern ridge."

Clothahump peered in the indicated direction. Yes, there was a dark mass back there, which had materialized suddenly. It was blacker than any of the scattered cumulo-nimbus that hung in the afternoon sky like winter waifs. The cloud foamed down the face of the ridge, rushing toward the Pass.

"That's not a cloud," said Caz, seeking with eyes sharper than those of other creatures. "Plated Folk."

"What kind?" asked Clothahump, already confident of the reply.

"Dragonflies, a few large beetles. All with subsidiary mounted troops, I fear. Many other large beetles behind them."

"They should be no trouble," murmured Clothahump. "But I wonder."

Aveticus crossed the Gate and joined them.

"What do you make of this, sir?"

"It appears to be the usual aerial assault."

Aveticus nodded, glanced back toward the plain. "If so, they will fare no better in the air than they have on the ground. Still . . ."

"Something troubling you then?" said Clothahump.

The marten eyed the approaching cloud confusedly. "It is strange, the way they are grouped. Still, it would be peculiar if they did not at least once try something different."

Yells sounded from behind the Gate. The warmlanders own aerial forces were massing in a great spiral over the camp. They were of every size and description. Their kilts formed a brilliant quiltwork in the sky.

Then the spiral began to unwind as the line of bats and birds flew over the Gate to meet the coming threat. They intercepted the Plated Folk fliers near the line of combat.

As soon as contact was made, the Plated Folk forces split. Half moved to meet the attack. The second half, consisting primarily of powerful but ponderous beetles, dipped below the fight. With them went a large number of the more agile dragonflies with their single riders.

"Look there," said Mudge. "Wot are the bleedin' buggerers up to?"

"They're attacking ground troops!" said Aveticus, outraged. "It is not done. Those in the sky do not do battle with those on the ground. They fight only others of their own kind."

"Well, somebody's changed the rules," said Jon-Tom, watching a tall amazonian figure moving across the wall toward them.

Confusion began to grip the advance ranks of warmlanders. They were not used to fighting attack from above. Most of the outnumbered birds and bats were too busy with their own opponents to render any assistance to those below.

"This is Eejakrat's work," muttered Clothahump. "I can sense it. It is magic, but of a most subtle sort."

"Air-ground support," said the newly arrived Flor. She was staring tight-lipped at the carnage the insect fliers were wreaking on the startled warmlander infantry.

"What kind of magic is this?" asked Aveticus grimly.

"It's called tactics," said Jon-Tom.

The marten turned to Clothahump. "Wizard, can you not counter this kind of magic?"

"I would try," said Clothahump, "save that I do not know how to begin. I can counter lightning and dissipate fog, but I do not know how to assist the minds of our soldiers. That is what is endangered now."

While bird and dragonfly tangled in the air above the Pass and other insect fliers swooped again and again on the ranks of puzzled warmlanders, the sky began to rain a different sort of death.

The massive cluster of large beetles remained high out of arrowshot and began to disgorge hundreds, thousands of tiny pale puffs on the rear of the warmlander forces. Arrows fell from the puff shapes as they descended.

Jon-Tom recognized the familiar round cups. So did Flor. But Clothahump could only shake his head in disbelief.

"Impossible! No spell is strong enough to lift so many into the air at once."

"I'm afraid this one is," Jon-Tom told him.

"What is this frightening spell called?"

"Parachuting."

267

The warmlander troops were as confused by the sight as by the substance of this assault on their rear ranks. At the same time there was a chilling roar from the retreating Plated Folk infantry. Those who'd abandoned their weapons suddenly scrambled for the nearest canyon wall.

From the hidden core of the horde came several hundred of the largest beetles anyone had ever seen. These huge scarabaeids and their cousins stampeded through the gap created by their own troops. The startled wolverines were trampled underfoot. Massive chitin horns pierced soldier after soldier. Each beetle had half a dozen bowmen on its back. From there they picked off those warmlanders who tried to cut at the beetle's legs.

Now it was the warmlanders who broke, whirling and scrambling in panic for the safety of the distant Gate. They pressed insistently on those behind them. But terror already ruled their supposed reinforcements. Instead of friendly faces those pursued by the relentless beetles found thousands of Plated Folk soldiers who had literally dropped from the sky.

The birds and their riders, mostly small squirrels and their relatives, fought valiantly to break through the aerial Plated Folk. But by the time they had made any headway against the dragonfly forces confronting them the great, lumbering flying beetles had already dropped their cargo. Now they were flying back down the Pass, to gather a second load of impatient insect parachutists.

Glee turned to dismay on the wall as badly demoralized troops streamed back through the open Gate. Behind them was sand and gravel-covered ground so choked with corpses that it was hard to move. The dead actually did more to save the warmlander forces from annihilation than the living.

When the last survivor had limped inside, the great Gate was swung shut. An insectoid wave crested against the barrier.

Now the force of scarabaeids who'd broken the warmlander front turned and retreated. They could not scale the wall and would only hinder its capture.

Strong-armed soldiers carrying dozens, hundreds of ladders took their places. The ladders were thrown up against the wall in such profusion that several defenders, while trying to spear those Plated Folk raising one ladder, were struck and killed by another. The ladders were so close together they sometimes overlapped rungs. A dark tide began to swarm up the wall.

Having no facility with a bow, Jon-Tom was heaving spears as fast as the armsbearers could supply them. Next to him Flor was firing a large longbow with deadly accuracy. Mudge stood next to her, occasionally pausing in his own firing to compliment the giantess on a good shot.

The wall was now crowded with reinforcements. Every time a warmlander fell another took his place. But despite the number of ladders pushed back and broken, the number of climbers killed, the seemingly endless stream of Plated Folk came on.

It was Caz who pulled Jon-Tom aside and directed his attention far, far up the canyon. "Can you see them, my friend? They are there, watching."

"Where?"

"There . . . can't you see the dark spots on that butte that juts out slightly into the Pass?"

Jon-Tom could barely make out the butte. He could not discern individuals standing on it. But he did not doubt Caz's observation.

"I'll take your word for it. Can you see who 'they' are?"

"Eejakrat I recognize from our sojourn in Cugluch. The giant next to him must be, from the richness of attire and servility of attendants, the Empress Skrritch."

"Can you see what Eejakrat is doing?" inquired a worried Clothahump.

"He looks behind him at something I cannot see."

"The dead mind!" Clothahump gazed helplessly at his sheaf of formulae. "It is responsible for this new method of fighting, these 'tactics' and 'parachutes' and such. It is telling the Plated Folk how to fight. It means they have found a new way to attack the wall."

"It means rather more than that," said Aveticus quietly. Everyone turned to look at the marten. "It means they no longer have to breach the Jo-Troom Gate. . . ."

XVI

"Is it not clear?" he told them when no one responded. "These 'parachute' things will enable them to drop thousands of soldiers *behind* the Gate." He looked grim and turned to a subordinate.

"Assemble Elasmin, Toer, and Sleastic. Tell them they must gather a large body of mobile troops. No matter how bad the situation here grows these soldiers must remain ready behind the Gate, watching for more of these falling troops. They must watch only the sky, for, if we are not prepared, these monsters will fall all over our own camp and all will be lost."

The officer rushed away to convey that warning to the warmlander general staff. Overhead, birds and riders were holding their own against the dragonfly folk. But they were fully occupied. If the beetles returned with more airborne Plated Folk troops, the warmlander arboreals would be unable to prevent them from falling on the underdefended camp.

Attacked from the front and from behind, the Jo-Troom Gate would change from impregnable barrier to mass grave.

Once out on the open plains the Plated Folk army would be able to engulf the remnants of the warmlander defenders. In addition to superior numbers, which they'd always possessed, the attackers now had the use of superior tactics. Eejakrat had discovered the flexibility and imagination dozens of their earlier assaults had lacked.

Not that it would matter soon, for the inexorable pressure on the Gate's defenders was beginning to tell. Now an occasional Plated Folk warrior managed to surmount the ramparts. Isolated pockets of fighting were beginning to appear on the wall itself.

" 'Ere now, wot d'you make o' that, mate?" Mudge had hold of Jon-Tom's arm and was pointing northward.

On the plain below the foothills of Zaryt's Teeth a thin dark line was snaking rapidly toward the Gate.

Then a familiar form was scuttling through the milling soldiers. It wore light chain-mail top and bottom and a strange helmet that left room for multiple eyes. Despite the armor both otter and man identified the wearer instantly.

"Ananthos!" said Jon-Tom.

"yes." The spider put four limbs on the wall and looked outward. He ducked as a tiny club glanced off his cephalothorax.

"i hope sincerely we are not too late."

Flor put aside her bow, exhausted. "I never thought I'd ever be glad to greet a spider. Or that to my dying day I'd ever be doing this, *compadre*." She walked over and gave the uncertain arachnid a brisk hug.

Disdaining the wall, the modest force of Weavers divided. Then, utilizing multiple limbs, incredible agility, and built-in climbing equipment, they scrambled up the sheer sides of the Pass flanking the Gate. They suspended themselves there, out of arrow range, and began firing down on the Plated Folk clustered before the Gate.

This additional firepower enabled the warmlanders on the wall to concentrate on the ladders. Nets were spun and dropped. Sticky, unbreakable silk cables entangled scores of insect fighters.

Dragonflies and riders broke from the aerial combat to swoop toward the new arrivals clinging to the bare rock. The Weavers spun balls of sticky silk. These were whirled lariatlike over their heads and flung at the diving fliers with incredible accuracy. They glued themselves to wings or legs, and the startled insects found themselves yanked right out of the sky.

Now the birds and bats began to make some progress against their depleted aerial foe. There was a real hope that they could now prevent any returning beetles from dropping troops behind the Gate.

While that specific danger was thus greatly reduced, the most important result of the arrival of the Weaver force was the effect it had on the morale of the Plated Folk. Until now all their new strategies and plans had worked perfectly. The abrupt and utterly unexpected appearance of their solitary ancient enemies and their obvious rapport with the warmlanders was a devastating shock. The Weavers were the last people the Plated Folk expected to find defending the Jo-Troom Gate.

Directing the Weavers' actions from a position on the wall by relaying orders and information, via tiny sprinting spiders colored bright red, yellow and blue, was a bulbous black form. The Grand Webmistress Oll was decked out in silver armor and hundreds of feet of crimson and orange silk.

Once she waved a limb briskly toward Jon-Tom and his companions. Perhaps she saw them, possibly she was only giving a command.

The warmlanders, buoyed by the arrival of a once feared

but now welcomed new ally, fought with renewed strength. The Plated Folk forces faltered, then redoubled their attack. Weaver archers and retiarii wrought terrible destruction among them, and the warmlander bowmen had easy targets helplessly ensnared in sticky nets.

A new problem arose. There was a danger that the growing mountain of corpses before the wall would soon be high enough to eliminate the need for ladders.

All that night the battle continued by torchlight, with fatigue-laden warmlanders and Weavers holding off the still endless waves of Plated Folk. The insects fought until they died and were walked on emotionlessly by their replacements.

It was after midnight when Caz woke Jon-Tom from an uneasy sleep.

"Another cloud, my friend," said the rabbit. His clothing was torn and one ear was bleeding despite a thick bandage.

Wearily Jon-Tom gathered up his staff and a handful of small spears and trotted alongside Caz toward the wall. "So they're going to try dropping troops behind us at night? I wonder if our aerials have enough strength left to hold them back."

"I don't know," said Caz with concern. "That's why I was sent to get you. They want every strong spear thrower on the wall to try and pick off any low fliers."

In truth, the ranks of kilted fighters were badly thinned, while the strength of their dragonfly opponents seemed nearly the same as before. Only the presence of the Weavers kept the arboreal battle equal.

But it was not a swarm of lumbering Plated Folk that flew out of the moon. It was a sea of sulfurous yellow eyes. They fell on the insect fliers with terrible force. Great claws shredded membranous wings, beaks nipped away antennae and skulls, while tiny swords cut with incredible skill.

It took a moment for Jon-Tom and his friends to identify

the new combatants, cloaked as they were by the concealing night. It was the size of the great glowing eyes that soon gave the answer.

"The Ironclouders," Caz finally announced. "Bless my soul but I never thought to see the like. Look at them wheel and bank, will you? It's no contest."

The word was passed up and down the ranks. So entranced were the warmlanders by the sight of these fighting legends that some of them temporarily forgot their own defensive tasks and thus were wounded or killed.

The inhabitants of the hematite were better equipped for night fighting than any of the warmlanders save the few bats. The previously unrelenting aerial assault of the Plated Folk was shattered. Fragmented insect bodies began to fall from the sky. The only reaction this grisly rain produced among the warmlanders beneath it was morbid laughter.

By morning the destruction was nearly complete. What remained of the Plated Folk aerial strength had retreated far up the Pass.

A general council was held atop the wall. For the first time in days the warmlanders were filled with optimism. Even the suspicious Clothahump was forced to admit that the tide of battle seemed to have turned.

"Could we not use these newfound friends as did the Plated Folk?" one of the officers suggested. "Could we not employ them to drop our own troops to the rear of the enemy forces?"

"Why stop there?" wondered one of the exhilarated bird officers, a much-decorated hawk in light armor and violet and red kilt. "Why not drop them in Cugluch itself? That would panic them!"

"No," said Aveticus carefully. "Our people are not prepared for such an adventure, and despite their size I do not think our owlish allies have the ability to carry more than a single rider, even assuming they would consent to such a proposition, which I do not think they would.

"But I do not think they would object to duplicating the actions of the Plated Folk fliers in assailing opposing ground forces. As our own can now do."

So the orders went out from the staff to their own fliers and thence to those from Ironcloud. It was agreed. Wearing dark goggles to shield their sensitive eyes from the sun, the owls and lemurs led the rejuvenated warmlander arboreals in dive after dive upon the massed, confused ranks of the Plated Folk army. The result was utter disorientation among the insect soldiers. But they still refused to collapse, though the losses they suffered were beginning to affect even so immense an army.

And when victory seemed all but won it was lost in a single heartrending and completely unexpected noise. A sound shocking and new to the warmlanders, who had never heard anything quite like it before. It was equally shocking but not new to Flor and Jon-Tom. Though not personally exposed to it, they recognized quickly enough the devastating thunder of dynamite.

As the dust began to settle among cries of pain and fear, there came a second, deeper, more ominous rumble as the entire left side of the Jo-Troom wall collapsed in a heap of shattered masonry and stone. It brought the great wooden gates down with it, supporting timbers splintering like fire-crackers as they crashed to the ground.

"Diversion," muttered Flor. "The aerial attack, the para-chutists, the beetles . . . all a diversion. *Bastardos;* I should have remembered my military history classes."

Jon-Tom moved shakily to the edge of the wall. If they'd been on the other side of the Gate they'd all be dead or maimed now.

Small white shapes were beginning to emerge from the

ground in front of the ruined wall. Waving picks and short swords they cut at the legs of startled warmlander soldiers. Like the inhabitants of Ironcloud they too wore dark goggles to protect them from the sunlight.

"Termites," Jon-Tom murmured aloud, "and other insect burrowers. But where did they get the explosives?"

"Little need to think on that, boy," Clothahump said sadly. "More of Eejakrat's work. What did you call the packaged thunder?"

"Explosives. Probably dynamite."

"Or even gelignite," added Flor with suppressed anger. "That was an intense explosion."

Sensing victory, the Plated Folk ignored the depradations of the swooping arboreals overhead and swarmed forward. Nor could the hectic casting of spears and nets by the Weavers hold them back. Not with the wall, the fabled ancient bottleneck, tumbled to the earth like so many child's blocks.

It must have taken an immense quantity of explosives to undermine that massive wall. It was possible, Jon-Tom mused, that the Plated burrowers had begun excavating their tunnel weeks before the battle began.

Without the wall to hinder them they charged onward. By sheer force of numbers they pushed back those who had desperately rushed to defend the ruined barrier. Then they were across, fighting on the other side of the Jo-Troom Gate for the first time in recorded memory. Warmlander blood stained its own land.

Jon-Tom turned helplessly to Clothahump. The Plated Folk soldiers were ignoring the remaining section of wall and the few arrows and spears that fell from its crest. The wizard stood quietly, his gaze focused on the far end of the Pass and not on the catastrophe below.

"Can't you do something," Jon-Tom pleaded with him. "Bring fire and destruction down on them! Bring . . ."

277

Clothahump did not seem to be listening. He was looking without eyes. "I almost have it," he whispered to no one in particular. "Almost can . . ." He broke off, turned to stare at Jon-Tom.

"Do you think conjuring up lightning and floods and fire is merely a matter of snapping one's fingers, boy? Haven't you learned anything about magic since you've been here?" He turned his attention away again.

"Can almost . . . yes," he said excitedly, "I can. I believe I can see it now!" The enthusiasm faded. "No, I was wrong. Too well screened by distortion spells. Eejakrat leaves nothing to chance. Nothing."

Jon-Tom turned away from the entranced wizard, swung his duar around in front of him. His fingers played furiously on the strings. But he could not think of a single appropriate song to sing. His favorites were songs of love, of creativity and relationships. He knew a few marches, and though he sang with ample fervor nothing materialized to slow the Plated Folk advance.

Then Mudge, sweaty and his fur streaked with dried blood, was shaking him and pointing westward. "Wot the bloody 'ell is that?" The otter was staring across the widening field of battle.

"It sounds like . . ." said Caz confusedly. "I don't know. A rusty door hinge, perhaps. Or high voices. Many high voices."

Then they could make out the source of the peculiar noise. It was singing. Undisciplined, but strong, and it rose from a motley horde of marchers nearing the foothills. They were armed with pitchforks and makeshift spears, with scythes and knives tied to broom handles, with woodcutters' tools and sharpened iron posts.

They flowed like a brown-gray wave over the milling combatants, and wherever their numbers appeared the Plated Folk were overwhelmed.

"Mice!" said Mudge, aghast. "Rats an' shrews in there, too. I don't believe it. They're not fighters. Wot be they doin' 'ere?"

"Fighting," said Jon-Tom with satisfaction, "and damn well, too, from the look of it."

The rodent mob attacked with a ferocity that more than compensated for their lack of training. The flow of clicking, gleaming death from the Pass was blunted, then stopped. The rodents fought with astonishing bravery, throwing themselves onto larger opponents while others cut at warriors' knees and ankles.

Sometimes three and four of the small warmlanders would bring down a powerful insect by weight alone. Their makeshift weapons broke and snapped. They resorted to rocks and bare paws, whatever they could scavenge that would kill.

For a few moments the remnants of the warmlander forces were as stunned by the unexpected assault as the Plated Folk. They stared dumbfounded as the much maligned, oft-abused rodents threw themselves into the fray. Then they resumed fighting themselves, alongside heroic allies once held in servitude and contempt.

Now if the warmlanders prevailed there would be permanent changes in the social structure of Polastrindu and other communities, Jon-Tom knew. At least one good thing would come of this war.

He thought they were finished with surprises. But while he selected targets below for the spears he was handed, yet another one appeared.

In the midst of the battle a gout of flame brightened the winter morning. There was another. It was almost as if . . . yes! A familiar iridescent bulk loomed large above the combatants, incinerating Plated Folk by the squadron.

"I'll be damned!" he muttered. "It's Falameezar!"

"But I thought he was through with us," said Caz.

"You know this dragon?" Bribbens tended to a wounded leg and eyed the distant fight with amazement. It was the first time Jon-Tom had seen the frog's demeanor change.

"We sure as hell do!" Jon-Tom told him joyfully. "Don't you see, Caz, it all adds up."

"Pardon my ignorance, friend Jon-Tom, but the only mathematics I've mastered involves dice and cards."

"This army of the downtrodden, of the lowest mass of workers. Who do you think organized them, persuaded them to fight? Someone had to raise a cry among them, someone had to convince them to fight for their rights as well as for their land. And who would be more willing to do so, to assume the mantle of leadership, than our innocent Marxist Falameezar!"

"This is absurd." Bribbens could still not quite believe it. "Dragons do not fight *with* people. They are solitary, antisocial creatures who..."

"Not this one," Jon-Tom informed him assuredly. "If anything, he's *too* social. But I'm not going to argue his philosophies now."

Indeed, as the gleaming black and purple shape trudged nearer they could hear the great dragon voice bellowing encouragingly above the noise of battle.

"Onward downtrodden masses! Workers arise! Down with the invading imperialist warmongers!"

Yes, that was Falameezar and none other. The dragon was in his sociological element. In between thundering favorite Marxist homilies he would incinerate a dozen terrified insect warriors or squash a couple beneath massive clawed feet. Around him swirled a bedraggled mob of tiny furry supporters like an armada of fighter craft protecting a dreadnought.

The legions of Plated Folk seemed endless. But now that the surprise engendered by the destruction of the wall had passed, their offensive began to falter. The arrival of what amounted to a second warmlander army, as ferocious if not as well trained as the original, started to turn the tide.

Meanwhile the Weavers and fliers from Ironcloud continued to cause havoc among the packed ranks of warriors trying to squeeze through the section of ruined wall to reach the open plain where their numbers could be a factor. The diminutive lemur bowmen fired and fired until their drawstring fingers were bloody.

When the fall came it was not in a great surge of panic. A steady withering of purpose and determination ate through the ranks of the Plated Folk. In clusters, and individually, they lost their will to fight on. A vast sigh of discouragement rippled through the whole exhausted army.

Sensing it, the warmlanders redoubled their efforts. Still fighting, but with intensity seeping away from them, the Plated Folk were gradually pressed back. The plain was cleared, and then the destroyed section of wall. The battle moved once again back into the confines of the Pass. Insect officers raged and threatened, but they could do nothing to stop the steady slow leak of desire that bled their soldiers' will to fight.

Jon-Tom had stopped throwing spears. His arm throbbed with the efforts of the past several days. The conflict had retreated steadily up the Pass, and the Plated combatants were out of range now. He was cheering tiredly when a hand clamped on his arm so forcefully that he winced. He looked around. It was Clothahump. The wizard's grip was anything but that of an oldster.

"By the periodic table, I can see it now!"

"See what?"

"The deadmind." Clothahump's tone held a peculiar mixture of confusion and excitement. "The deadmind. It is not in a body."

"You mean the brain itself's been extracted?" The image was gruesome.

"No. It is scattered about, in several containers of differing shape."

Jon-Tom's mind shunted aside the instinctive vision and produced only a blank from the wizard's description. Flor listened intently.

"It talks to Eejakrat," Clothahump continued, his voice far away, distant, "in words I can't understand."

"Several containers . . . the mind is several minds?" Jon-Tom struggled to make sense of a seeming impossibility.

"No, no. It is one mind that has been split into many parts."

"What does it look like? You said containers. Can you be more specific?" Flor asked him.

"Not really. The containers are mostly rectangular, but not all. One inscribes words on a scroll, symbols and magic terms I do not recognize." He winced with the strain of focusing senses his companions did not possess.

"There are symbols over all the containers as well, though they mostly differ from those appearing on the scroll. The mind also makes a strange noise, like talking that is not. I can read some of the symbols . . . it is strangely inscribed. It changes as I look at it." He stopped.

Jon-Tom urged him on. "What is it? What's happening?"

Clothahump's face was filled with pain. Sweat poured down his face into his shell. Jon-Tom didn't know that a turtle could sweat. Everything indicated that the wizard was expending a massive effort not only to continue to see but to understand.

"Eejakrat . . . Eejakrat sees the failure of the attack." He swayed, and Jon-Tom and Flor had to support him or he would have fallen. "He works a last magic, a final conjuration. He has . . . has delved deep within the deadmind for its most powerful manifestation. It has given him the formula he needs. Now he is giving orders to his assistants. They are bringing materials from the store of sorceral supplies. Skrritch watches, she will kill him if he fails. Eejakrat promises her the battle will be won. The materials . . . I recognize some. No, many. But I do not understand the formula given, the purpose. The purpose is to . . . to . . ." He turned a frightened face upward. Jon-Tom shivered. He'd never before seen the wizard frightened. Not when confronted by the Massawrath, not when crossing Helldrink.

But he was more than frightened now. He was terrified.

"Must stop it!" he mumbled. "Got to stop him from completing the formula. Even Eejakrat does not understand what he does. But he . . . I see it clearly . . . he is desperate. He will try anything. I do not think . . . do not think he can control . . ."

"What's the formula?" Flor pressed him.

"Complex . . . can't understand . . ."

"Well then, the symbols you read on the deadmind containers."

"Can read them now, yes . . . but can't understand . . ."

"Try. Repeat them, anyway."

Clothahump went silent, and for a moment the two humans were afraid he wouldn't speak again. But Jon-Tom finally managed to shake him into coherence.

"Symbols . . . symbols say, 'Property.' "

"That's all?" Flor said puzzledly. "Just 'property'?"

"No . . . there is more. Property . . . property restricted access. U.S. Army Intelligence."

Flor looked over at Jon-Tom. "That explains everything; the parachutes, the tactics, the formula for the explosives to undermine the wall, maybe the technique for doing it as well. *Los insectos* have gotten hold of a military computer."

"That's why Clothahump tried to find an engineer to combat Eejakrat's 'new magic,' " Jon-Tom muttered. "And he got me instead. And you." He gazed helplessly at her. "What are we going to do? I don't know anything about computers."

"I know a little, but it's not a matter of knowing anything about computers. Machine, man or insect, it has to be destroyed before Eejakrat can finish his new formula."

"What the fuck could that devil have dug out of its electronic guts?" He looked back down at Clothahump.

"Don't understand..." murmured the wizard. "Beyond my ken. But Eejakrat knows how to comply. It worries him, but he proceeds. He knows if he does not the war is lost."

"Someone's got to get over there and destroy the computer and its mentor," Jon-Tom said decisively. He called to the rest of their companions.

Mudge and Caz ambled over curiously. So did Bribbens, and Pog fluttered close from his perch near the back of the wall. Hastily, Jon-Tom told them what had to be done.

"Wot about the Ironclouders, wot?" Mudge indicated the diving shapes of the great owls working their death up the Pass. "I don't think they'd 'old you, mate, but I ought to be able to ride one."

"I could go myself, boss." Clothahump turned a startled gaze on the unexpectedly daring famulus.

"No. Not you, Pog, nor you, otter. You would never make it, I fear. Hundreds of bowmen, a royal guard of the Greendowns' most skilled archers, surround Eejakrat and the Empress. You could not get within a quarter league of the deadmind. Even if you could, what would you destroy it with? It is made of metal. You cannot shoot an arrow through it. And there may be disciples of Eejakrat who could draw upon its evil knowledge in event of his death."

"We need a plane," Jon-Tom told them. "A Huey or some other attack copter, with rockets."

Clothahump looked blankly at him. "I know not what you

describe, spellsinger, but by the heavens if you can do anything you must try."

Jon-Tom licked his lips. The Who, J. Geils, Dylan: none sang much about war and its components. But he had to try something. He didn't know the Air Force song. . . .

"Try something, Jon-Tom," Flor urged him. "We don't have much time."

Time. Time's getting away from us. There's your cue, man. Get there first. Worry about how to destroy the thing then.

Trying to shut the sounds of fighting out of his thoughts, he ran his fingers a couple of times across the duar's strings. The instrument had been nicked and battered by arrows and spears, but it was still playable. He struggled to recall the melody. It was simple, smooth, a Steve Miller hallmark. A few adjustments to the duar's controls. It *had* to work. He turned tremble and mass all the way up. Dangerous, but whatever materialized had to carry him high above the combat, all the way to the end of the Pass.

Anyway, Clothahump's urgency indicated that there was little time left now either for finesse or fine tuning.

Just get me to that computer, he thought furiously. Just get me there safely and I'll find some way to destroy it. Even pulling a few wires would do it. Eejakrat couldn't repair the damage with magic . . . could he?

And if he was killed and the attempt a failure, what did it matter? Talea was dead and so was much of himself. Yes, that was the answer. Crash whatever carries you and yourself into the computer. That should do it.

Time was the first crucial element. Though he did not know it, he was soon to learn the other.

Time . . . that was the key. He needed to move fast and he didn't have *time* to fool with machines that might or might not work, might or might not appear. Time and flight. What song could possibly fill the need?

Wait a minute! There was something about time and flight slipping, slipping into the future.

His fingers began to fly over the strings as he threw back his head and began to sing with more strength than ever he had before.

There was a tearing sound in the sky, and his nostrils were filled with the odor of ozone. It was coming! Whatever he'd called up. If not the sung-for huge bird, perhaps the British fighter nicknamed the Eagle, bristling with rockets and rapid-fire cannon. Anything to get him into the air.

He sang till his throat hurt, his fingers a blur above the strings. Reverberant waves of sound emerged from the quivering duar and the air vibrated in sympathy.

A deep-throated crackling split the sky overhead, a sound no kin to any earthly thunder. It seemed the sun had drawn back to hide behind the clouds. The fighting did not stop, but warmlander and insect alike slowed their pace. That ominous rumble echoed down the walls of the Pass. Something extraordinary was happening.

Vast wings that were of starry gases filled the air. The winter day turned warm with a sudden eruption of heat. Hot air blew Jon-Tom against the rampart behind him and nearly over, while his companions scrambled for something solid to cling to.

Atop the wall the remaining warmlander defenders scattered in terror. On the cliffsides the Weavers scuttled for hiding places in the crevices and crannies as a monstrous fiery form came near. It touched down on the mountainside where the remaining half of the wall was worked into the naked rock, and twenty feet of granite melted and ran like syrup.

"WHAT HAVE YOU DONE!" roared a voice that could raise a sunspot. The remaining stones of the wall trembled, as did the cells of those still standing atop it. "WHAT HAVE YOU WROUGHT, LITTLE HUMAN!"

"I . . ." Jon-Tom could only gape. He had not materialized the plane he'd wished for or the eagle he'd sung to. He had called up something best left undisturbed, interrupted a journey measurable in billions of years. It was all he could do to gaze back into those vast, infinite eyes, as M'nemaxa, barely touching the melting rock, fanned thermonuclear wings and glared down at him.

"I'm sorry," he finally managed to gasp out, "I was only trying . . ."

"LOOK TO MY BACK!" bellowed the sun horse.

Jon-Tom hesitated, then took a cautious step forward and craned his neck. Squinting through the glare, he made out a dark metallic shape that looked suspiciously like a saddle. It was very small and lost on that great flaming curve of a spine.

"I don't . . . what does this mean?" he asked humbly.

"IT MEANS A TRANSFORMATION IN MY ODYSSEY; A SHORT-CUT. LITTLE MAN BENEATH THE STARS, YOU HAVE CREATED A SHORTCUT! I CAN SEE THE END OF MY JOURNEY NOW. NO LONGER MUST I RACE AROUND THE RIM OF THE UNIVERSE. ONLY ANOTHER THREE MILLION YEARS AND I WILL BE FINISHED. ONLY THREE MILLION, AND I WILL KNOW PEACE. AND YOU, MAN, ARE TO THANK FOR IT!"

"But I don't know what I did, and I don't know how I did it," Jon-Tom told him softly.

"CONSEQUENCE IS WHAT MATTERS, CAUSATION IS BUT EPHEM-ERAL. EMPYREAN RESULTS HAVE BEEN ACHIEVED, LITTLE MAN OF NOTHINGNESS.

"AS YOU HAVE HELPED ME, SO I WILL HELP YOU. BUT I CAN DO ONLY WHAT YOU DIRECT. YOUR MAGIC PUTS THIS SHIELD ON MY BACK, SO MOUNT THEN, GUARDED BY ITS SUBSTANCE AND BY YOUR OWN MAGIC, AND RIDE. SUCH A RIDE AS NO CREATURE

OF MERE FLESH AND BLOOD HAS EVER HAD BEFORE NOR WILL HENCE!''

Jon-Tom hesitated. But eager hands were already urging him toward the equine inferno.

"Go on, Jon-Tom," said Caz encouragingly.

"Yes, go on. It must be the spellsong magic that's protecting us," said Flor, "or the radiation and heat would have fried all of us by now."

"But that little lead saddle, Flor..."

"The magic, Jon-Tom, the magic. The magic's in the music *and the music's in you.* Do it!"

It was Clothahump who finally convinced him. "It is all or nothing now, my boy. We live or we die on what you do. This is between you and Eejakrat."

"I wish it wasn't. I wish to God I was home. I wish...ahhh, fuck it. Let's go!"

He could not see a barrier shielding the streaming nuclear material that was the substance of M'nemaxa, but one had to be present, as Flor had so incontrovertibly pointed out. He cradled the battered duar against his chest. That barrier had momentarily lapsed when M'nemaxa had touched down, and a thousand tons of solid rock had run like butter. If it lapsed again, there would not even be ashes left of him.

A series of stirrups led to the saddle, which was much larger up close than it had appeared from a distance. He mounted carefully, feeling neither heat nor pain but watching fascinated as tiny solar prominences erupted from M'nemaxa's epidermis only inches from his puny human skin.

It was little different in the saddle, though he could feel some slight heat against his face and hands.

"Just a minim, guv'," said a voice. A small gray shape had bounded into the saddle behind him.

"Mudge? It's not necessary. Either I'll make it or I won't."

"Shove it, mate. I've been watchin' you ever since you stuck your nose int' me business. You don't think I could let you go off on your own now, do you? Somebody's got t' watch out for you. This great flippin' flamin' beastie can't be 'urt, but a good archer might pick you off 'is back like a farmer pluckin' a bloomin' apple." He notched an arrow into his bowstring and grinned beneath his whiskers.

Jon-Tom couldn't think of anything else to say: "Thanks, Mudge. Mate."

"Thank me when we get back. I've always wanted t' ride a comet, wot? Let's be about the business, then."

The serpentine fiery neck arched, and the great head with its bottomless eyes stared back at them. "COMMAND, MAN!"

"I don't know . . ." Mudge was prodding him in the ribs. "Shit . . . giddy up! To Eejakrat!"

Whether the message was conveyed by the word or the mental imagery connected with it no one knew. It didn't matter. The vast wings seared the earth and a warm hurricane blasted those who were beneath. Those wings stretched from one side of the canyon to the other, and the Ironclouders, seeing it race toward them, scattered like gnats.

A swarm of dragonfly fighters rose to meet them, the Empress' private aerial guard. They attacked with the mindless but admirable courage of their kind.

Mudge's bow began its work. The soldiers riding the dragonflies fell from their mounts and none of their arrows reached the sun riders. Those that were launched impacted on the body or wings or neck of M'nemaxa and were vaporized with the briefest of sizzling sounds.

"Fly past them!" Jon-Tom ordered. "Down, over there!" He gestured toward the blunt butte rising fingerlike near the rear of the Pass. Beyond lay the mists of the Greendowns.

Jon-Tom's attention shifted to concentrate on a single figure standing before a pile of materials and a semicircle of metal forms. Dragonflies and riders tried to break through to do battle with swords, but wings and hooves touched them, and their charred remnants fell earthward like so many sizzling lumps of smoking charcoal.

The imperial bodyguard sent a storm of arrows upward. Not one passed the belly of that flaming body. Jon-Tom was watching Eejakrat. He held his own spear-staff tightly, ready to pierce the sorcerer through.

Then his attention was diverted. In the air above the computer floated two faintly glowing pieces of stone. They were so tiny he noticed them only because of their glow. Behind the sorcerer danced the fearful, iridescent green shape of the Empress Skrritch.

What devastating magic so terrified the imperturbable Clothahump? What was Eejakrat about to risk in hopes of winning a lost war?

"Down," he ordered M'nemaxa. "Down to the one surrounded by maggots and evil, down to destroy!"

A whispery sorceral mumbling, rapid and desperate, sounded from the crest of the butte. Eejakrat had panicked. He was rushing the incantation, as others had done before him, though he knew nothing of them. The two glowing shards of stone moved through the air toward the onrushing spirit fire and its mortal riders, and toward each other. Stones and spirit would meet at the same point in the sky.

They were no more than fifty yards from it and as many more from the butte's summit when M'nemaxa suddenly gave forth a thunderous whinny. The infinite eyes glowed more brightly than the stones as the two came almost together a couple of yards in front of them.

There was a faint, hopeless scream from Eejakrat below, a desperate croaking Jon-Tom deciphered: "Not yet . . . too near, too close, not *yet!*"

Then the world was spinning farther and farther below them like a flower caught in a whirlpool.

Gone was the Troom Pass. So too was the butte where Eejakrat had gesticulated frantically before the Empress Skrritch. So were the milling mob of Plated Folk plunging to war and the insistent battle cries of the warmlanders.

Gone were the mists of the distant Greendowns and noisome distant Cugluch, gone too the mountain crags that towered above insignificant warriors. Soon the blue sky itself vanished behind them.

They still rode the spine of the furiously galloping M'nemaxa, but they rode now through the emptiness of convergent eternity. Stars gleamed bright as morning around them, unwinking and cold and so close it seemed you could reach out and touch them.

You *could* touch them. Jon-Tom reached out slowly and plucked a red giant from its place in the heavens. It was warm in his palm and shone like a ruby. He cast it spinning back free into space. A black hole slid past his left foot and he pulled away. It was like quicksand. He inhaled a nebula, which made him sneeze. Behind him Mudge the otter seemed a distant, diffuse shape in the stars.

He breathed infinity. The wings and hooves of M'nemaxa moved in slow motion. A swarm of motile, luminescent dots gathered around the runners, millions of lights pricking the blackness. They danced and swirled around the great horse and its riders.

Where the world had no meaning and natural law was absent, these too finally became real. Gneechees, Jon-Tom thought ponderously. Only now I can see them, I can see them.

Some were people, some animals, others unrecognizable; the afterthoughts, the memories, the souls and shadows of all intelligent life. They were all the colors of the rainbow, a spectrum filled with life, both mysterious and familiar.

He began to recognize some of the forms and faces. He saw Einstein, he saw his own grandfather. He saw the moving lips of now dead singers he had loved, and it was as if their music swelled around him in the ultimate concert. He noted that the faces he saw were not old, and showed no trace of death or suffering. In fact the famous physicist's eyes glittered like a child's. Einstein had his violin with him. Hendrix was there, too, and they played a duet, and both smiled at Jon-Tom.

Then he saw a face he knew well, a face full of fire and light. He concentrated on that face with all his strength, trying to pull it into his brain through his eyes. The face was distinct and warm; it seemed to float toward him instinctively. His whole being glowed with love as it neared him, and suddenly when it touched his lip a flame ignited inside him and he almost lost his seat. It was the Talea gneechee, he knew, and he surrounded it with his entire will.

"We must go back. Now!" he roared at the fiery stallion.

"YOU MUST KNOW THE WORDS, LITTLE MAN, OR REMAIN WITH ME UNTIL THE END OF MY JOURNEY."

What song? Jon-Tom thought. There seemed no music equal to the immensity of space and stars all around him. Every song he had ever heard dried up on his tongue.

The Talea gneechee seemed to stir someplace deep inside him, and he looked out at the cold blue distance ahead. It was time to go back where he belonged. He couldn't be specific, but he suddenly had a real sense of where he belonged in life and he knew he could get there.

His mouth opened and his fingertips caressed the duar. A new sound rose, a new voice came both from the duar and from his mouth, and though he had never heard it before he knew it was, finally, his true voice.

Stars spun faster around him, the universe seemed wrenched

for an instant. His head throbbed and his throat burned with the strange wordless song that poured from him like a river a million times stronger than any earthly river.

Now blue sky hurried toward them, then the snowy caps of mountains. The boundary was back—the luscious, palpable limit of existence. He felt more alive than he had ever in his life.

"Cor, wot a friggin' ride!" Mudge's joyous voice came from behind him.

"Love you, Mudge!" screamed Jon-Tom, ecstatic to hear that familiar sound.

"You're crazy—where the 'ell we been?"

Everywhere, Jon-Tom thought, but there was no way to say it.

"THE COURSE OF MY JOURNEY HAS BEEN FOREVER CHANGED," bellowed M'nemaxa. "I HAVE HAD TO CHANGE MY DIRECTION BECAUSE OF THE EVIL IN YOUR WORLD AND NOW MY ROUTE IS ALMOST THROUGH. COME WITH ME TO THE OUTSIDE, LITTLE MAN, YOUR WORLD IS FULL OF DOOM. I WILL SHOW SUCH THINGS AS NO MORTAL SHALL EVER AGAIN SEE."

"Wot's 'e talkin' about, guv'nor?"

"Eejakrat's magic, Mudge. Clothahump knew that they could not control it, and it has created devastation so utter that even M'nemaxa had to detour around it. It's happened before, but in my world. Not here. Look."

The mushroom cloud that billowed skyward from the far end of the Troom Pass was not large, but it was considerably darker and denser than any of the mists behind it.

Below them now the last of the Plated Folk army, those who'd been lucky enough to be trapped in the middle of the Pass, were surrendering, turning over their weapons and going down on all sixes to plead for mercy.

Beneath the now fading mushroom cloud that marked the failure of Eejakrat's imported magic, the butte he'd stood upon had vanished. In its place there was only an empty, radioactive crater. The bomb Eejakrat had been in the process of creating had been a relatively clean one. What remained would serve as a warning to future generations of Plated Folk. It would block the Pass far more effectively than had the Jo-Troom Gate.

Flaming wings slowed. Mudge was deposited gently back on top of the wall. Jon-Tom thanked the flaming being but would not return with him.

"THREE MILLION YEARS!" M'nemaxa boomed, his neighing shaking boulders from the cliffsides of the canyon.

"ONLY THREE MILLION. THANK YOU, LITTLE HUMAN. YOU ARE A WIZARD OF UNKNOWN WISDOM. FAREWELL!"

The vast fiery form rose into the air. There was an earsplitting explosion that rent the fabric of space-time. The gap closed quickly and M'nemaxa had gone, gone back to resume his now truncated journey, gone back to the everywhere otherplace.

Bodies, furred and otherwise, swarmed around the returnees—Caz, Flor, Bribbens holding his bandaged right arm where he'd taken a sword thrust. Pog fluttered excitedly overhead, and warmlander soldiers mixed queries with congratulations.

The battle had ended, the war was over. Those Plated Folk who had not perished in the modest thermonuclear explosion at the far end of the Pass were being herded into makeshift corrals.

Jon-Tom was embarrassed and nervous, but Mudge glowed like M'nemaxa himself from the adjulation of the crowd.

When the excitement had died down and the soldiers had gone to join their companions below, Clothahump managed to make his way up to Jon-Tom.

"You did well, my boy, well! I'm quite proud of you." He smiled as much as he could. "We'll make a wizard of you yet. If you can only learn to be a bit more specific and precise in your formulations."

"I'm learning," Jon-Tom admitted without smiling back. "One of the things I've learned is to pay attention to what lies *behind* a person's words." He and the wizard stared into each other's eyes, and neither gave ground.

"I did what I had to do, boy. I'd do it again."

"I know you would. I can't blame you for it anymore, but I can't like you for it, either."

"As you will, Jon-Tom," said the wizard. He looked past the man and his eyes widened. "Though it may be that you condemn me too quickly."

Jon-Tom turned. A petite, slightly baffled redhead was walking toward them. He could only stare.

"Hello," Talea said, smiling slightly. "I must have been unconscious for days."

"You've been dead," said a flabbergasted Mudge.

"Oh cut it out. I had the strangest dream." She looked down at the canyon. "Missed all the fighting, I see."

"I saw you . . . out there," Jon-Tom said dazedly. "Or a part of you. It came to me and I knew it was you."

"I wouldn't know about that," she said sharply. "All I know is that I woke up in a tent surrounded by corpses. It scared the shit out of me." She chuckled. "Did worse to the attendants. Bet they haven't stopped running.

"Then I asked around for you and got directions. Is it true what everyone's saying about you and M'nemaxa and . . ."

"Everything's true, nothing's false," Jon-Tom said. "Not anymore. Whatever entered me I sent back to you, but it doesn't matter. What is is what matters, and what is, is you."

"You've gotten awfully obscure all of a sudden, Jon-Tom."

He put his hands on her shoulders. "I suppose we have to stay together now." He smiled shyly, not able to explain what had happened in Elsewhere. She looked blank. "Don't you remember what you said to me back in Cugluch?" he asked.

She frowned at him. "I don't know what you're talking about, but that's nothing new, is it? You always did talk too much. But you're wrong about one thing."

"What's that?"

"I do remember what I said back in Cugluch," and she proceeded to give him the deepest, longest, richest kiss he'd ever experienced.

Eventually she let him go. Or was it the other way around? No matter.

Caz and Flor sat on the ramparts nearby, hand in paw. Jon-Tom shook his head, wondering at that blindness that conceals what is most obvious. Bribbens had disappeared, doubtless to make arrangements for reaching the nearest river. Falameezar was able to help the boatman with that, being a river dragon. That is, he was when he wasn't too busy reeducating his rodent charges about their responsibilities and rights as members of the downtrodden proletariat. Clothahump had gone off to discuss the matters of magic with the other warmlander wizards.

"What now, Jon-Tom?" Talea looked at him anxiously. "I guess now that you've mastered your spellsinging you'll be returning to your own world?"

"I don't know." He studied the masonry underfoot. "I'm not so sure you could say I've *mastered* spellsinging." He plucked ruefully at the duar. "I always seem to get what I need, not what I want. That's nice, but not necessarily reassuring.

"And for some reason being a rock star or a lawyer doesn't seem to hold the attraction it once did. I guess you could say I've had my horizons somewhat expanded." Like to include infinity, he told himself.

She nodded knowingly. "You've grown up some, Jon-Tom."

He shrugged. "If experiences can age you, I ought to be the equivalent of Methuselah by now."

"I'll see what I can do about keeping you young. . . ." She ran fingers through his hair. "Does that mean you'll be staying?" She added quietly, "With me, maybe? If you can stand me, that is."

"I've never known a woman like you, Talea."

"That's because there aren't any women like me, idiot." She moved to kiss him again. He edged away from her, preoccupied with a new thought.

"What's the matter? Not coy enough for you?"

"Nothing like that. I just remembered something that's been left undone, something that I promised myself I'd try to do if given the chance."

They found Pog hanging from a spear rack in the middle of the remaining wall. The warmlanders were beginning to disperse, those not remaining behind to guard the Plated Folk forming into their respective companies and battalions preparatory to beginning the long march home. Some were already on their way, too tired or filled with memories of dead companions to sing victory songs. They were traveling west toward Polastrindu or southward to where the river Tailaroam tumbled fresh and clear from the flanks of the Teeth.

The sun was setting over the fringes of the Swordsward. The poisonous silhouette of the mushroom cloud had long since been carried away by the wind. Their kilts flashing as brightly as their wings, squads of aerial warmlanders in arrowhead formations were winging back toward their home roosts. A distant line of silk-clad shapes showed where the Weavers were wending their way northward along the foothills, and a dark mass was just disappearing over the northern crest of the mountains in the direction of fabled Ironcloud.

"Hello, Pog."

"Hi, spellsinger." The bat's voice was subdued, but Jon-Tom no longer had to ask why. "Some job ya did. I'm proud ta call ya my friend."

Jon-Tom sat down on a low bench near the spear rack. "Why aren't you out there celebrating with the rest of the army?"

"I attend to da needs of my master, you know dat. I wait for his woid on what ta do next."

"You're a good apprentice, Pog. I hope I can learn as well as you."

"What's dat supposed ta mean?" The upside-down face turned to stare curiously at him.

"I'm hoping that Clothahump will accept me as an apprentice wizard." The duar rested in his lap and he strummed it experimentally. "Magic seems to be the only thing I have any talent for hereabouts. I'd damn well better learn how to discipline it before I kill myself. I've just been lucky so far."

"Da master, da old fart-face, says dere's no such ting as luck."

"I know, I know." He was slowly picking out a tune on the duar. "But I'm going to have to work like hell if I'm going to attain half the wisdom of that senile little turtle." He started to hum the song that had come to him back in the tent on that day of fury not long ago, when a certain famulus had been thoughtful enough to comfort him and lay down the life laws.

"I appreciated what you said to me that time in the tent, when I came out of the stupor Clothahump was forced to put me into. You see, Pog, Clothahump cared about me because he knew I might be able to help him. Caz and Flor and Bribbens cared about me because we were dependent on one another.

"But the only ones who cared about me personally, really cared, turned out to be Talea, and you. We've got a lot in common, you and I. A hell of a lot in common. I never saw it before because I couldn't. You were right about love, of course. I thought I wanted Flor.'' Talea said nothing. ''What I really wanted was someone to want me. That's all I've ever wanted. I know that's what you want, too.''

Now he began to sing out, loud and clear. Suddenly there was a shimmering in the air around the bat. It was evening now, and the wall was growing dark. Camp fires were beginning to spring up on the plain where Plated Folk and warmlander for the first time in thousands of years were beginning to talk to one another.

''Hey, what's going on?'' The bat dropped from his perch, righted himself, and flapped nervous wings.

The bat shape was flowing, shifting in the evening air.

''That was my falcon song, Pog. I've got to get my spellsinging specific, Clothahump says. So I'm giving you the transformation you wanted from him.''

Talea clung tight to Jon-Tom's arm, watching. ''He's changing, Jon-Tom.''

''It's what he wants,'' he told her softly, also watching the transformation. ''He gave me understanding when I needed it most. This is what I'm giving in return. The song I just sang should turn him into the biggest, sleekest falcon that ever split a cloud.''

But the shape wasn't right. It was all wrong. It continued to change and glow as Jon-Tom's expression widened in disbelief.

''Oh God. I should've waited. I should've held off and waited for Clothahump's advice. I'm sorry, Pog!'' he yelled at the indistinct, alien outline.

''Wait,'' said Talea gently. Her grip tightened on his arm and she leaned into him. ''True, it's no falcon he's becoming. But look—it's incredible!''

The metamorphosis was complete, finished, irrevocable.

"Never mind, never mind, never mind!" sang the transformed thing that had been Pog the bat. The voice was all quicksilver and light. "Never mind, friend Talea. Be true to Clothahump, Jon-Tom. You'll get a wing on it, you will."

A flock of fighters, eagles perhaps, crossed the darkling sky from east to west. A few falcons were scattered among them. Perhaps one was Uleimee.

"Meanwhile you've made me very happy," Pog-that-once-was assured the spellsinger.

Jon-Tom realized he'd been holding his breath. The transformation had stunned him. Talea called to him softly and he turned and found her waiting arms.

Above them the change which had been Pog searched with keen eyes among the winged shapes soaring toward the distant reaches of the warmlands. It saw a particular female falcon emerging with others of her kind from a thick cloud, saw with eyes far sharper than those of any bat, or owl, or falcon.

Leaving the two humans to their own destinies, and rising on suddenly massive wings, the golden phoenix raced for that distant cloud, the sun setting on its back like a rare jewel.

By
ALAN DEAN FOSTER

__THE MAN WHO USED THE UNIVERSE

(E90-353, $2.95, U.S.A.)
(E30-870, $3.75, Canada)

Power is his passion, his plaything, but what is his ultimate aim? Kees vaan Loo-Macklin is a born killer, the criminal prodigy who seized the reins of an intergalactic underworld, then sold out to go legit. Even then he could see there was no future on Evenwaith with its poisoned atmosphere and cities sheathed in glass and steel tubes; no safe harbor, and the ever-present threat of interstellar war. So he reached out to the Nuel, his natural enemies. Only one alien dares to suspect vaan Loo-Macklin's real motivation— is it greed, personal power, revenge?

__ALIEN

by Alan Dean Foster *(E30-577, $3.25)*

Astronauts encounter an awesome galactic horror on a distant planet. But it's only when they take off again that the real horror begins. For the alien is now within the ship, within the crew itself. And a classic deathtrap suspense game begins.

THE WILDERNESS OF FOUR series

by Niel Hancock

This series takes you back into time before time. Here you discover the origins of the titanic struggle that wracked the world before man and beast were hostile strangers. You will meet many of the same characters who enthralled you in Niel Hancock's CIRCLE OF LIGHT saga, characters revealing their youthful brashness, and unspeakable wickedness.

MORE GREAT BOOKS
from WARNER